SHAMANKA

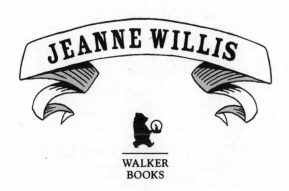

JEANNE WILLIS

WALKER
BOOKS

First published 2007 by Walker Books Ltd
87 Vauxhall Walk, London SE11 5HJ

This edition published 2013

2 4 6 8 10 9 7 5 3 1

Text © 2007 Jeanne Willis
Inside illustrations © 2007 Walker Books Ltd
Cover illustration © 2013 Joe Wilson at début art

The right of Jeanne Willis to be identified as author of this work
has been asserted by her in accordance with the Copyright,
Designs and Patents Act 1988

This book has been typeset in Bembo.

Printed and bound in Great Britain by Clays Ltd, St Ives plc

British Library Cataloguing in Publication Data:
a catalogue record for this book is available from the British Library

ISBN 978-1-4063-5082-1

www.walker.co.uk

MONDAYS ARE MURDER

TANYA LANDMAN

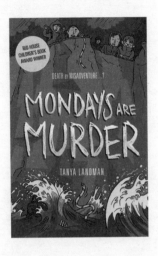

Death by misadventure...?

When Poppy Fields goes on an activity holiday to
a remote Scottish island, she is looking forward to a
week of climbing, hill-walking and horse riding. But
things take a disastrous turn when their instructor
has what appears to be a fatal abseiling accident.
When Poppy discovers that his rope was cut, and
more of the instructors start to have "accidents", she
and best friend Graham suspect foul play and decide
to investigate.

"With a convincing twist in the tail this is a really
satisfying story." *Carousel*

DRAGONBORN

TOBY FORWARD

In a world where magic has become wild, and evil is afoot, can the forces for good prevail?

When the great wizard Flaxfield dies, his apprentice Sam is left without a master. As the wizards gather for his Finishing, Sam does not know whom to trust and whom he should fear. He sets off alone with only his dragon Starback for company, little realizing the perils that lie in wait. This powerful opening book of the Flaxfield Quartet is an adventure story told with great lyricism and power.

"Toby Forward has created a world and characters uniquely his own." *School Librarian*

For *Sylvie Jane Wilcock,*
because she's magical.

With thanks to *Cher Adeyinka,*
who knows a trick or two.

THE MAGICIAN'S OATH

As a magician, I promise never to reveal the secret of any illusion to a non-magician without first swearing them to the Magician's Oath. I promise never to perform any illusion for any non-magician without first practising the effect until I can perform it well enough to maintain the illusion of magic.

Signed _____

WE MEET AT LAST

You might think you are alone, but I can see you. You can't see me because I'm in disguise, but one day you *will* see me. You might even see straight through me. After all, you have spectacular hidden powers.

You do realize you have hidden powers, don't you? We all have them, but most people are too lazy or too stupid to use them. Not you though; you have great potential.

Shortly, you will no longer be where you are now. There's no need to get up. You don't have to move a muscle. I will simply wave my wand and shift the scenery around ... like so!

You are sitting in the front row of a grand old theatre. I've given you the best seat so you won't miss a trick. There will be many tricks because this is a magic show, and I have volunteered you for the main act. While this may come as a shock, please remain calm. Do not attempt to leave during the interval. If you do, you will miss out on a whole lot more than the ice cream lady.

There are people around you rustling and fidgeting, waiting for the show to begin. They want to be surprised and fooled by magic. They're weary of this world and its harsh rules. They yearn to be taken to a place where the impossible happens; where elephants hide under teacups and ladies smile when they're sawn in half. Oh, to be able to forget about sorrow and suffering and rise above gravity! Or to become invisible. Or to produce anything you desire out of thin air. How happy we would be.

Hush! The lights are dimming. There is a roll of drums. As the curtain begins to rise, the chattering stops. Children with their own hopes and dreams merge into one child in the darkness, eyes drawn to the centre of the stage by the hypnotic spotlight; you are no longer aware of your surroundings or yourself.

There's a thunder crack! A puff of scarlet smoke! You are mesmerized as it uncurls like a phantom serpent. As the smoke clears, a strange figure in a mask emerges from an impossibly small cauldron; how did the Masked Magician ever fit inside it?

There's no time to puzzle it out or you will miss what happens next. The magician produces a rope out of nowhere and throws it into the air. Somehow, this rope – which you know to be bendy – stands upright and hovers with no visible anchor.

The Masked Magician whistles into the wings. A monkey disguised as a boy (or could it be a boy disguised as a monkey?) bounds across the stage and climbs to the top of the rope. You wonder how it's possible for him to do this without the rope collapsing; can the laws of nature really be broken?

The Masked Magician instructs the creature to come down at once. It refuses.

It climbs higher and higher, then vanishes ... just like that! Perhaps you blinked at the wrong moment. You thought your eyes were open, but you blinked.

Again, the magician asks the invisible monkey to come back down. It just cackles and hurls tomatoes, which splatter on the stage. It must be up there still, this monkey–boy; tomatoes don't just fall from theatre roofs.

The Masked Magician pulls out a cutlass, climbs the rope and slashes wildly with the flashing blade. There are curdling screams as a shower of severed limbs thump into the cauldron below.

A little girl is bundled out of the theatre by her mother; this is not suitable entertainment for children. Where are the rabbits? The top hats? The pretty silks?

But *you* are not afraid; you're fascinated. You're watching to see how the illusion is done. You're certain it's an illusion and you hold your eyelids open with your thumb and finger so that you won't blink. The Masked Magician climbs back down the rope to a cacophony of hisses and boos; the audience is outraged by the barbaric slaughter of the small assistant.

The magician shows no remorse and, with a wand, stirs the limbs in the cauldron adding squashed tomatoes all the while. Is the poor creature to be cooked?

Watch carefully and you will see a foot begin to twitch,

then an arm, then a hand, then out leaps the monkey, alive and well! The whole theatre sighs with relief. There is laughter, applause, disbelief...

"How? How? *How?*"

The magician floats to the front of the stage, stops right in front of you and bows deeply. Two glittering eyes stare into yours, boring through the slits in the mask. A shiver plays along your spine. You have been singled out for attention and, while you feel uneasy, isn't it exciting?

Here is the truth: the whole show has been put on just for you. Now the Masked Magician beckons with a long, gloved finger. You rise from your seat and walk onto the stage as if in a trance.

We meet at last! I am the Masked Magician, allow me to shake your hand. Your palm is sweating. It leaves an imprint on my glove. Don't be nervous, I'm happy to answer your questions. Who am I? What do I want from you?

All will be revealed. But only if you join me on a quest which will take you to the four corners of the Earth. This journey has only ever been attempted once by a child, but she was wiser and braver than any adult that ever lived – at least she was until you came along.

Her name was Sam Khaan and she learnt the truth about magic the hard way. This is your chance to take the easy route. Shortly, you will re-trace her footsteps. I will be with you throughout the journey, disguised as a camel or a cloud or a cat, depending on circumstances. In case you lose sight of me in my ever-changing guises, here are my travel tips – observe them or be damned.

1. As you travel through these unchartered pages, keep your mind open but your mouth closed. This will keep the sand out and the secrets in.
2. Lay your soul bare, but wear a big hat in the hot sun or your brain will bake.
3. Watch out for anacondas and anagrams. Remember: An *anaconda* is the name of a snake that twists itself around you. An *anagram* is a name that twists around itself, like a snake.

Now you know what's afoot, you can either put this book down like a coward and forget I exist, or you can turn the page and we will set off around the globe. I hope you will join me because you really are wonderful company and a lot more fun than your friends.

First you must relax. Loosen your clothing and let your shoulders drop. Let the rest of the world and all its sounds and distractions fade into the background. Concentrate on my voice, the voice of the Masked Magician. Breathe slowly and deeply. In … and out. In … and out. Drifting away … drifting … drifting.

On the count of three, I will take you back in time to when Sam Khaan was almost thirteen and living in abject misery with her mad, bad, sad Aunt Candy in London. Here we go.

One … two … three.

HOW TO PUSH A CUP THROUGH A TABLE

The masked magician places a coin on the table, lifts up a cup and brings it down hard over the coin. The cup goes right through the table and drops from underneath it.

THE SECRET

You need: a plastic cup, a paper napkin, a coin, a table

1. Sit at the table with your audience facing you.
2. Place the cup over the coin and wrap the cup in the napkin.
3. Lift the cup and tell the audience to concentrate on the coin.
4. Secretly drop the cup onto your lap, still holding the napkin, which should be in the shape of the cup. This is known as an "ashra" device – the audience thinks the cup's still inside it.
5. Place the napkin "cup" back on the table, grab the audience's attention and smash your hand down on it.
6. Drop the real cup from your lap.
7. Show the audience there is no hole in the table and the coin is still there!

MAD BAD, SAD AUNT CANDY

We have travelled back in time to 1985. We're in London, looking through the back window of a top floor flat in a crumbling house in St Peter's Square. We can't see through the front windows; they're boarded up. The panes were smashed in a fit of rage and they were never replaced. You'd think the flat was unoccupied if you looked up at it from the street – but it's not.

There is a dreadful commotion going on. The neighbours can't hear it, because there are no neighbours. A woman is screeching at Sam. The voice you can hear is Aunt Candy's but I'm afraid it's a little slurred.

"You've been practising your dirty magic tricks behind my back all along haven't you, Spam? Remove that hat! If there's a rabbit under it, I swear I'll skin you both alive!"

Aunt Candy hates magic but she loves gin. She's been drinking it for breakfast. She gets drunk because she's unhappy, but the drink doesn't make her forget; it makes her remember, and then she hates Sam even more.

Why does Aunt Candy hate her? Sam has no idea. She is a good child, grateful for a roof over her head (even if it does leak). She lives with her aunt because she has no mother and her father has disappeared to the ends of the earth – or so she's been told.

Aunt Candy is demanding to know why Sam is dressed in that *ludicrous* ringmaster's hat, that *nasty* velvet cloak and that *ridiculous* silver leotard. The leotard is baggy, partly because it belongs to Aunt Candy and partly because Sam is so thin; she has to survive on scraps. If she were properly fed, she might be pretty, but Aunt Candy couldn't stand that. She's already jealous of Sam's green eyes and her blue–black hair, which has a tantalizing streak of natural blonde.

She knocks Sam's hat off with her umbrella and pokes her in the ribs.

"I hate you, *hate* you! Did I say you could borrow my stage clothes, Spam? Take them off before I hurl. They remind me of my stupid, wanton sister."

Sam leaps to her mother's defence.

"Why must you say such wicked things about her?"

Aunt Candy has good reason to hate Sam's mother, Christa, but she won't tell her why. She staggers into the front room, wrestles the cap off the gin and dabs some behind her ears like perfume, as if to remind herself she was glamorous once. She takes a long swig. It sounds like bath water gurgling down a plughole.

"Your mother never wanted you!" she snorts. "You were an accident, Spam. When you were born, she took

14

one look at you and died of shame. Your own father left the country! Face it, daaahling. You're not very popular, are you?" She has told Sam many stories about her parents, none of which are the same.

"But the last time I asked, you said my father went abroad because he was an intrepid explorer. Why won't you tell me the truth, Aunt Candy?"

Aunt Candy sprawls around on the sofa.

"I was trying to spare your pain," she sneers. "But if you want the truth, you can have it. Your father wasn't an intrepid explorer, he was a womanizer. A trickster! A back street bungler, and his name was – wait for it, because it's quite hilarious – his name was *Bingo Hall*!" She laughs until she coughs. "And here's the crunch! Your mother went looking for him in the jungle and was eaten by a crocodile – *snap, snap*! That's why we never visit her grave, may she rest in pieces!"

"You're making it up!" cries Sam.

"Oh, there, there. All right, she wasn't eaten by a cwocodile. She went to Wonga Wagga and married a cannibal so you have lots of lickle cannibal brothers and sisters."

"Aunt Candy, you're lying."

"There's no fooling you, Spam, is there?"

Aunt Candy has rolled onto her stomach so her head is hanging off the sofa. Her legs are doubled up behind her at such a spine-snapping angle, she's actually folded herself in half. The gin bottle is held between her toes and she is tipping alcohol into her mouth with her feet. The reason she can assume this grotesque position is because she used to be a contortionist, performing under the dubious title of Candy, The Human Cobra. Sam shakes her head in despair.

"You know what, Aunt Candy? I don't care if my brothers and sisters are cannibals. If only you'd invite them to stay, at least I'd have someone to play with."

"Well, ha, ha. They're not coming. Your darling mummy *didn't* marry a cannibal. Auntie made it all up. Seriously – and this is the truth – your daddy murdered her and she came back as a zombie to haunt him!"

Aunt Candy slides off the sofa. Her blonde, nicotine-stained wig has slipped sideways. Her scarlet lipstick is smeared into a lop-sided gash. She lurches towards Sam, eyes rolling, hands outstretched as if she is about to strangle her.

Just then, a ginger ape leaps out from behind the sofa, bares its teeth at Aunt Candy and snatches off her wig. This is Lola, Sam's pet orang-utan. If it wasn't for Lola, Sam would have died long ago. Aunt Candy clutches her head and screams.

"Get that flea-ridden beast away from me! I'll have it destroyed!"

"Lola doesn't have fleas, Aunt Candy. The only time she *ever* had fleas was after she borrowed your hairbrush, remember?"

Sam's voice is low and calm, which annoys her aunt even more. Her face turns purple. She tries to rearrange her few remaining wisps of real hair in the mirror, shrieks at her bald patch, then blunders back into the kitchen and jams a tea cosy over her head. Now she threatens Sam with a teapot.

"How *dare* you encourage that monkey to mock me!" she splutters. "I've put up with you for all these years and what thanks do I get? Rudeness and tricks! I never wanted you here!"

"So you keep telling me, Auntie. In which case, why did you take me in?"

Sam steps backwards to avoid being jabbed with the spout of the teapot. She's asked Aunt Candy this question many times before but has never had a satisfactory answer.

"Your *only* friend, the orange monkey, turned up with you on my doorstep like rubbish blown in from the street," she snaps. "Could I shoo her away? No! She barged past me and put you to bed in my knicker drawer. She wouldn't even let me throw you out of the window. I've been stuck with you ever since."

Sam folds her arms defiantly.

"Lola isn't a monkey and she isn't smelly. She's an ape and she's been a better mother to me than you ever have."

This much is true. Aunt Candy showed no interest in caring for Sam when she was a baby. She worked in a night club and any money that she earned went on clothes and beauty treatments, in the hope that one day the man she loved would come back and marry her; but he never did. Meanwhile, Baby Sam had to sleep in the knicker drawer. Aunt Candy gave her no cot, no comfort and no love. I think she had none left to give.

Luckily, Lola was very maternal. She loved Sam as if she were her own baby. She fed her with a bottle, combed her silky, dark hair and knew just where to rub if she had wind. She bathed her in a washing-up bowl and carefully powdered her. She put her to bed in the knicker drawer and if she cried, she would rock her in her long, strong arms until she fell asleep. She never left Sam's side – she daren't, for fear that Aunt Candy would kill her.

Sam hardly ever cried. She was too young to realize how much she had to cry for; but on the odd occasion when she did, Lola would amuse her with magic tricks she'd learnt from her previous owner. His name will become familiar to you soon.

For now, it's enough to know that Lola could make a pebble appear from nowhere, then – *puff!* – she would make it disappear, and little Sam would gurgle with delight. Lola could make a white daisy turn into a pink one, and once she turned a frog into a raspberry bun. It was a good illusion. Lola was so silent and dextrous, the lady on the bench next to theirs (to whom the bun belonged) never saw her take it.

As Sam grew older, Lola taught her how to do these tricks for herself. She had a natural instinct for it. Making a coin disappear was child's play; she mastered it before she could walk. As a toddler, her sleight of hand was so good she could fool you into thinking a paper cup could be pushed through a solid oak table.

By the time Sam was four, she could put three silk ribbons in her mouth and when she pulled them out –

abracadabra – they would be neatly knotted together. Soon, she was creating her own illusions. She fitted secret compartments into matchboxes and made magic hoops out of coat hangers. She practised for hours in front of a mirror until each trick was perfect. As she had no human company, it was her only source of amusement. Apart from Lola, magic was the one thing that made her happy.

Sadly, Sam couldn't share that happiness with Aunt Candy. She had to learn to keep her tricks up her sleeve. Once, when she was nine, Sam made the mistake of thinking she could endear herself to her aunt by showing off her magic skills and produced a baby mouse from under the lid of the butter dish.

It was a sweet mouse, a neat illusion, and the butter wasn't spoilt; but instead of greeting it with applause, Aunt Candy flew into a rage. She threw the dish and the mouse out of the window, locked Sam in the broom cupboard and made her promise never to do magic again.

If Lola hadn't found the key, she'd have been left in the cupboard all night.

From that day forward, Sam only dared to practise magic in secret; her aunt had no idea what an expert she'd become until just now.

Earlier today, Aunt Candy had announced that she was going to the pub and wouldn't be back before six. Thinking she had the house to herself, Sam had gone into Aunt Candy's bedroom and borrowed her old circus clothes. Completing the outfit with a ringmaster's hat she found in the back of the wardrobe, Sam had covered the kitchen table with a sparkly cloth and performed her latest illusions in front of Lola.

She was just coming to the finale when Aunt Candy came home early, caught her in the act and became hysterical. That's when we arrived and began to watch them through the window.

Lola has been shut in the kitchen. Sam is backing away from the teapot, and wigless, drunken Aunt Candy is forcing her to march backwards up the stairs that lead to the attic.

"I told you, no magic! No magic … ever!"

She kicks the attic door open and pushes Sam inside.

"*Please*… Let me out! I didn't mean any harm," Sam pleads.

Aunt Candy is merciless. She locks the door, puts the key down her cleavage and goes back to the pub.

Sam is left alone in the dark.

How to speak Motu

ENGLISH	MOTU
Ape	Ataiai
Bag	Puse
Big Magic	Bada Karaia
Box	Maua
Boy	Meru
Chant	Sing-Sing
Death	Dina
Father	Tamana
Girl	Kekeni
Good	Namo
Grandchild	Tubuna
Grandfather	Papa Tumbuna
Guide	Hakaua
Hello	Ororo
Hornbill	Kokomo
Journey	Laola
Mother	Sinana
Shaman	Hegeregere
Trick	Idia-Edia
One	Ta
Two	Rua
Three	Toi

YAFER TABUH

If you look through the keyhole into the attic you won't be able to see much. The skylight is so filthy, everything inside is thrown into silhouette: broken candelabra, limbless dolls, books, more books, and boxes full of – what?

Sam is curled up against a battered leather trunk with her head in her hands. She's crying. This is a rare event; she's not one for self-pity. There's a butterfly trapped in a cobweb in the window and she's sad that it died with only a thin sheet of glass between death and freedom.

She feels guilty. Last night, she dreamed about a butterfly trapped in an attic. Now she's punishing herself for ignoring her dream and failing to rescue it.

Sam is plagued by dreams that often turn out to be premonitions. They're most vivid when she's on the blurry edge of half-asleep, half-awake, just as she is now. Her sobs turn to shudders which slowly ebb away. Her eyelids flicker. She lays her head on her wrist and – though it may be just the rush of her own pulse – she's certain she can hear a primitive drum beat:

Bom-*bom bomba,* **bom**-*bom bomba,* **bom**-*bom bomba!*

The drum beat is getting louder and louder. Bright pictures come into Sam's head – a fitful dream? A vision? Call it what you will, it's as real as anything. Beads of perspiration appear on her brow but she has no fever. The sun is steaming. There's an intoxicating smell of wild orchids.

She fans herself. Leaf-sweat drips off the sago palm trees and plops like musical notes into the green-blue water of the Sepik River. The raucous call of the Torresian crow announces the arrival of the witch doctor; he's beating a drum trimmed with fur.

The witch doctor's name is Yafer Tabuh. He's smaller than he looks, but his presence is huge. The bird of paradise feathers in his headdress are two metres high. He wears a necklace threaded with hornbill beaks the size of bananas. He has a pair of boar's tusks thrust through his nostrils and his copper-coloured skin is tattooed with crocodile scales.

Here he comes, leaning on a stick with a monkey-head handle; the one he inherited from his grandfather. He's not alone. A youth in a bush hat follows in his footsteps. It's the witch doctor's son, but you wouldn't guess to look at him.

The son is tall and slender. His skin is the colour of olives. His eyes are green, and although his hair is dark, it's sleek and straight and flows over his elegant shoulders like a mane. He has his mother's English nose and he is breathtakingly handsome. As far as the witch doctor is concerned though, his son's good looks count for nothing; he is not pleased with him.

Resting against the bank of the river among the mandrake roots is a dugout canoe – a mwa sawah. There's nothing to distinguish it from any other canoe apart from its familiar passenger; an orang-utan. It's Lola, only younger. Sam recognizes her immediately and waves excitedly in her sleep.

The witch doctor tells his son to get into the canoe but the boy is reluctant. His father speaks to him firmly in his tribal tongue, which is Motu. Sam has never heard the language before, but this is dreamtime and, somehow, she understands every word.

"You will always be my number one son, but you are *sceptical*!" groans the witch doctor. "Have you forgotten the day you came to me with your pet orang-utan dead in your arms and begged me to bring her back to life? Unless my memory fails me, I removed the poisoned dart from her chest, chanted my chant and resurrected her. Is she not sitting in that canoe, grinning away in a very lifelike manner or have I gone mad?"

The boy replies in excellent English, "She's alive and grinning, Father, and I'm sure you're not nearly as mad as you look."

"But *still* you do not believe in my ancient magic!" The witch doctor sulks.

The lad folds his arms and tries to explain himself.

"It's not that I don't *believe*. It's just that my dear departed mother taught me to question everything in the western way. I can't help wondering if Lola wasn't quite as dead as I thought, and that her amazing recovery was brought about by an antidote which you cleverly mixed, rather than as a result of spells and chanting, that's all."

Yafer Tabuh shakes his head so hard, the beaks on his hornbill necklace clack together like machine-gun fire.

"ALL?" he shrieks. "That's *ALL*? He who questions the witch doctor's magic has no faith! When I die, you will not be fit to step into my shoes!" The fact that he isn't wearing any shoes is neither here nor there. "I have no other child to instruct in the ancient magic," he rants. "It will die with me; the villagers will die without me and so will this whole way of life. Do you want that on your conscience, number one son?"

The boy bows his head. "No, Father. I'll be the next witch doctor if you insist, and I'd have every faith in your power if you could answer me one tiny little question."

Yafer Tabuh throws his hands in the air.

"Always questions! What *now*?"

His son looks him straight in the eye.

"If you truly brought Lola back to life with your ancient magic, why couldn't you do the same for Mother?"

There's an awkward silence. The witch doctor twiddles the boar's tusks in his nose, until his nostrils flare so wide you could stuff an orange up each one. He snorts as he paces up and down, muttering to himself in Motu.

"My own son suspects I allowed his mother to die because my *magic* was weak? Yet I loved his mother more than he loves himself … this just won't do! For all our sakes, I must send him to the four corners of the Earth and work Big Magic on him." He unties the goat skin pouch from around his waist and throws it into the canoe. "My son, in answer to your question, it is pointless asking *me* any questions, because you do not trust my answers. Get into the mwa sawah!"

The boy wants to refuse; he likes living here. It's a pleasant life, pottering round the rainforest. There are no man-eating tigers. Although the rain gets a bit boring and a holiday abroad would be nice, he suspects this isn't what his daddy has in mind.

He dare not disobey him. Although he doubts his father's ability to raise the dead, he's seen him flatten enemy crops with a wave of his hand. He's seen him raise a storm on a sunny day and, once, he saw him kill a crocodile by fixing it with a nasty glare. The witch doctor isn't to be messed with, so the son climbs into the canoe next to Lola and awaits instructions.

"Because you are so very fond of questions, you are to go on a quest," announces the witch doctor. "Inside this goatskin pouch you will find, among other things, a notebook. In the notebook is a list of Very Important People I want you to meet."

"Friends of yours?" asks the son.

"Some are scholars, some are scientists, some are magicians; but none are who they seem. Ask them what you like, but be sure to find the answers to these three questions: What is magic? What is illusion? What is real?"

The son is puzzled; why those particular questions?

Yafer Tabuh rolls his eyes. "If you find the answers to them, you will no longer question my power. You will have absolute faith in me and return home bearing the greatest gift you could ever give your father."

"A new set of drums?" queries the boy.

"No."

"Some strappy sandals?"

"No!"

The boy stops being flippant and tries again. "A wise and wonderful young candidate to replace your good self?"

The witch doctor grins broadly, exposing his teeth which have been filed into points. "Ha! You have knocked the coconut right on the head."

His son sighs deeply. He doesn't want to be a witch doctor when he grows up. The hours are too long, the training's too hard and he doesn't like the uniform. He's always dreamed of being an anthropologist like his mother. Or a crab fisherman. Or a poet. Yet here he is, at the tender age of eighteen, being told that he must be the next witch doctor or else.

He has one last attempt at getting out of it.

"You won't need me to replace you, Father," he says. "When you die, you can bring yourself back to life, surely? Do I have to go right now? You're not *that* old!"

The witch doctor stamps his foot. "I am getting older by the second. Hurry up and leave!"

The boy is just about to pull on the oar when he thinks of yet another question to trouble his father with.

"What if I *fail* to find the answers to the three questions?"

"You can never come home."

Never coming home seems rather melodramatic, even by his father's standards. Number one son laughs uproariously, but he soon shuts up when he realizes the witch doctor isn't joking. His face falls and although his upper lip is stiff and British, his bottom lip quivers slightly.

"What, *never*? But where will I live? What will I do?"

"That is for you to find out. Now, I don't want to hear another word. Off you go. Keep paddling. That's the way…"

As the boat bearing the witch doctor's son drifts down the Sepik River past the Spirit House decorated with the skulls of tribal ancestors and begins its journey into the unknown, Sam opens her eyes. She's almost awake, the images are fading but she can still hear the splash of the canoe paddle – or is just the sound of the water tank suspended on the attic wall?

She's disorientated. She sits up. The movement causes the catch on the trunk to flick up and the lid flies open.

What's inside? A goatskin pouch with a crocodile-claw clasp. It's just like the one the witch doctor gave to his son. Dare she touch it? What if the pouch is like Aladdin's lamp or Pandora's box? What genie, what dark force, might lurk within?

The lure is too great. As Sam snaps open the pouch, it exhales like a lung and the attic fills with the sun-baked dream-smell of the banks of the Sepik River. Its contents spill out onto her lap – a shard of human bone, an oyster shell containing three pearls, and a tortoiseshell locket.

Inside the locket is a faded photograph of a white woman in sensible shorts. She has a baby boy sitting on her hip, wearing a big smile and an even bigger bush hat. Who are they? Relatives of Aunt Candy's perhaps?

In the bottom of the pouch is an ancient, tattered notebook bound with snakeskin. The pages are made of the crudest hand-pulped, sundried paper sewn together with sinew. Sam flicks through them with her thumb, revealing an animated whirr of notes, spells and diagrams, all rendered with a quill in fading berry juice.

The book falls open near the middle, marked with a piece of card. This is modern card, strictly out of place in this antique volume. Sam turns it over. It is a black and white photograph of a handsome man in a magician's outfit pulling a rabbit out of a hat. It's signed with a flourish: The Dark Prince of Tabuh.

Sam's heart thumps. The second she sees him, she *knows* who he is; he's the witch doctor's son. He has the same eyes, the same English nose and now that he has no hat on, she can see that he has a curious blond streak in his dark hair – just like hers.

Could he possibly be her long-lost father? The more Sam stares at his face, the more she's convinced. Aunt Candy lied! Her father isn't Bingo Hall. He isn't a backstreet bungler; he's the Dark Prince! But how did his photo end up in this notebook, in this attic?

Is he dead or alive? Where and why and who is the Dark Prince of Tabuh?

She gazes at the open pages of the notebook. There

is an incantation; it's written in blood because this is a resurrection chant. It's in Motu and, although Sam is awake and this isn't a dream, she understands every word.

She reads the chant aloud and as she does so, she hears the faraway voice of the witch doctor joining in, as if they're singing a solemn duet. She stands up and, taking the shard of yellow bone in her hand, she continues to chant. As she chants, she points the bone at the skylight. *Flick, flick, flick.* The butterfly flutters. Shocked, Sam drops the bone. Has the chant worked? She examines its wings. It's still again now. Was it just the breeze through the gap in the glass that made it seem alive just then? Maybe it was never dead, just dying. Maybe it still has a little life left in it.

She rescues the butterfly from the tatty web and cradles it in her hand. Still not certain if it's dead or alive, she stands on a pile of books and, taking the goatskin pouch and its contents with her, climbs out of the skylight onto the roof. She opens her fingers and a gust of wind carries the butterfly away. Did it fly or did it fall? How can we ever know? Sam sits down, her head full of questions:

1. Is the Dark Prince of Tabuh really my father?
2. Is my grandfather really a witch doctor?
3. How do I get down from this roof?

She needn't worry about the last question. If you look at the chimney pot to your left, you will see a furry face sticking out, covered in soot; it's Lola. She's climbed up the inside of the chimney to rescue Sam. There is mutual hugging and smacking of lips, then Sam grabs the notebook and the goatskin pouch and slides down the drainpipe on Lola's back.

They climb back into the flat through the bathroom window and go to bed. Sam lies down on her thin mattress on the floor of the poky boxroom. She can't sleep; she's too excited. She rewinds the dream she had in the attic, replaying it over and over in her head. She sighs and puts her arm around Lola, who is dozing on the sooty pillow.

"I wish you could speak, Lola. Then you could tell me if you really did belong to the son of a witch doctor. In which case, how come you're here with me in London? As for being resurrected, I'm sure *that* can't be true."

Even so, she can't help parting the fur on Lola's chest to see if there might just be a scar left by a poisoned dart... There *is* a scar! But it could be an old fleabite. Sam pulls the blankets over them both.

"Lola, we mustn't say a word to Aunt Candy – not yet."

"Oo–oo."

They're asleep when Aunt Candy comes rolling home. She is crashing about in the kitchen, looking in cupboards and drawers for Lola.

"I know you're here somewhere, smelly monkey! Are you in the fridge? No!"

She can't work out how something the size of an orang-utan could have escaped. The kitchen door is still locked. The window is still closed.

"Ah…" she slurs. "I know your li'l game!" She sticks

her head up the chimney. "Mon–keeee! I know you're up there!"

Her glass of gin fills with soot. Oblivious, she takes a swig and stomps up to the attic, cursing. She rummages among the cinders in her cleavage for the key, kicks open the door and peers into the darkness.

"Spam? Are you there, Spam? It's Auntie Candy!"

No reply.

"If you don't come out this instant, I'll put you in an orphanage. I'll put you in a … zoo! No, I'll put you in a bucket and throw you down the toilet."

Sam, as you know, is no longer there. Aunt Candy is too sozzled to work out how she got away, but she suspects that her scheming little niece and the ape are in cahoots – they must be separated. The orang-utan is a ginger menace.

It will have to go.

How to Palm a Coin

Palming is a technique for holding or concealing small objects in the hand. With practice, the hand containing the palmed object appears to be completely empty.

1. Hold the coin between the muscle which forms the base of thumb and fleshy area of palm beneath the little finger.
2. Use slight pressure to keep the coin in place.
3. From most angles the hand should appear relaxed and natural.

SCHOOL AND SPARROWS

I f you listen hard, you may hear a sound like a pig being slaughtered in Aunt Candy's bedroom. Do not fret; it's nothing so barbaric. It's just Aunt Candy snoring. She's fallen asleep in her day clothes again, poor old love.

She can't lie in a bed like a normal person. Being a contortionist, she finds it uncomfortable. All the bits that hold her together have lost their elastic, so she has to sleep folded up in a rum barrel, which amplifies every porky grunt and squeak.

In her youth, Candy was brown-eyed and slender with the silkiest, ice-blonde hair. She had a 23-inch waist and wonderful knees. Everywhere she went, she turned heads; now it's just stomachs.

There are photographs to prove she was beautiful once. Strangely, there are none of Christa. Sam has never seen a photo of her mother. Given that Christa and Candy were sisters, she used to hope her mum looked as lovely as Candy did before the drink destroyed her.

Apparently not. Aunt Candy always insists that Christa was so hideous she broke the camera lens. She claims that Christa was such an ugly baby the midwife slapped her mother. Sam doesn't believe it; every girl wishes her mother to be beautiful and she is no exception.

The snoring continues. While Aunt Candy is out for the count, Sam sits up in bed with Lola and studies the witch doctor's notebook by the dawn light. It's the first chance she's had to look at it properly. The bulb in her bedside lamp broke years ago. Aunt Candy is too mean to replace it so it's impossible for her to read after dark.

Unfortunately, even the brilliant sunrise fails to illuminate some of the words. The handwriting is faded in places and there are bookworm holes too. Among other things, she notices incomplete chants for luring goats into cooking pots, unfinished dance movements for raising storms and only half the ingredients needed to make a volcano erupt. Sam sighs.

"It's so frustrating, Lola. Say we wanted to make Mount Etna erupt? Well, we can't. It says here to grind the nose of a red kangaroo and mix it into a paste with Bogong moths baked in sand. Only I can't see how many moths we need. The writing's blurred and it's no good trying to guess. Too few moths and the volcano might not even come to the boil. Too many and the universe could explode."

Fortunately the Dark Prince of Tabuh had attached several sheets of fresh paper at the end of the notebook complete with his own notes written clearly in biro. As well as jotting down the three questions his father had given him, there are ideas for new tricks, sketches for magic box designs and a few personal scribbles, including a heart doodled with the initial *C*.

If the *C* stood for Christa, he must have loved her mother once. But if he wasn't an Intrepid Explorer or the philandering Bingo Hall, why did he leave? Why would he abandon his motherless child? Did he really not want her, or was there some other mysterious reason that Aunt Candy had failed to mention? Sam is determined to find out.

She flicks through the book to see if she can discover the list of Very Important People the witch doctor wanted his son to visit. At first, she can't find it – it's hiding between the first page and the inside cover, which for some reason are stuck together.

Slowly, carefully, she prises them apart. She's almost done it when suddenly, Aunt Candy screams in her sleep and Sam tears the bottom of the page. The last name on the list is obliterated for ever.

Ah, well. Perhaps she was never meant to read it; all the others are intact. Each one has a map and a thumbnail portrait next to it. There's no room to show you here, which is a shame because the drawings are hilarious.

However, there's no reason why you can't see the list. It might not seem to be in any particular order – it's neither alphabetical nor geographical – but there's a *magic* order. The list is bewitched; the names shift positions when the book is closed. At certain times, certain names call attention to themselves, but only if they're read by the intended person.

Here they all are, except for the last name, which, as you

know, was torn. Make of it what you will. The names will crop up again and again.

Mrs Reafy

Athea Furby

Father Bayu

Ruby Featha

Bahut

Bart Hayfue

Mr Fraye

Hubert Faya

Effie Ray

Yorba Hufat

Beau Farthy

Fu Bar Yotah

Tuhab

Ruth Abafey

Fey Ra

Abu Yarfhet

We will now leap forward a week. With the aid of the magician's notes Sam has built a false compartment into the orange crate she uses as a bedside cabinet. She's hidden the witch doctor's notebook and the goatskin pouch inside. Aunt Candy still hasn't forgiven her for escaping from the attic. She's thought of a devious way of getting rid of Lola while Sam's at school today.

School is not a happy place for Sam. She has no friends. It's not that the other children are deliberately cruel; they just think she's odd and leave her alone. They huddle in little gangs in the playground and play games she doesn't know the rules for. Or they talk about television programmes she knows nothing about. Aunt Candy has no TV. No radio. No computer.

Sam can never bring anyone home in case they tell the rest of the class about her drunken aunt and her poky bedroom. Then there's the problem of her clothes.

Although Sam dresses in the correct school colours – red and grey – her uniform is by no means standard; it's made from chopped-down versions of Aunt Candy's old circus outfits. All the other girls wear plain red-wool blazers, but Sam's is made from silk and shot through with glitter. None of the teachers comment on her uniform, but the children do. Not to her face; they're afraid of her in the way that some of us are scared of spiders no matter how many times we're told they mean us no harm.

Sam isn't bothered about being friendless; she's used to it. She enjoys her lessons, but the subject she *really* likes to study is People. She watches them constantly and makes notes, such as these:

a) When people like something, their pupils dilate.

b) People often scratch themselves when they are lying.

c) Tugging the earlobes means people are nervous.

She has been observing body language since she was a baby. Aunt Candy hardly ever spoke to her, and when she did, she slurred. Lola can't talk human, so Sam learnt to read facial expressions instead, partly to make up for the lack of conversation, but also for self-defence.

If the muscles in Aunt Candy's jaw twitched, it meant she was about to scream. If the vein in her temple throbbed, it was a three-second warning that she was about to throw a vase at Sam's head. Being able to predict this gave her a chance to duck out of the way.

Sam can read people's emotions even if they try to

disguise them. Body language always gives them away: a scratch of the head, a twitch, a slightly unnatural grin. She notices and can calculate their state of mind with frightening accuracy.

It's morning break now, and she's in the playground observing a group of children. Without hearing their conversation, she can tell they're concerned about something they've found under the rose bushes by the art block. They don't want to touch it; whatever it is must be dead. And it's a small creature because they're crouching over it. They look sorry for it, so it must be an animal that looks sweet in death, rather than a dried frog or a squashed rat. As they keep looking up at the window, she guesses it's a bird that crashed into the glass pane and broke its neck.

She's right. It's a sparrow. One of the smallest girls is stroking its head with a pencil. She doesn't like to touch it with her hands.

"Aw, poor little fing. Wot a shame. Wish I could bring it back to life."

"Do you?" says Sam.

The girls turn and look up at her, not quite sure why she's there. They didn't hear her coming.

"Go away, you. It's our dead bird," says Smallest Girl.

Sam kneels down and studies the bird.

"I could bring it back to life if you like."

Smallest Girl stares at Sam and pulls a face.

"No, you can't. It's dead, look!" She prods it with her pencil again. "It's gone stiff." She rolls the bird over in the dust, its eyes glazed, feet in the air.

"Yeah, it's stiff," says her friend. "You can't bring it back to life, unless you're Jesus."

"Or a magician," says Smallest Girl.

Sam scoops the dead bird into her hands. It weighs almost nothing.

"Ugh, dead birds have fleas. My nan told me," says the friend of Smallest. Sam smiles.

"I can make it come back to life."

"You're lying," say the girls in unison. "Liar, liar."

They dance around her in a ring. Other children stop what they're doing and wander over; they want to know what Sam Khaan is lying about. She reckons she can bring that dead bird back to life? Yeah, right! Like to see her try. Go on, Khaan, prove it!

"All right, I will." She puts the bird in her lunchbox.

"Ugh! She's gonna eat it!" interrupts Smallest.

Sam ignores her and tells everyone present to meet her under the birch tree after lunch. "I will make this dead sparrow fly."

No one believes her but they all want to see her fail, so Smallest Girl, all her friends and all their friends spread the word: the weirdo in the funny uniform is going to perform a miracle. She'll probably just chuck the dead bird over the fence and say it flew, pretend it came alive. Yeah, that's what she'll do. Not like she's Jesus, is it? No.

By lunchtime, the whole of the lower school has heard about it. They are all meandering down to the birch tree at the bottom of the field, trying not to arouse suspicion among the staff on playground duty. "No, we're not up to nuffing, miss!" "We're not going anywhere, sir." "Down to the birch tree? No, sir!"

Sam is waiting for them; she knows the resurrection chant off by heart. If it doesn't work, she has Plan B up her sleeve. She arranges the dead sparrow on a pad of grass inside her lunchbox in preparation.

The first group of kids arrives. Smallest Girl and friends sit at her feet like disciples. Some boys arrive. They don't want to sit down but Smallest Girl whines at them, "Sit down, will ya? Else I can't see!"

"Yeah, sit down!" yells the crowd.

They gather and gather. Sam didn't think there'd be quite so many.

"Get on with it," says Trevor Randle from Year 9. "Or I'll kick your lying butt."

"Watch!" commands Sam. She removes the lid from her lunchbox and throws it into the air – it vanishes. Already their eyes and their brains are confused; they were expecting one thing, but something else happened. Now they don't know what to expect, and Sam has their full attention.

Everyone stops messing around. What has she done with the lid? It can't have just disappeared – or can it? They are so busy worrying about the lid, they can't catch up with what she's doing next. They're always a few seconds behind and that's all the time she needs. She shows them the contents of the box.

"See the poor sparrow! It is dead. It is cold and stiff. I would like a volunteer to touch it to prove that it is not merely asleep. Any fool can wake the sleeping, but *I* can wake the dead." No one in the audience moves. Sam fixes her eyes on Trevor Randle. "You believe it's dead then?"

"No, but I ain't touching it. It might have fleas."

Smallest Girl pushes herself up.

"Oh, *I'll* do it. I want fleas. You get a day off school." She strokes the bird's head with her finger and shudders slightly. "It's dead all right, poor fing."

Sam nods. "It *is* dead … but not for much longer."

She cups the broken corpse in her hands, lowers her voice and begins to chant in Motu. She thought they might heckle, but they don't; they're *still* looking for the lunchbox lid. Now she's chanting in an ominous language they don't understand. The resonance and rhythm lulls their minds to the point of numbness.

Suddenly, she opens her hands and the sparrow flutters into the sky. There's a collective gasp. Some of the girls shriek. No one was expecting that, least of all Trevor Randle. For all his jeering and bravado, he doesn't like it at all; it frightens him.

"No way did that happen. That's sick."

Smallest Girl brushes grass from her skirt "Wassup, Trev? I fink it's nice. I'm glad the sparra' came back to life."

The boy is riled. "What are you saying, little mad girl? Things don't come back from the dead."

"Forget it, Trev," says his mate. "It's a trick. It wasn't dead, it can't have been."

"*Was* dead," mumbles Smallest Girl.

Trevor shoves his friend hard in the chest. "It was dead; now it ain't!"

"P'raps it's gone to heaven," says Smallest, which only makes Trevor angrier.

"Shut *up*! Unless you want to go to heaven an' all … do ya?" He points angrily at Sam. "You're evil, man. I want you out of this school. I'm gonna grass you up, pikey!"

Two other lads hold him back, but he catches one of them on the chin. A fight breaks out. All the boys bundle in, feet and fists flailing. Blazers rip. Eyes are poked. Buttons pop. First a resurrection, then a ruck; it's a lot more exciting than double Maths.

Smallest Girl runs off to fetch a teacher before someone gets maimed; she knows she'll get house points for Telling. Sam steps back, retrieves the lid from the inside of her blazer and puts it back on her lunchbox; no one notices.

Seconds later, a red-faced teacher arrives to break up the fight. He marches Trevor Randle by the collar to the headmistress's office and it is there that the boy grasses on Sam. "It was Sam Khaan started it, miss. She brought a dead bird back to life. Ask anyone."

Every pupil confirms his story so the headmistress has no choice but to phone Sam's carer, Miss Candy Khaan, and ask her to come up to the school. The phone rings while Candy is in her rum barrel; she is furious at being woken.

Aunt Candy arrives at the school on her rusty old bike with her wig on backwards and totters into the headmistress's office. "What have you done *now*?" She screams at Sam.

The headmistress describes the incident on the school field; the bringing back to life of the dead sparrow. The school doesn't allow resurrections; it mustn't happen again.

Aunt Candy stamps her feet in irritation. "It's a trick. An illusion. Search her!"

Sam shifts uneasily. Aunt Candy glares at her, the vein in her temple throbbing. "Come along, Spam! Show Miss Looney what you're hiding."

The headmistress fiddles with her glasses nervously. "*Langley*. My name is Miss Langley." She's fond of Sam and not in the least bit fond of Aunt Candy, but she has a duty to get to the bottom of this, so she asks Sam to turn out her pockets.

Sam places the contents of her top pocket on Miss Langley's desk; a biro and a coin. She empties the bottom pocket; there's nothing in there except a pack of cards. Miss Langley tries to make light of things. "Not gambling, I hope."

"No, miss."

"Good girl."

Aunt Candy bangs her fist on the desk and screeches. "*Good girl?* She's a liar! A cheat! Check her *inside* pockets. Let's take her blazer off!" Without warning, she marches over to Sam, yanks her blazer off, turns it upside down and shakes it.

Miss Langley panics. "Miss Khaan, I really don't think that's appropria—"

A very dead sparrow drops out of Sam's pocket onto the carpet. Another second and she'd have managed to hide it behind a cushion, but the attack was too sudden.

"See?" shrieks Aunt Candy. "There was no resurrection!

45

The brat pocketed the dead bird and released a live one hidden in her blazer. Cane her, Miss Looney!"

"Oh, no, we don't have a cane."

Aunt Candy looks very disappointed. "Don't have a cane? Well, what *do* you have? Got any thumbscrews?"

Miss Langley shakes her head.

"No thumbscrews?" yells Candy, "No wonder there's no discipline! And I have to say the hygiene in this school is appalling, Miss Looney."

"The hygiene?"

"There is a dead bird on your rug. I'm not keeping my niece at this filthy, feeble school a day longer. Come, Spam! We're leaving."

"But, Aunt Candy, I don't want to leave."

Despite Miss Langley's pleas for calm, Aunt Candy grabs Sam's hand and drags her outside. Then she sits on the bike, puts her feet on the handle bars and refuses to pedal. "You can push me all the way home, Spam, then you can have your surprise."

It is Sam's birthday today. The occasion is never celebrated, but today is her thirteenth. Ever the optimist, she wonders if Aunt Candy might have bought her a card for once. Or a small gift. Or baked her a cake.

But what are the chances of that happening?

HOW TO SPOT A LIAR

If someone is lying, their body language is sure to give them away. Here's how.

1. They avoid eye contact.

2. They touch their face, throat and mouth a lot.

3. They scratch their nose or behind their ear.

4. They wear a false smile (if it's a real smile, the eyes become squished).

5. If they say, "I love it!" after receiving a gift and only smile after they've said it, they're lying.

6. A guilty person gets defensive.

7. A liar may unconsciously place objects (books, coffee cup, etc.) between themselves and you.

8. A liar uses your last words to answer questions: "Did you hit John?" "No, I did not hit John."

9. A guilty person may speak too much and add unnecessary details to convince you.

10. If you think someone's lying, change the subject. They'll instantly relax, whereas an innocent person will want to go back to the previous subject.

EFFIE RAY

Lola has gone. Sam searches everywhere, but an orang-utan isn't easy to lose. She isn't on the roof or in the attic or sleeping in the trees of the communal gardens in St Peter's Square. Sam calls her name over and over, but she doesn't come.

"Surprise!" snorts Aunt Candy. "Lola's not here. She's never coming back. Get over it."

Sam's stomach sinks. Her eyes prickle with tears but she refuses to let them fall. "What have you done with her?"

Aunt Candy is walking around on all fours with her back arched like a demented crab.

"I've sent her to a lovely zoo. You can't keep an orang-utan in a little flat, it's cruel. An orang-utan needs to be with its hairy friends, doing monkey things."

"Which zoo? Tell me which zoo!"

Aunt Candy raises her eyebrows. "What's it called now? Let me think... Ah, I remember. It's The Zoo for Nosy Parkers."

It doesn't take an expert in body language to know that Aunt Candy is lying. Sam feels like kicking her feet out from under her, but she doesn't; she's not a violent person.

"Why did you get rid of her? Just to hurt me?"

Aunt Candy looks mortally offended. "I got rid of her because she's been teaching you tricks – I hate tricks. I've asked you not to do them, but you carry on behind my back and I won't have it."

"But *why* do you hate magic so much?"

Aunt Candy won't answer, so Sam decides to risk everything and mentions the F-word.

"Is it to do with my father, the *magician*?"

She guesses it is, because suddenly Aunt Candy's knees buckle. She collapses, cracks her head on the floor and lies there cackling hysterically.

"Magician? Your father isn't a magician. No, no, no. Whatever gave you that idea? He's Bingo Hall. He's an explorer. A murderer. A vicar … a postman."

"No, he isn't; he's the Dark Prince of Tabuh."

At the mention of his name, Aunt Candy starts frothing at the mouth. "No, no! He's a grave digger, a dustman, a donkey!" She flips onto her stomach and lashes out like a serpent. "How d'you know he's the Dark Prince? Who told you, WHO TOLD YOU?"

It would be so easy for Sam to admit that she's found the witch doctor's notebook and seen her father's photo, but she wants to keep that to herself.

"I'm psychic," she says. "I dreamt about my father. He has a blond streak, just like mine, doesn't he, Aunt Candy?

I know I'm right. Now, where's Lola? If you lie to me, I'll know. My dreams will tell me where she is." Sam is exaggerating about her dreams. They won't tell her where Lola is but she wants Aunt Candy to think they will, to freak her out. She hopes it will make her confess and it does.

"All right, you meddling little runt!" she snaps. "I didn't put your stupid ginger friend in a zoo. I sent her to a laboratory where she will help the nice scientists with their experiments."

"But they'll put her in a cage – they'll hurt her! How *could* you, Aunt Candy?"

"Easy! I phoned the laboratory and a man collected her in an armoured van."

Lola would never go anywhere with a stranger, but unfortunately Aunt Candy knew that. "I slipped a tablet into her banana," she confesses. "She was taken away on a stretcher. Looked ever so peaceful."

Sam is not a violent person but she's so upset about Lola, she grabs Aunt Candy by the ears and tries to shake the truth out of her.

"Which laboratory. Where is it?!"

Aunt Candy's chins wobble like a turkey wattle. She seizes Sam's lapels and wrestles her to the ground. There's a lot of slapping and kicking, and in the struggle, her wig slips off and a strand of her real hair ravels round one of Sam's blazer buttons. As Sam struggles to her knees, the trapped hair is ripped out of Aunt Candy's scalp. She clutches her head, screams; then, in a pincer movement, snatches hold of Sam's ponytail and drags her towards the boxroom.

"So you like hair-pulling, do you Spam? I like hair-pulling. Come, brat! Into your poky room and stay there!" She pulls the door shut and shoves a chair under the handle so Sam can't escape. "Your cheeky, chimpy chum can't save you now! You can stay there until you are a good brat, which will be … *never!*"

Sam hammers on the door. "Let me out! Let me out!" But it's useless. Aunt Candy storms off, slumps on the sofa and sips gin through a straw the width of a hosepipe.

Never one to sit there doing nothing, Sam has opened the witch doctor's notebook and is reading how to make a doll in the shape of her worst enemy. According to the pictures, the doll can be used to inflict anything from measles to murder on the person it represents. Mercifully, all Sam wants to do is prevent Aunt Candy from following her; she's decided to run away. She must rescue Lola, then find her father. She wants to ask him why he abandoned her as a baby. If he had good reason and is a good man, she hopes he'll give her a home. If he is bad or dead, she will mourn him and move on; perhaps she'll find some other relative willing to adopt her.

She's made a scary model of Aunt Candy from sticky putty scraped out of the window. For the spell to work, the book says she must incorporate her enemy's nails or hair into the doll. Aunt Candy's nails are false but she's unwillingly donated some hair. Sam unwinds it from her blazer button and uses it to make a topknot which she pins to the doll's head. To stop Aunt Candy following her, she follows the instructions to the letter and binds the doll's ankles together with cotton. Then she sits the doll on the sill and packs her rucksack.

Before packing the goatskin pouch, Sam takes out the locket and smiles at the photo of the woman carrying the baby boy on her hip. If the boy is the Dark Prince, she must be his mother – which means she's Sam's grandmother. She ties the locket around her neck and says a final goodbye to her home in St Peter's Square. There's nothing to keep her here, but even so it's a wrench – it's all she's ever known. Sometimes, no matter how bad things are, we stick with what we know because it's less frightening than what we don't. But there's no hope for her or Lola if she stays.

She puts on the ringmaster's hat and gathers a few tricks. If she needs money, she can always perform illusions on a street corner somewhere. People will pay to see magic. Then she opens her bedroom window and climbs out. As she runs across the roof, some of the tiles clatter and smash on the pavement below. Aunt Candy tries to go after Sam, but she can't move her feet; her ankles appear to be glued together and she falls face down on the rug.

Is her temporary paralysis the effect of the witch doctor's doll or is it the first symptoms of a frozen cartilage, something many contortionists suffer from in their later years? It is not for me to say, but by the time it wears off – if it wears off – it will be too late for her to follow Sam. She has lost her and she is too insane, too drunk, to try and find her.

Aunt Candy bursts into tears; it wasn't meant to be like

this. If only Sam had been her child, she could have loved her, would have loved her. She did have a heart once.

By now, Sam is at Stamford Brook tube station. She's dumped Aunt Candy's bike and she's looking at the map, trying to figure out how to get to St Pancras so that she can catch the overground train to St Albans. Why does she want to go there? To visit a certain Mrs Reafy.

Sam has never met Mrs Reafy, but while she was locked in her room, she studied the witch doctor's list again, wondering idly if any of the people on it could help her find Lola or her father. The more she studied it, the more Mrs Reafy's name leapt off the page. As Sam touched it, her hand was thrown aside. It gave her an electric shock and when, for some reason, the room filled with the smell of boiling jam, she felt certain the witch doctor was trying to tell her something and found herself talking to him out loud.

"So, Grandpa, I take it I should visit this lady? I wish your handwriting was clearer. Does she live in St Aubins or St Albans? Oh, well, I'll just have to look her up in a phone book."

Returning to his list, she'd noticed a portrait next to Mrs Reafy's name, depicting a wild-haired woman swinging a potato – or possibly a pendulum – over a diamond buried in the sand. From this drawing, Sam guessed that Mrs Reafy was skilled at locating missing objects, in which case she might be able to find lost apes and absent fathers. It was a long shot, but as she didn't have a shorter one, she planned to go and see her.

Back to now. Sam is on the tube and she's been passing the time by practising coin tricks, making them appear and disappear. Now she must change onto the Piccadilly Line which she does with no trouble at all. She's travelling without a ticket but it's easy to fool the inspector with an old one she found on the floor; she's been taught sleight of hand by a gifted orang-utan after all.

Sam sits on the only seat available in the carriage, opposite an old lady who keeps staring at her hat. Sam smiles briefly then averts her eyes, hoping to be left alone; but the old lady pokes her with a walking stick and pipes up.

"Don't I know you, dear? You look so familiar."

Sam doesn't know the woman but she recognizes her walking stick. Where had she seen it before? The handle has a monkey's head carved into it.

"It was my grandfather's," says the old lady. "Monkeys aren't to everybody's taste, but I've always had a soft spot for our close relatives."

"Me too," says Sam. "I had a pet orang-utan. She was like a mother to me."

The old lady purses her lips. "Really? You don't look like you were brought up by an orang-utan. You have quite nice manners for a child."

"Lola had perfect manners," says Sam, wistfully.

The old lady puts her head on one side. "Had? Don't you have her any more? What happened, did she pass away?"

Who knows why it's so easy to pour out your life story to strangers on trains, but it is. In less time than it takes to write down, Sam tells the woman that she's run away from home to look for Lola and that she's off to St Albans to see if Mrs Reafy can find her.

"You won't get to St Albans today," says the old lady. "No trains until tomorrow. There's a strike." She suggests that Sam goes home to her parents. Sam tells her that's out of the question.

"My mother's dead and my father's done a disappearing act; he's a magician, you know."

"A *magician*?" The old lady rolls the word around in her mouth like a humbug. "I thought your father might have been a ringmaster, judging by your hat. There again, only a fool would judge a person by their hat. It's what goes on *under* it that's important." She prods Sam's seat with her stick.

"I sat opposite a magician once on this train, in this same compartment. I'll never forget him. His magician's outfit was far too big, but he was so fit and young and handsome, he took my breath away; either that or I was allergic to his rabbit."

"He had a rabbit?"

The old lady shrugs. "Rabbits, doves…? I'm guessing. Whatever he had in his trunk, it was alive and fidgeting." She sighs deeply. "He spoke to me, my magician. He had a voice like melting chocolate. All the men on the train hated him; he made their shoulders look narrow and their hair look thin."

"Did he mention his name?" asks Sam.

"No, dear. He just said it was his first time in London and asked if I knew a good place for a penniless magician to perform. I suggested Covent Garden."

"Why?"

"Have you never been? There are fire-eaters, mime artists, all manner of entertainers; it's famous for them. He took my advice and went there. I often wonder what happened to him."

Covent Garden is the next stop. Given that there's no chance of making it to Mrs Reafy's today, Sam decides to get out. Maybe one of the street performers knows her father. The old lady nods and smiles. "Even if no one's heard of him, you'll while away a pleasant afternoon."

Sam shakes her hand. "Thanks, Mrs…? I'm sorry, I don't know your name."

"That's because I didn't tell it to you, Sam. But since you ask, it's Effie Ray. Quickly or you'll miss your stop."

Sam waves goodbye. It's only when she's in the lift that she realizes Effie Ray knew her name – but how? She's sure she didn't tell her. But it's so easy to forget exactly what we've said to complete strangers.

THE MAGIC SUGAR CUBE

The masked magician asks a volunteer to pick a number between 1 and 10 and write it on a sugar cube.

The cube is dropped into a glass of water and the volunteer's hand is held over it.

When the volunteer's hand is turned over – hey presto – the number is written on it. How?

THE SECRET

You need: a pencil, a sugar cube and a glass of water

1. Ask the volunteer to pick a number.
   Write it onto the sugar cube.
   (Press hard!)

2. Hold the cube between your thumb
   and finger and say, "Now I will put
   the cube in the glass!"

3. Press the cube as hard as possible so
   the number transfers onto your thumb.

4. Drop the cube into the water and hold
   the volunteer's hand above it, making sure

   your thumb is in their palm
   so the number from your finger
   transfers onto their hand.

BART HAYFUE

Covent Garden isn't disappointing. It has a market, interesting shops and a large, cobbled square. There's a man selling jumping beans from a suitcase, a Chinese girl on a unicycle, and a fire-eater. As a ribbon of roaring flames shoots from his mouth, there is loud applause, and he hands his hat around.

Sam has run away with no money. She watches the fire-eater as he juggles three flaming torches for a fresh audience. She daren't interrupt him to ask if he's ever met the Dark Prince of Tabuh in case he burns himself; she'll wait for him to finish. Meanwhile, she will try to earn some cash of her own.

Normally, she's self-conscious about her clothes but in Covent Garden the combination of sparkly red jacket, shiny green flares and a ringmaster's hat doesn't look out of place at all. Everyone simply assumes that Sam is another street entertainer, so when she pulls out a pack of cards and shuffles them in a flying arc, several tourists wander over to see what she is up to.

"Ladies and gentlemen, there is nothing up my sleeves … except my arms!"

She performs several basic tricks – the kind she mastered when she was six – but the tourists are genuinely amazed when she finds the Queen of Hearts whilst blindfolded. They're confounded when she produces the missing Ace of Spades from inside a small boy's wellington boot, and delighted when she turns a grey pigeon into a white one. They drop money into her hat. Some are pennies, but most are pounds. Perhaps the tourists are being generous because she's so young. Whatever the reason, she makes eight pounds in as many minutes; it's the richest she's ever been.

Sam is hungry for more. She hasn't eaten since she left home, so she puts her hat back on and pulls out her cards again. She's about to shuffle them when she hears an angry voice.

"Oi, dilly, dilly! Get off my pitch or you shan't be Queen!"

She can't work out who's speaking. The nearest person is the Jumping Bean Man and he has a Mexican accent; this one's definitely cockney.

"Yeah, *you*. Off you go to Banbury Cross. Clear off!"

The voice appears to be coming from a statue of a Victorian pie-seller. It wasn't there a moment ago, or had she been too engrossed in her magic to notice it? She stares at the figure; it can't have spoken – it's made from stone.

Then suddenly the statue blinks. Sam leaps back, cracks her head against a lamppost and sits down hard on her hat. The pie-seller rushes forward to help her up, shedding clouds of grey powder.

"Sorry, Jumping Joan. This is what happens when Simple Simon meets a pieman."

Sam dusts herself down and punches her hat back into shape.

"I'm fine, really. You made me jump, that's all."

The statue laughs, but not unkindly. The pink of his mouth looks luminous and fleshy against his flinty face.

"I made you jump? Occupational hazard, I'm afraid. S'wot I do for a living." He reaches inside his concrete-coated apron and shows her his business card.

BART HAYFUE
LIVING STATUE

Parties, weddings, barmitzvahs

Sam is impressed. "How do you manage to stand so still, Mr Hayfue?"

"Practice, love. Been doing this since the Stone Age. The trick is to wriggle your toes to keep the blood circulating, otherwise you pass out."

"I want to have a go," says Sam. "Tell me if I blink."

Bart gives her his tray of stone pies. She fixes her face and her limbs, stands as still as she can and holds her breath. After a few seconds, he snaps his fingers near her nose.

"Ha, you blinked! You gotta be prepared or all the Contrary Marys will see straight through your disguise. They'll pinch you, tickle you; anything to get a reaction. But if you can ignore it, you'll fool them as easy as three blind mice."

Sam tries again and this time Bart is full of encouragement.

"Pretty good, Polly Flinders. You'll be warming your pretty little toes on my pitch next, only please don't. This spot used to be a good 'un but now I can't move for fire-eaters, jugglers and magicians – not that I'm *supposed* to move, of course."

Sam assures him he can have his pitch back right now. She didn't realize she was standing in his spot. She just needed the money for food.

"You could do with fattening up," he grins. "Fancy a pie, Lucy Locket?"

The ones on his tray look decidedly inedible. Sam pokes one and wrinkles her nose.

"Not *those*. I meant a real pie from the caff. They do a nice one with four and twenty blackbirds and there's Tuppenny Rice for pudding. They bung half a pound of treacle on it, but it's too much for one person, you'll go pop. We'll ask for two spoons and share, all right?"

Sam asks why he keeps quoting nursery rhymes and he explains that when he was a baby, he had a terrible accident. His mother put his cradle at the top of a tree but unfortunately it had been a particularly windy day and the bough broke. Sam smiles. "And down you came, cradle and all, I suppose?"

"You heard about it then?" says Bart. "I bumped my head, you know. Wrapped it in vinegar and brown paper and went to bed, but the damage was done. I've been stuck in nursery rhyme mode ever since. Mother wasn't one to sit on her tuffet. She called Doctor Foster but there was heavy flooding where he lived – Gloucester as I recall – and the poor bloke stepped in a massive puddle and never turned up. So much for the National Health Service, eh?"

Sam has never heard such a load of nonsense. "You're just making all this up aren't you, Bart?"

"Am I? Who are you to say what's fact and what's fiction? For all you know, you're just a character in a book."

"A likely story."

They walk down a side street to the café, away from the smart restaurants. This is where the market traders eat. Although the pies are frozen and there's margarine on the white, ready-sliced bread, Sam has never tasted anything better. She almost kids herself that she's happy but, of course, how can she be when Lola is trapped in a cage somewhere.

Bart, who has made a career out of watching people watching him, watches her. He sees the sadness floating across her eyes in a beautiful pea-green boat.

"What's up, Bo? Lost your sheep?"

She puts her fork down. "Bart, there's something I need to ask you."

"Go on, then. But you'll have to speak up coz I'm stone deaf. *Stone deaf!*" He snorts at his own joke but it doesn't raise a smile. Sam isn't in the mood.

"Bart, did you ever come across a magician called the Dark Prince of Tabuh?"

Bart almost chokes on his gristle. "Blimey ... the Dark Prince? I haven't heard that name in a while."

Yes, Bart had met him. Years ago, mind. He'd met him right here, in Covent Garden. The Dark Prince had just come over from abroad. He'd been working on an ocean liner – one of those cruise ships – but had to leave in a hurry because ... well, he never said why. He was a good-lookin' lad, only he was wearing a magician's outfit that looked like it belonged to a fat bloke. His name wasn't really the Dark Prince, of course. No, that was just his stage name.

"Did he tell you his real name?"

Bart hits himself on the head with his pudding spoon to jog his memory.

"Let me see. Was it Tommy Tucker? No! It was a regular, English name. Was it Bobby Shaftoe? Only he'd been to sea and he was bonny. No, no, his real name was John. John Tabuh – that was it! Why do you ask, d'you know him?"

Sam touches the locket around her neck. "He's my dad. I'm trying to find him. He left when I was a baby."

Bart blinks slowly. Fake stone-dust floats off his eyelashes and lands in his pastry. "I'll tell you what," he says. "Fathers don't just say 'Bye, Baby Bunting' and leave for no reason. Maybe he just went hunting to fetch you a rabbit skin."

"No, if that was the case, he'd be back by now. Aunt Candy told me he was an explorer but I found his photo and his magician notes and ... I *dream* about him."

"I've never had a dream," says Bart. "Not when I'm asleep, anyway. Not even when I was a little boy under a haystack. When I'm sleeping, it's as if the curtains fall and the show's over. There's no encore of events that happened in my life. I only ever have dreams in the day when my eyes are open, when I'm standing still. Maybe I'm dreaming now." He freezes in his chair; his fork halfway to his lips, his mouth fixed in mid-chew. One second he is a man of flesh, the next he is stone. Sam taps his bowl with her fork.

"Bart ... Bart!"

He shakes his head like a dog with wet fur and becomes human again. "Where was I? Has the clock struck one? Has the mouse run down?"

Bart gathers his thoughts and picks up the invisible thread that might lead to John Tabuh. The last time he saw him he was performing tricks where the Jumping Bean Man now stands. Good tricks they were, like he'd been doing them for far longer than his years. John couldn't have been much older than ... what, eighteen?

How did he come to be there? Well, he never said

much, but he did mention he'd met an old lady on the Piccadilly Line who'd told him to get out at Covent Garden. Sam's mouth drops open.

"That's what happened to me! An old lady on the train told me to come here too. I wonder if it was the same person? That would be too much of a coincidence, surely? Unless it's some kind of magic?"

Bart shakes his head. "Not magic, just maths. Coincidences are one a penny, two a penny. It's a small world and a very repetitive one. A very repetitive one. I bet your old lady sits in the same seat on the same train every day and has done for donkey's years. The odds are that ninety-five per cent of old ladies talk to strangers on trains, rising to ninety-nine per cent if the stranger is handsome. If he happens to be a magician, Covent Garden is bound to crop up in conversation, so, statistically, the chances of the same lady talking to you and your dad are much higher than you think."

Sam would have preferred a magical answer to a mathematical one. She toys with a sugar cube and takes out a pencil. "So, Mr Statistics, what are the odds of me finding my father? Give me a number between one and ten."

"Three."

Sam writes it on the sugar cube, drops it in her glass of water and holds Bart's hand over it. "Only three? Are you sure?"

He nods and squeezes her hand. She turns it over. There's a number three written on his palm but he never put it there.

"How did *that* get…?"

"Magic, Bart. If *only* you'd said five. A three in ten chance of finding him is not good."

He wipes crumbs off his lips. "If you want my advice, leave him alone and he'll come home, wagging his tail behind him. On the other hand, if you go after him it might speed things up a bit."

Two schools of thought then, but Sam doubts her father will ever come home of his own accord.

"Have you any idea where he went, Bart?"

"The Old Bill moved him on coz he didn't have a licence for his monkey. So feeling sorry for the bloke, I ran after him and—"

"His monkey? Are you sure it wasn't an ape?"

"Am I a zoo keeper? Monkey, ape? I dunno. It was hairy and ginger and shuffling cards with its toes. Anyway, as I said, I ran after The Dark Prince and—"

"But that was *Lola*!" interrupts Sam, "My orang-utan!"

So now we know how Lola learnt to do magic. She helped John Tabuh with his act. If Sam's dreams are to be trusted, they'd left their home in the rainforest together to find the answer to three questions and somehow they ended up here. They didn't travel all that way in a mwa sawah; they'd been on a cruise ship. But why? And where did John learn to perform magic?

"I think you should find out," says Bart.

Sam pushes her plate to one side. "That's what I'm *try-ing* to do."

First, though, she has to find Lola; it's a matter of life and death. Mrs Reafy might be able to help her, but she can't get there until tomorrow because of the porters' strike. If only she could find her father, he'd know what to do.

Bart orders pudding, but Sam can't eat hers. Not because it's too hot or too cold or because it's nine days old. She's lost her father, her orang-utan and her appetite. Perhaps all is not lost, however...

"'Course, John had nowhere to stay, so I gave him the address of a warehouse he could doss in," says Bart. "My mate Kitty lived there at the time. She did a lot of wood carvings. Liked to keep herself to herself. What was her surname ... Fisher? No, not Fisher. It was Bastet."

Fortified by this new piece of information, Sam picks up her spoon and shovels a large helping of rice pudding into her mouth.

"Mad as a hatter, poor old Kitty," mutters Bart.

"Why mad?"

According to the living statue – who considered himself to be normal in every way – Kitty Bastet was mad because she claimed to be the reincarnation of an Egyptian priestess and worshipped cats; mad because she believed the ancient spirits communicated with her through automatic writing. Sam thinks she sounds wonderful.

"Don't you believe in spirits, Bart?"

"I once met a ghost eating toast – halfway up a lamppost. What's up, why the face?"

Sam looks at him rather strictly. "It's not kind to call your friend mad, Bart."

"She wasn't a close friend."

Kitty had what they call a split personality. Bart reckoned the "spirits" who spoke to her were the voices in her own head.

"Do you think Kitty would talk to me?" asks Sam. "Even if my father has moved out, she might know where he went. Does she still live at the warehouse?"

Bart has no idea. We're talking years ago, but Sam could always go and see. The warehouse is near Docklands. She'd need to get to West India Quay. He pulls out a piece of paper and draws her a map. She thanks him for everything, especially the pudding and pie, and he walks her to the station. He seems sorry to see her go.

"I won't kiss you goodbye," he says. "Georgie Porgie did that and made the girls cry. I don't want to see you cry. Anyone would think I was made of stone." And he gets down on one knee, clutching his hand to his heart. A tear rolls down his dusty cheek and sets like concrete. In a split second, Bart morphs from emotional to motionless.

Sam doesn't look back. She has a quick look at Bart's map but she's in such a hurry, she fails to notice it's drawn on ancient, hand-pulped paper. Mind you, the light is fading.

She changes trains several times. The warehouse is a long walk from West India Quay and by the time she arrives, it is dark. She's not at all sure this is where she should be. There's no warehouse – just scorched earth, scrubby wasteland and rubble.

Hang on … maybe this is the right place. There could have been a warehouse; she can make out where the old foundations used to be – but why isn't it here any more? The wasteland is deserted. There's an ominous chill rising from the wharf. Sam shivers; this is a ware-house grave. Kitty is no longer here, there's no point in staying. She decides to retrace her steps back to West India Quay, catch a night train and sleep at St Pancras station. She'll catch the first train to Mrs Reafy's in the morning.

It's late and dark, and she has a long way to go, so she begins to run. But something in the soil doesn't want her to leave; it trips her up. She falls, grazes both hands and cuts her knee open on sharp metal. As she crouches down to examine her wound, a hunched figure slips out of the shadows and moves quietly about its business.

It's coming towards her.

HOW TO TEAR A COIN IN HALF

You need: A large coin, tin foil, an envelope

1. Cut the corner off an envelope so you have a square pouch.

2. Cover the coin in tin foil and press so the coin is imprinted on the foil.

3. Open the foil, take out the coin, then refold the foil so it looks like a solid coin.

4. Show the fake coin to the audience, put it in the pouch and rip it up – they'll think you've torn the real one.

RUTH ABAFEY

Sam stands as still as Bart Hayfue to make herself invisible to the warehouse ghost. She sighs with relief as it brushes past her: this is no spectre; it's a tiny woman, scratching in the dirt like a shy night creature. A Moon Lady. She hasn't noticed Sam and talks softly to herself.

"Ah, milkweed! Milkweed in full bloom and it's a full moon."

She pulls the herb up by the roots, blows the soil off and places it in a woven basket. Sam wants to ask her about the warehouse, but if she speaks suddenly, it might scare her away. She decides to sing a lullaby; a lullaby is never threatening – unless it's sung by Aunt Candy.

In order not to frighten the Moon Lady, Sam sings airily, so that the words sound like night breeze or the patter of moth's wings. "Rock a bye baby, on the tree top, when the—"

The woman cocks an ear and mutters softly to herself. "Hark! Is that the call of the Torresian crow? Or is it the wind?

No, it is a *girl's* voice!" She straightens up like a rabbit trying to guess where the vixen is lurking. "Girl? Show yourself! Come out of the shadows and show yourself."

Sam waves her hand slowly. "Here I am… I hope I didn't scare you."

"No, no. Not scared – just wary until I get the measure of you." She shuffles closer. She's so short and hairy, Sam wonders if she's stumbled across a goblin. The woman looks her up and down. "Stay standing still, just like that. Then I can get on with it."

"Get on with what?"

"Measuring you, of course! Name, name, name?"

"Sam – Sam Khaan. What are you going to do with *that*?"

The Moon Lady has pulled a length of red cord from her pocket. Is Sam about to be strangled? She steps back, but the woman reaches out to her.

"Don't panic, Sam Khaan. I wouldn't hurt a fly. *Do harm to none* – that is the Wiccan Creed, the rules by which witches must abide." She smiles brightly.

Sam has got the measure of her too; she has nothing to fear. "Is that what you are? A witch?"

Yes, indeed. Her name is Ruth Abafey and she's a solitary hedgewitch. She has nothing to do with the devil, nor is she prone to dancing naked round a cauldron; she's a white witch.

She takes her red cord, measures Sam's right arm from shoulder to wrist then measures the left arm. She ties knots in the cord and asks Sam to remove her ringmaster's hat.

"Why?"

"To measure your skull, what else?" She climbs onto a pile of broken bricks to reach Sam's head and as she starts to measure, she notices the curious blonde streak in her hair.

"Hmmm," she says. "Well … that's *hereditary*."

To mark the circumference of Sam's head, she ties two knots in the cord, then she holds the knots together. "Big, but not big enough," she exclaims.

"Not big enough for my hat?"

"Not big enough to be a witch. Never mind, you'll grow."

Sam has no intention of becoming a witch, but then she remembers the putty doll she made and with great enthusiasm she tells Ruth Abafey how she bound the ankles together to stop Aunt Candy chasing after her.

"I ran away from home. She was very cruel. She got rid of my—"

The witch throws up her hands in horror and warns her about the dangers of playing with such dolls. "Beware of using a fith-fath against anyone, Sam Khaan! Whatever you wish for others, it will visit you three times over."

"I'm not sure the doll worked," Sam insists. "I just copied the idea from an old book."

"Books can be very dangerous things – especially old ones," tuts Ruth. "If your fith-fath was a good one, your aunt might have tripped and broken her neck."

The idea that she could have killed Aunt Candy never crossed Sam's mind.

"Think on!" says the witch. "If you wished to break her

neck, that wish will revisit you three times over. You'll be looking at life in a wheelchair at the very least." Ruth replaces the ringmaster's hat back on Sam's head. "What are you thinking, dear?"

"Do you really think I've killed Aunt Candy? I hate her, but I wouldn't want to kill her. I'd never kill anybody."

The witch pats her hand. "Listen, Sam Khaan. The good news and the bad news is that your aunt is still alive. I'll prove it if you like. You fell, didn't you? Show me your hands and knees."

Sam rolls up her trouser legs and holds out her palms. The witch examines her wounds.

"Ah, yes. Two little cuts and a graze. Three minor injuries – that's payback for temporarily paralyzing your aunt's ankles. I imagine she tripped, laddered her tights and possibly broke a nail. If you'd killed her, your head would have fallen off by now. Now lift your arms. Lift … lift!"

Sam lets Ruth pass the cord around her chest, all the while thinking how odd it is to be standing here in the dark allowing a tubby little witch to measure her.

"Am I dreaming, Ruth?"

"Who knows, dear? It is not for me to say." She hands Sam the knotted cord. "For you. Keep it with you at all times. It represents the umbilical cord that connects you to your mother and the Mother of Everything."

"I haven't got a mother," says Sam flatly. "She's dead."

Ruth Abafey invites Sam to stay the night. She lives just over there – a short walk. It's *far* too dangerous for a girl to sleep in St Pancras station, she says. There are thieves and murderers, tricksters and junkies, legless beggars and merciless muggers. Even worse, the police might send her back to Aunt Candy.

It has to be safer to stay with Ruth. Tonight, Sam will ask if she knew anyone who lived in the warehouse. Tomorrow, hopefully armed with more clues, she'll go to Mrs Reafy's.

They walk the length of a disused railway line until it parts at the end like a giant zip. The witch takes such small steps that Sam has to walk in ridiculous slow motion to stay by her side. Suddenly, a ghostly reflection in the water catches her eye. She stops.

"Why do you stare?" asks the witch.

"Look at the moon!"

It's floating, face-up and mouth open, beneath the black surface of the wharf.

"It looks just like the face of the drowned woman I see in my dreams," says Sam. "I've had the same dream many times. It begins with a feeling that I'm falling, but I don't know who the woman is."

Ruth squats down and fishes for the moon with her fingers. "The moon is in the sky, yet it is in the water. It's an illusion, Sam Khaan. But the drowning woman in your dream was really in this wharf. I pulled her out myself. She was washed up against the reeds, where the moon is floating now."

It happened during the Summer Solstice – was it twelve years ago? Ruth was cutting bulrushes when she noticed the woman's body. She'd waded in up to her neck and dragged her onto the bank.

Was she dead? She had no pulse. Both nostrils were plugged with mud. Ruth had turned her over to drain the water out of her lungs but still she wouldn't breathe, so she gave her the kiss of life. Full of witch's breath, the woman spluttered and opened her eyes.

Not only was she half-drowned, this woman, she'd been badly burnt. In places her long brown hair had been singed to the scalp. She couldn't remember who she was or what had happened. She was in such shock, she'd lost her power of speech; she couldn't say where she'd come from.

"She must have jumped into the wharf from the top window of the burning warehouse, hit her head and floated downstream," says Ruth.

"The *burning* warehouse!" exclaims Sam. "How did the fire start?"

Ruth doesn't know. She'd smelled smoke and gone to investigate. No one else had noticed it; there were no houses nearby. The warehouse hadn't been used for storage since just after the war; it had been left to rot in the wasteland. There was no power supply, so the fire couldn't have been caused by an electrical fault.

On several occasions, Ruth had seen candlelight in an upper window and heard voices. Whoever lived there, she respected their privacy and they respected hers; she never saw them.

"But when you smelt smoke, you hurried and called the fire brigade, didn't you?"

Ruth stares hard at Sam, conscious that she's being accused.

"No, I just let it burn... Of *course* I called them! Honestly, the way you're looking at me, anyone would think it was your nearest and dearest trapped in that fire!"

Sam goes pale. She feels sick and dizzy and suddenly her legs buckle. Ruth tries to support her under the armpits, but it's like a duck trying to hold up a deer.

"Up you come! Have you been skipping meals? Don't worry, we're almost home. Try not to faint until we get inside. Deep breaths, dear. That's it, on we go!"

HOW TO LIGHT A SPENT MATCH

The masked magician searches for a match but can find only a dead one – yet when it is struck against the matchbox it lights as if by magic. How?

THE SECRET

It's all in the preparation. Simply take a new match, dip it in black ink, allow it to dry then dip it in some ash to create the illusion that it's been used.

THE SILVER RATTLE

They arrive at a wrought-iron shelter situated on a platform which is sinking into the earth. It's an old waiting room; it hasn't been used by the public since 1942. The clock stands still at three minutes past three.

Ruth bundles Sam inside and steers her into a wicker chair. Sam stares wide-eyed and clammy as the witch lights an oil lamp. The illuminated room is clean and neat and smells of drying herbs. A few coals glow in the grate. Ruth gives them a prod with a poker. "Why so weak and wan, dear? Is it lack of food? Or was it something I said?"

Sam is hungry and tired, but that's not the reason for her sudden collapse; she's afraid that the woman who jumped from the burning warehouse was Kitty Bastet – the one person who knew where her father might be. Did he die in the fire? She can't bring herself to ask. Ruth places a pot on the embers.

"I will heat up this soup and, by and by, you will unburden yourself to me, Sam Khaan."

The soup fills the waiting room with an intense, musky perfume; it's just plain old field mushrooms. Nothing odd, nothing hallucinogenic, but something is loosening Sam's tongue.

"I met a man called Bart Hayfue today. He had a friend who lived in the warehouse."

The witch stirs the soup and waits for Sam to continue.

"I came here to find her. She might be the woman in the wharf. Where is she now?"

"Who knows, dear? I brought her back here and nursed her. Physically, she improved – but mentally? Even if you found her, I'm not sure she'd make much sense. She used to sit for hours, pencil in hand, like a poet waiting for inspiration, but it never came. She never wrote a word or spoke, but I tell you this; she wasn't mute."

"How do you know?"

"She babbled in her sleep."

Perhaps it wasn't Kitty. Perhaps she was just a stranger who'd lost her mind. But what if the babbling was Ancient Egyptian? Hadn't Kitty believed she was the reincarnation of an Egyptian priestess? And when this woman had sat at her blank page, was she trying to communicate with the witch or the spirits?

Ruth removes the pan from the fire and pours the soup into a bowl. It's so hot Sam scalds her mouth, so she pauses, spoon in hand.

"Memories can come back though. Maybe she can remember everything now, Ruth."

"But she isn't here to ask, is she? The last time I saw her, it was three minutes past three in the morning. I went to find her a coot's egg for breakfast; when I came back, she was gone."

"No note, nothing?"

"Well ... there was *something*." Ruth squirrels around in a drawer and puts something in Sam's palm. It's a gold cat charm. "She left this under my pillow. By way of a thank you, I suppose. Funny, she remembers her manners but forgets her own name."

"It's Kitty Bastet," announces Sam. The babbling, the automatic writing, the worshipping of cats; she can be no other.

The witch raises her eyebrows. "Bastet, you say? It sounds like a stage name. Was she an actress?"

"An artist. She carved things out of wood. If only I knew where she was, she might be able to help me find my father. I *have* to find him. He's the only family I have."

"Oh? Don't you even have a grandfather?"

There's an uncomfortable pause. Sam hadn't mentioned Yafer Tabuh because she's still not sure if he really exists. She's seen him in her dreams and heard him when she chanted the resurrection chant, but what if that means she just hears voices in her head like mad Kitty?

"I'm not sure if he's dead or alive. Either way ... oh, he's on the other side of the world."

Ruth lets it pass. "Why bother to find your father? You've managed without him for all these years."

"Yes, but only because Lola looked after me so well." Sam explains about Lola: how she was like a mother to her and how she's in a laboratory somewhere, lost and alone. "If I could find my father, he might be able to help me rescue her." She braces herself. "You don't think he was trapped in the warehouse fire, do you?"

Ruth stares at the ceiling, ignoring her gaze. Sam is sure she's hiding something.

"You know, don't you! He's *dead*, isn't he? That's why he never came for me!"

The witch flaps her hands in nervous agitation. "You mustn't jump to conclusions! I did see someone leaving the burning warehouse, but it was a lady. She ran out and slammed the door. I thought she'd gone to raise the alarm."

This wasn't the same woman that Ruth had discovered half-drowned. The one running away was blonde. So, there were *two* women in the warehouse.

"But no man?"

"Not that I saw. But as I got closer to the building, I thought I heard a baby cry. It might have been a cat, but I couldn't see for the smoke."

Ruth had run to nearest phone box but when she got there, it had been vandalized. It was Sunday, none of the shops were open but, finally, she'd found a café and persuaded the owner to call the fire brigade. Unfortunately, by the time they arrived there was nothing left to save; everything had turned to ashes.

"All they found was a silver rattle."

The rattle might have belonged to a baby who had grown up and moved out years before there was a fire. Or maybe there was no baby. Maybe Ruth *had* heard a cat.

"Maybe, dear."

The witch's expression changes subtly – for a second, she averts her gaze like someone who's said too much. Most of us would have missed this little nuance, but not Sam.

"*Why* don't you think it was a cat, Ruth?"

The soup works both ways. The witch, who has kept this secret for so long, finally spills.

"I met someone who recognized the rattle. Sometime after the fire, I found a young man standing in the dark, just as I found you. I didn't approach him. I just busied myself with my basket. Such a handsome man, so elegant, so—"

"So what did he say? I'd have said something if a witch was hovering."

Ruth purses her lips. "I wasn't *hovering*, I was being patient. Mindful of his privacy. It's a gift, is patience!" She snatches Sam's bowl and disappears into the kitchen to wash it up. Finally, she returns.

"He asked about the fire. How it had happened. He'd been in Scotland at a wedding. He'd come to collect his baby from someone in the warehouse. They'd promised to look after her until he came back. He had no idea everything had gone up in smoke."

Ruth had been right; there had been a baby in the warehouse and the man's eyes had filled with unspeakable anguish as he forced himself to ask, "Did anyone survive?" When he heard that a blonde woman was spotted running from the scene, his eyes flashed and he said, "If only *she'd* been in the box instead!"

It may seem like a mad thing to say, but it wasn't, as

you'll discover. When he learnt about the other woman – the dark one – he'd smiled hopefully and asked. "The lady you rescued from the wharf – is she all right?"

The witch couldn't say; the woman had lost her memory and disappeared without trace. If she *had* tried to rescue the baby, there was no sign of it; there was no little body in the wharf. Was there any chance that the blonde woman had the baby in her arms?

No, all that remained was the silver rattle. The man had asked to see it. He insisted, in case it didn't belong to his baby. Sadly, he recognized it immediately, held it to his chest and roared like a wounded animal.

"His heart was broken," sighs Ruth Abafey. "More soup, dear?"

Sam shakes her head. She's trying to make sense of the facts. If the woman who jumped into the wharf from the burning warehouse was Kitty and she'd been looking after the man's baby, that man had to be her father. Sam leaps out of her chair.

"*I* was the baby in the fire, wasn't I?"

Ruth hides a knowing smile behind her hand. Sam doesn't need to see it; she knows she's right.

"But how did I survive?"

"More soup!" insists the witch.

Here is why John Tabuh never came back for Sam; I am the Masked Magician and it falls upon me to tell you that, having spoken to the witch, he truly believed that his baby daughter was dead. He didn't believe it at first though. Like everyone who's lost someone they love, he hoped it had all been a dreadful mistake and that, by some miracle, she'd been saved.

John watched the top flat in St Peter's Square for nights on end, listening for baby cries but he heard none. He saw no one. No one answered the door. The front windows were boarded up and he assumed, quite understandably, that its wicked tenant, Candy Khaan, had moved out – but it was just an illusion. She was there all along, in a drunken stupor. Sam was there too, her pitiful cries muffled in the knicker drawer.

He couldn't go to the authorities to see if anyone had signed Sam's death certificate; her birth had never been registered. There was no paper trail to say she'd ever existed. He couldn't go to the police because he had a dark secret: he'd entered the country on a stolen passport. He was wanted for murder.

John Tabuh was probably innocent. Probably? Usually a man can be sure if he's murdered someone, but not in this case. The manner of the victim's death was most bizarre; he couldn't help wondering if it had been caused by the Old Magic and panicked on two counts:

1. Was his father infinitely more powerful than he'd given him credit for?
2. Had he murdered the man himself and, unable to live with the guilt, grossly exaggerated his father's power in order to shift the blame?

Judge for yourself when you have more evidence. For now, the facts are that under very trying circumstances, John Tabuh exhausted every means of finding baby Sam alive and returned to the witch in a state of unbearable grief.

"If only they'd found her body," he cried. "My father might have brought her back to life."

He'd told the witch about the alleged resurrection of Lola and asked if she thought it could have happened in reality. Did she know any magic strong enough to wake the dead? Could he buy such a spell from her? He was sceptical, he said, but he'd been told to ask questions.

Sam's brain is whirring. It strikes her that not only has she followed her father's footsteps onto the Piccadilly Line and through Covent Garden, but also into Ruth Abafey's waiting room. Has she been sent on a quest too?

It's beginning to look that way. She only left home to find Lola and the Dark Prince but it seems Fate has other plans – or is it Fate? The witch must be reading her mind because she suddenly claps her hands, declares that Fate is a fickle thing and tries to change the subject.

Sam's not having it. "I know Fate is fickle but can it be *deliberately* altered?"

The witch is evasive. "It can be – if you're good with a needle."

"I wish you'd give me a straight answer instead of resorting to riddles," groans Sam.

Ruth Abafey wags a finger at her. "You won't get the right answers unless you ask the right questions. That's where your father went wrong."

Sam has three questions she'd like answers to:

1. Who rescued her from the fire?
2. How did she end up living with Aunt Candy?
3. Where is Kitty now?

But these questions are not the Big Three. They're not the ones the witch doctor told his son to ask; the ones that would reveal the truth about resurrection. Having nothing to lose, she questions Ruth. "What is magic? What is illusion? What is real?" she asks.

Here is the witch's reply:

"I know many antidotes to poison, but I have never brought anyone – man, woman or beast – back from the dead. Resurrection is against the laws of nature. Witches work with nature, we never go against it. Although magic can achieve wonderful things, it cannot create miracles. Witches do not have the power of life over death."

But do witch doctors? Sam mentions the dead butterfly, the resurrection chant. She recites it softly to herself. Ruth Abafey closes the window hastily. "It was the draught, not your incantation."

Sam smiles; the witch protests too much. "So, Ruth, you know of no spell that can bring a person back to life?"

"Spells are cast to focus the human mind. It is the mind that is powerful; therein lies the magic, my dear."

Note that she doesn't say it's *impossible* to bring someone back from the dead – just that it goes against the moral code of witches. And while she says that magic cannot create miracles, she doesn't deny they may occur. Unfortunately, that's not how John Tabuh interpreted it. When Ruth refused to give him a resurrection spell, he thought three things:

1. She has the spell but is too mean to give it to me.
2. She doesn't trust me with it because I'm as useless as my father thinks I am.
3. There is no such spell, resurrection is impossible and my father is a liar.

All of which was rather negative, but don't be too harsh on him; he had a lot in his mind – far more than you realize because you don't know the half of it yet.

"Where did my father go after he left here?" asks Sam. "Did he say?"

It seems that he wanted to continue his search for Kitty in the hope that she could shed some light on the fate of his daughter. He'd told Ruth he was off to visit a friend of his father's, someone with a reputation for finding missing persons; a certain Mrs Reafy.

"But that's who I was on my way to see!" exclaims Sam.

"There's a surprise," yawns Ruth. "It's three minutes past three in the morning. I'll sleep in this chair, you can borrow my bed and tomorrow you can be on your way."

Sam tosses and turns on the witch's mattress, thinking of her father and Lola and wishing she could find them and say, "Hey, I'm alive! Now we can all be happy."

But are *they* still alive? Maybe her dreams would tell

her – but how can she dream if she can't sleep? Perhaps it would help if she read for a while. She picks up the witch doctor's notebook and tries to open it, but the pages refuse to turn. She has no choice but to study the list on the inside cover again. Right at the top, jostling for position with Mrs Reafy, are three other names.

Effie Ray, Bart Hayfue and Ruth Abafey.

Recipe for Magic Protective Oil

While many essential oils have healing properties, it's important to focus your intent to enhance this recipe magically. Witches define magic as the ability to create change by force of will; in other words, you may get what you wish for if you really put your mind to it.

You need:

A small sterile bottle, clearly labelled

3 tablespoons base oil (sweet almond or wheatgerm)

3 teaspoons frankincense

1 teaspoon juniper berries

1 teaspoon fennel

3 drops of rue

Method:

1. Gather ingredients during a full moon.

2. Pour the base oil into the bottle.

3. Add rest of ingredients.

4. Replace lid. Store in a cool, dark place until needed.

5. Anoint your temple with a thin smear, also your third eye and wrists.

6. Go about your intent with courage.

WARNING: DO NOT DRINK

MRS REAFY

It's Wednesday morning and, according to the witch, Wednesday is the best day to travel.

Just to make sure, she's anointed Sam with home-made Magic Protective Oil. Is it really magic? The more you believe it, the more potent it becomes – or so I'm told. If you truly believe, it'll make you feel invincible. Your enemies will notice this and because you appear so powerful, they'll leave you alone and pick on someone weaker. This oil will also protect you from fierce animals. Even if you are frightened the herbs will disguise the smell of fear and they'll go and tear the throat out of some other poor wretch.

The train journey to St Albans is not particularly treacherous unless you eat the stale sandwiches from the buffet car. Even so, the witch won't take any risks with her young friend. At sunrise, Sam awakes to find her arranging five coloured candles at various compass points on the floor. She lights them with a taper.

"Don't tell me. You haven't paid your electricity bill

and you've been cut off," says Sam. It happened to Aunt Candy all the time.

Ruth pulls a face. "I'm *casting* a circle, a space between the worlds where a witch does her work. Each candle represents one of five elements: air, fire, water, earth and spirit, and—"

"My friend Bart says there're no such things as spirits," Sam interrupts. "Do you really think there's a spirit world?"

"See for yourself."

The witch beckons her into the circle. Sam walks around it anti-clockwise – Ruth throws her hands up in the air.

"No, not *widdershins*! Clockwise! Sit in the centre!"

Sam sits and waits and waits, then a voice which she knows to be Ruth's but which sounds much further away murmurs in her ear.

"Close your eyes. Sink slowly down, down, to the centre of the Earth…"

Sam melts through the floorboards, through the floury foundations of the waiting room, through the layers of grey clay veined with pale tubes. At first she thinks they're worms, but these are the roots of Yggdrasil, the Tree of Life.

She falls further, past the layer of tilth sieved by moles, past seams of prehistoric silt, past mausoleums of prehistoric creatures, until she is beneath the taproot of the tree.

Here is a chamber beneath the arc of roots; an organic cathedral. There's a table with a sheet of paper on it. Write your name down, Sam Tabuh. Knock three times on the table. To your left there is a doorway covered by a blue veil. Ask your spirit guide to appear.

Knock. Knock. Knock.

Sam watches and waits for the veil to twitch. There's no breeze, yet the corner is lifting slightly. Someone's coming. She hears the faint pounding of the drum, or is it the molten thump of the Earth's heart?

"My name is Freya."

It's a woman's voice, but no one's there. Did Sam blink or is she invisible? Open your eyes. Sam is back in the waiting room staring into the candle flame that represents Earth. For the first time, she understands what she's made from; just as cakes are made from flour, sugar, eggs and butter, she is made from earth, water, fire and air. She is stardust and seawater. These are the basic ingredients needed to make every creature from hippos to humans, but what is the magic ingredient that makes her *Sam* – is that spirit? Is Freya her spirit guide?

Ruth stares pointedly at Sam's locket. "The Norse goddess of love was called Freya. Her symbol was a shell."

Armed with her witch's cord, protective oil and the possibility of a kindly spirit watching over her, Sam is pointed in the direction of West India Quay. As she leaves the waiting room, she feels a rare urge to fling her arms around Ruth Abafey – but she doesn't. She's been starved of human touch for so long, the idea makes her feel peculiar. Even so, she's grown fond of this lady. No one has ever looked after her so carefully – apart from Lola – and while it's wonderful to be loved by an ape, it's not the same as being loved by one of your own species.

"I wonder if we'll ever see each other again, Ruth?"

"Sure, sure. In some form or another." The witch

presses a twenty pound note into Sam's hand as if she were her favourite grandchild and sends her on her way.

The journey to St Albans passes without event. If Sam hadn't had to wait so long for a bus from the station, she'd have been standing outside Mrs Reafy's ages ago. She'd found her address in a public phone book easily enough and has an excellent sense of direction.

She knocks. She hears someone slamming a pan down on a stove, then slippered footsteps. The door opens and there's Mrs Reafy clutching a wooden spoon coated in hot jam, her hair bristling with static as if she'd recently shoved her finger in a socket.

"Burnt!" she snaps. "The saucepan's ruined. What do you want? Lost your tongue?"

"No, I've lost my orang-utan."

Sam had learnt after years of dealing with Aunt Candy that if a person is in a rage, the best way to diffuse the situation is to say something unexpected.

"Lost your *orang-utan*?"

"Yes. And my father."

Mrs Reafy pushes her raspberry-spattered spectacles back up her nose and sniffs. "That was careless, wasn't it? You're sure they didn't run off together?"

Sam frowns. This is no joking matter and she explains that although she doesn't have an appointment, it is an *emergency*.

"Where did you find me, Yellow Pages?"

The pages in the witch doctor's notebook are rather yellow, so she nods and Mrs Reafy lets her in.

The smell of burnt sugar is overpowering. It looks as if there's been a massacre in the kitchen. There are thick clots all over the floor, red smears on the windows and what look like bloody fingerprints on the tea towels. It's only jam, but it's amazing how far it can spread once it gets out of control.

"I blame this oven," says Mrs Reafy. "We don't get along at all." After a short while in her company, Sam realizes that Mrs Reafy refers to every object in the house as if it has a personality. She even refers to her kettle as the son of the devil and scolds it when it blows a fuse.

"He hates me! He's showing off because you're here." She raps the kettle on the lid then spends the next five minutes scrubbing the sticky spoon as if it's a sulky child with jam round its face. Sam wonders if she behaves like this because she's lonely, but it soon becomes clear that Mrs Reafy *does* get a reaction from everything she touches. It's this – she tells Sam – that gives her the paranormal ability to contact missing persons.

She takes Sam into the living room and explains that certain objects absorb the emotions of the people they belong to. She can read these emotions; if she holds something belonging to a missing person, she often receives a mental snapshot of where they are. Sam is fascinated.

"How do you do it? Is it magic?" She pulls a coin out from behind Mrs Reafy's ear, wraps it in kitchen paper and tears it in half. It's a good trick but her audience is not impressed.

"Magic? Oh, please. Psychometry isn't a cheap trick. It's a rare gift, a talent I was born with it. Either you have it or you don't."

Sam's not convinced. "If it's not magic, there must be some scientific explanation, surely?"

"Must there?" huffs Mrs Reafy. "I disagree. Magic is a swear word used by idiots to describe things science cannot explain. I find it offensive and so does my spoon."

"But how can a spoon have feelings?"

"It's made from wood, wood has a heart," says Mrs Reafy. "The wood in *this* spoon came from an eaglewood tree in which there lived a crow. One day, the crow's eggs were broken and the cry of the crow and the yolk from her broken eggs seeped into the wood. When the wood was carved into this spoon, the crow's cry remained in every fibre, right down to the handle."

"Poor spoon," says Sam.

"Not poor spoon, poor *crow*!" insists Mrs Reafy. "*She* was the one who had her eggs broken, and what does this spoon do for a living? It breaks eggs! It offends the spirit of the crow. See how everything connects? In respect for the crow, I have demoted this spoon to jam-stirring duties only. I won't let it near an egg and that's why it's cross with me. The cooker felt sorry for the spoon and between them, they cooked up a plot to burn my jam." She raps the spoon loudly on the table as if to punish it. "This missing orang-utan of yours – what does it look like?"

It's tempting to say "Just like you!" because Mrs Reafy's stomach protrudes, her hair is bright orange and her arms are surprisingly hairy. The features that make an orang-utan beautiful are not those most woman aspire to – the whims of fashion are cruel.

"Lola is a redhead with brown eyes and a charming smile," says Sam. "She likes working with children and she can do magic tricks. Does that help?"

"What I need," says Mrs Reafy, "is something that belongs to her."

Sam gives her Lola's toy monkey. Mrs Reafy examines its glass eyes and checks its stuffing. Having done so, she sits it on her lap, holds it under the armpits and closes her eyes. After a moment, she's full of inspiration.

"Lola is a much loved pet. She came from far away … from a rainforest … Borneo … or is it Sumatra?"

Sam groans inwardly. This is nothing more than educated guesswork. Orang-utans only come from Borneo and Sumatra; the revelation is hardly psychic. But what she says next makes the hairs on Sam's neck stand up.

"Lola was orphaned … rescued as a baby by a woman studying tribespeople. Lola travelled with her across a stretch of water … to a different forest. I am not certain of its name… I am not getting anything else."

"Please try!" says Sam. "Do you see a little boy with her at all?"

Mrs Reafy blinks rapidly. "Wait! I see a sharp object … a dart? A boy is crying…"

"That's him! Is he wearing a bush hat?" asks Sam, unable to contain herself.

Mrs Reafy opens her eyes and glares at her. "You've interrupted my flow. It'll take ages to get back to where I was. I need *silence*. Go to the kitchen and wipe up the jam."

Reluctantly, Sam leaves the room.

How to Use a Pendulum

Pendulums can be used to detect water, divine the sex of unborn babies, diagnose illness and find lost objects or people.

1. To make a pendulum tie a finger ring onto a fine thread about 30–45 cm long.

2. Hold the end lightly between the thumb and first two fingers of one hand at shoulder height.

3. Tell the pendulum to move back and forth – do not try to make it swing by using your hand.

4. You'll find that it moves as directed, slightly at first, then with increasing speed.

5. Focus your mind. Tell the pendulum to stop. The swing should quickly reduce until the pendulum is still.

6. Try telling it to move in different ways – left to right, diagonally, clockwise, etc.

7. Practise until you understand how it moves and the effects your mental intentions have on it.

EXPERIMENT

Get three cups and turn them upside down on a table. Ask a friend to hide a coin under one of them. Now hold a pendulum over each cup and see if you can tell where the coin is. The pendulum isn't magic; the movements are caused by unconscious muscle movements in the body, arm and hand. But if you found the coin, there might be something magical about you; the movements might be produced by your strange, super-sensory awareness.

THE PENDULUM SWINGS

S am is on her hands and knees scrubbing jam off the lino
when the psychometrist comes in, looking agitated.
Her hair looks as if she's been rubbing it with a balloon.

"What's wrong, Mrs Reafy?" asks Sam. "Am I using the
wrong cloth? Do its fibres contain the tears of a lamb that
has lost its mother?"

Mrs Reafy slumps down on a chair, her ape-like arms
dangling by her sides, her eyes staring ahead. Sam drops
the cloth in dismay.

"Is it Lola? Please don't tell me she's dead."

"Not dead, no ... but she has *known* death."

Well, yes. Lola's mother had died. Is that what Mrs
Reafy is referring to? Seemingly not, for she begins to
mutter about poisonous darts and a man in a headdress
chanting, and how the orang-utan had *known* death but
beyond all fathoming had come ... back ... to ... life.

"I've done the most terrible thing!" she wails. "I'm an
ignorant, silly woman."

"You're not that silly."

Mrs Reafy lowers her eyes and fumbles with the woolly monkey.

"But I am! I once told a desperate man that I had it on the *utmost* authority that the dead couldn't be brought to life, but now I'm not sure. Not after what I've just seen."

"What have you seen?"

It had been a flashback of Lola's resurrection so vivid that Mrs Reafy had gone into shock. Sam shakes her by the shoulders. "Is Lola still alive? Do you know where she is?"

Mrs Reafy just wrings her hands and wails, "Oh, what have I done? If I'd believed in resurrection I'd never have set the police on that poor man, but he would keep asking me such alarming questions about death!"

You don't need telling who that man was and nor does Sam, but Mrs Reafy has to be told.

"That man was my father!"

Mrs Reafy is in no state to explain what happened, so allow me, the Masked Magician, to put you in the picture. John Tabuh came to see if Mrs Reafy could use her paranormal gifts to locate Kitty. Although she was on his father's list, he suspected she might be a fraud. Being a magician, he knew the tricks of the trade and suspected that her method of finding people had little to do with psychic power and lots to do with manipulating the person looking for them.

It's surprisingly easy to extract information from people

without them realizing. You then recount the facts and they're astounded by your accuracy, astonished as to how you know so much about them; it must be magic! It's not; it's a fortune-teller's trick.

John's logical mind told him that any success Mrs Reafy had in finding Kitty would be achieved by using the fortune-teller's technique along with a bit of secretive research. Foolishly, he never gave her a chance to prove him wrong. While it's a good idea to find out if a person is genuine or not, the way John went about it was a particularly bad one.

He'd arrived at her house after dark with an elaborately painted box the size of a coffin which he'd pushed from the station on a trolley. To avoid attention, he'd covered the box with a cloth and, having found the right address, he parked it on the drive and introduced himself.

Bowled over by John Tabuh's handsome face and magnificent, flowing mane, Mrs Reafy had become positively girlish and leapt at the chance to help him. The mood didn't change until he suddenly remembered the three questions. But, instead of just asking Mrs Reafy if she knew what was magic, what was real and what was illusion, he decided to find out another way.

Out of nowhere John produced a pink silk glove. He asked if she could tell him the location of the lady it belonged to, adding that she'd been brutally murdered by someone he knew. If she could prove herself by doing this he would pay her handsomely to find Kitty.

Somewhat taken aback, Mrs Reafy dutifully sat down

in the side room, pink glove in hand, and closed her eyes. What she saw filled her with dread. In her mind (or did she spot it through the curtains?), she thought she saw a coffin on her drive; inside it lay a woman's body. Shaking with fright, she opened her eyes a fraction. Now she saw John Tabuh in a very different light; he'd fooled her into thinking that because he was beautiful, he was good. Yet he'd left a corpse on her drive!

When John asked her if she had the power to bring someone back from the dead, Mrs Reafy convinced herself he was trying to get away with murder and called the police. John Tabuh was mortified.

"I've done nothing wrong! All I'm guilty of is grieving for my daughter."

Mrs Reafy put two and two together, made five and decided that he'd probably murdered his daughter too. She began to scream. John Tabuh had no choice but to run away with his box on wheels before the law arrived.

If only he'd given Mrs Reafy the silver rattle to hold instead of the pink glove. Maybe she could have told him where Sam was and they would have been reunited years ago. Sam heaves a great sigh.

"Who was the woman in the box, Mrs Reafy? Any ideas?"

"Whoever it was, she had good hair." She pats her electrified fringe until it crackles; but it won't stay down. "I don't know who she was, Sam. Now I'm thinking maybe the coffin wasn't a coffin; just a trunk for his luggage. Maybe the dead woman was just a tailor's dummy

– is anyone in your family a dressmaker?"

"I don't know. My mother might have been but she died when I was a baby."

"Really?"

"That's what Aunt Candy told me. Not that I trust her. She's one of the reasons I ran away. Now I'm homeless and I have to find my father. Do you know where he went?"

"No, but perhaps I can find out. Do you have anything of his that I could hold?"

There are the articles in the witch doctor's pouch, but Mrs Reafy thinks they'd give a false reading. The item must belong exclusively to him. A photo doesn't count, so there's nothing she can use to find him via psychometry.

"You can't trace Lola either? Not even through her monkey?"

No, she'd tried, but for some reason she could only see Lola's past, not her present.

"I could try the pendulum," announces Mrs Reafy. "But I'm only accurate as far as the British Isles. If your father's left the country, we're stuffed. But we might find the orang-utan."

She fetches an atlas, lays it on the table and smoothes it flat. "How odd. Look at that. It's covered in red dots."

"There's jam on your glasses," says Sam.

The psychometrist removes her spectacles and rubs them on her cardigan sleeve. She takes a pendulum out of her handbag and holds it over the map of Great Britain. Nothing happens.

"Wait…"

The pendulum begins to move, slowly at first – over the north of England – but then it swings in ever increasing circles. The circle grows wider and wider until it is whirling above Mrs Reafy's head, like a lasso.

"Look out!" The pendulum whips out of her hand, flies across the room and cracks the window pane.

"That," pants Mrs Reafy, "means he's gone abroad."

"And Lola?"

Mrs Reafy doesn't reply. The experience has exhausted her; she's fallen into a deep, deep sleep. Sam picks up the pendulum and examines it. It's a wedding ring threaded on a length of fishing line; that's all there is to it. So how does it work? For all she knows, Mrs Reafy just swung it round her head and let go for dramatic effect. She prods the sleeping woman gently. "Can you tell me how this pendulum works, please?"

Rudely interrupted from her slumber, Mrs Reafy's eyes dart wildly about the room as she struggles to compose herself. "Wah... What?"

"How does the pendulum work?"

"It's to do with electricity. We're full of the stuff. Some of us more than others."

She tries again in vain to smooth her hair down, but it bristles and sparks like fuse wire. "A good pendulum swinger like myself produces over a hundred millivolts. In fact, I'm so electric I can illuminate a light bulb just by holding it."

She removes the bulb from her desk lamp and holds it in her hand. "Let there be light!"

The bulb flickers and glows. Sam wants to try. With a faint smirk, Mrs Reafy hands over the bulb – nothing will happen. Sam grasps it by the neck. There's a bright flash and it shatters. For a moment they stare in shock at the jagged shards, then Mrs Reafy breaks the silence.

"You *squeezed* it, silly girl!"

Sam knew she hadn't. Maybe the bulb was old and would have blown anyway. She offers to clear away the glass but Mrs Reafy has already grabbed a dustpan and is sweeping the floor furiously. The friction of her tights and the nylon brush against the synthetic carpet causes a streak of lightning to shoot through her armpit hair; she drops the dustpan and groans.

"*You* should stick to fairy lights."

The fact that Mrs Reafy is highly electric still doesn't fully explain the mysteries of the pendulum though.

When she finally stops sparking, Sam asks again, "But *why* does the pendulum swing?"

"None of your business. It works like dowsing except that pendulums are vertical instruments."

Sam had heard of dowsing. As you may know, it's a method of finding water using a stick called a divining rod. Mrs Reafy has one hanging on the wall made from a willow crotch. She takes it down from its hook and gives it to Sam.

"Test it out in the garden. See if you can locate the sewers while I try to find your ape."

"I'd rather stay here."

"I'd rather you didn't. You are putting me off."

Mrs Reafy's garden is completely overgrown. The branches on the right have joined hands with the branches on the left, forming an arched roof. It is festooned with creepers, which droop like post-Christmas paper chains. The sky is only visible through a few open chinks.

Half-heartedly, Sam holds the divining rod in front of her and walks forward, stepping over twisted roots thicker than her arms. It's drizzling and, because it's a warm day, the foliage sweats and the perfume of rank blossom struggles to escape through the tree canopy above.

There is something so familiar about that smell; and the *drip, drip, drip* of the rolling rain splashing against the leaves is like the noise of oars cutting through the slow waters of the Sepik River. Now she hears the *ark, ark, ark* of the Torresian crow. But there is no crow; it's Mrs Reafy calling, "*Arkley!*"

Lola is in Arkley.

How to B a ventriloquist

While it's possible to say most of the alphabet without moving your lips, to be a good ventriloquist, you need to master the letter *B*. Here's how:

1. Relax your mouth.
2. Pronounce the sound *DER* but only use the tip of your tongue, as in *LER*. Only allow brief contact with the tip of your tongue behind your teeth.
3. Think *B*, not *D*.
4. Whisper it.

MR FRAYE

L ola is in danger. According to Mrs Reafy's pendulum, she's being held captive at a laboratory called the Grimm Experimental Centre. Sam must go to Arkley immediately. But not alone – what chance would a young girl have of persuading the scientists to release an orangutan they'd paid good money for? None at all. This is why Mrs Reafy offers to drive Sam to meet her brother, Mr Fraye. He has a certain talent that might come in useful.

Sam rides in the front seat, toying with the divining rod, a gift from Mrs Reafy who still felt very guilty about misjudging John Tabuh. If she'd helped him to find Sam, he'd never have left the country. The rod may seem like no compensation for all Sam's suffering, but maybe Mrs Reafy knows it will save her life one day.

Sam is greeted by Mr Fraye's wife, who invites her to wait for him in the garden. He won't be a moment.

It has stopped raining. Sam waits alone in the garden. Unlike Mrs Reafy's jungle, it's beautifully kept. The flowers are arranged in order of height. The stripes on the lawn are mathematically precise. The path twists and turns like a lazy anaconda sunning itself on the grass.

Three arches divide the garden into sections; who knows what lies beyond? It's a large plot but not as large as it seems: mirrors have been strategically placed in niches in the walls. At first, Sam doesn't realize. As she wanders down the path with the divining rod held out in front of her, she comes face to face with her twin sister. But it's just her reflection.

She walks on past wigwams of runner beans but as she turns left by the potting shed, she feels a tug on the end of the rod; it's trembling. She holds out her hand to make sure the movement isn't being caused by her own tremors; no, steady as a rock. She hears a sweet, warbling voice coming from under the willow.

"Damper … getting damper."

The divining rod is drawn to the voice. Like a dog after a rabbit, it drags her straight through the dripping curtains of the willow branches.

"Getting damper … wet … wet … soaking!"

As Sam battles her way out, the rod pulls her towards an ornamental pond and there, perched on a bridge, is a plump, collared dove. It bobs up and down and speaks in that same, soft voice, "Hello. My name is Freya."

A parrot can mimic and so can a jackdaw but can a dove? Why would it say its name is Freya? Do all birds have names or is this dove the embodiment of the spirit guide who announced herself under Yggdrasil, the Tree of Life?

"Pleased to meet you, Sam!" A be-whiskered gentleman has appeared at her side from behind a statue. He holds out his hand and beams broadly. He smells nicely musty, a mixture of peat, pipe smoke and lawn clippings. "I'm Mr Fraye ... so *very* pleased to meet you."

He pronounces his name as if it has an *r* on the end, so it sounds like "Freya".

Sam is disappointed; she wanted the dove to be her spiritual guardian. She's struggling to believe in spirits, but for a moment the dove seemed to be living, talking proof that there was another dimension beyond this world. It flies off.

"Charming," mutters Sam. "It might have said goodbye."

"Goodbyeeeeeeeee, Sam Tabuh." replies a wispy voice, high in the sky.

Sam is amazed. "How *does* it do that?"

Mr Fraye chuckles to himself. "It doesn't – I do."

He's a ventriloquist. He'd been throwing his voice to make it sound as if the dove could speak. He hopes he hadn't startled her; he was only seeking to amuse. "I've heard about your missing ape," he adds. "I have a plan."

"What kind of plan, Mr Fraye?"

The ventriloquist's pet terrier, which is bumbling around beside him, replies in a thick Cornish accent. "To rescue Lola, of course!"

Mr Fraye pulls a briar pipe out of his pocket and puffs on it. Aware that Sam is staring at him, he bangs the tobacco out on the heel of his slipper.

"You're quite right – filthy habit. Mrs Fraye doesn't like it either."

"It's not *that*," she insists. "I was just wondering if your pipe has a history. Only Mrs Reafy says that her wooden spoon is full of bird sorrow."

"My sister is a crackpot," Mr Fraye confides. "You mustn't set too much store by what she says. Psychometry, pendulums and such like? Hmm ... not convinced."

"Oh," says Sam, flatly. Maybe her father had been right. Maybe Mrs Reafy was a fraud.

Seeing her disappointment, Mr Fraye pipes up. "Hmm ... I shouldn't speak ill of my sister. All I'm suggesting is that she might have used something a little more ... conventional ... to find your missing friend. Did she ask you to leave the room at any point?"

Yes, twice. Sam had been sent to clean up jam and told to go into the garden.

"Does she have a computer?"

Well, yes. Mrs Reafy had said her PC was holy because the oil used to make it had come from the grave of the whale that swallowed Jonah. Mr Fraye rolls his eyes.

"Dear oh dear. She does have a vivid imagination. But ... hmm ... a quick look on the Internet could have revealed the addresses of several possible laboratories, could it not? Which my sister might have phoned, making certain enquiries about orang-utans, and what with orang-utans being extremely rare, it wouldn't be too difficult to find yours, would it?"

Yet Sam couldn't dismiss Mrs Reafy's paranormal abilities entirely. The night she stayed at Ruth's, she'd cuddled Lola's toy monkey and dreamt of a bleak building

– a laboratory perhaps – which lay beyond a cornfield in which there stood a scarecrow dressed in yellow. She doesn't mention this to Mr Fraye in case he thinks she's a crackpot like his sister. Instead, she asks about his rescue plan; will it involve ventriloquism?

"Ooh-arrgh!" agrees the terrier, whirling its tail like a propeller. "That it will!"

"Could you teach me to throw my voice?" asks Sam, laughing. "Is it difficult?"

Mr Fraye shakes his head. "Not once you've mastered *B* and *P*. It's all to do with tongue position and breathing."

"How did you make that dove speak from up in the sky?"

My Fraye strokes his Adam's apple. "By controlling certain muscles. You must … hmm … close the throat so that the air you need to make the voice is pinched." He gives her another demonstration and suggests an exercise to help her locate the right muscles. "Imagine you're lifting a heavy weight. As you strain to lift it, you say 'Ahhhh'. Making a sound when you are straining makes it go higher."

"Aghhhhh!"

Mr Fraye grins broadly, but is most encouraging. "Good! Practice, that's all you need. Now, try and say *B* without moving your lips. *B* is a bit of a dastard, I'm afraid."

Sam keeps practising. If you want to have a go at mastering ventriloquism for yourself – it may come in useful later – try the exercise at the front of this chapter. Kractice while you are in ged or going about your gusiness, but it is gest not to goo it in puglic in case keokle think you've geen grinking; keokle are very quick to judge.

Let's stop that now and find out exactly how Mr Fraye hopes to rescue Lola; there isn't a moment to lose. The plan is simple but cunning. Dressed as an RSPCA inspector, he will gain access to the laboratory and while he keeps the scientists talking, Sam will search for Lola. If she's there, the ventriloquism will come into play and her captor will be compelled to let her go. All will become clear.

Sam climbs into Mr Fraye's old Morris Minor and they drive into the countryside. The car is so sluggish, Sam feels it might be quicker to walk. Half an hour passes and the fields are all starting to look the same.

"Are we nearly there yet, Mr Fraye?"

The fields *are* the same. Mr Fraye is lost. The Grimm Experimental Centre isn't marked on his map and Mrs Reafy only indicated its whereabouts roughly. They've passed plenty of cornfields but none of them have scarecrows; perhaps Sam's dream *was* just a dream and not an enlightening piece of psychometric information. The road comes to a dead end. Mr Fraye stops the car, winds down the window and puffs thoughtfully on his pipe.

"I'm certain it's round about here … hmm."

"What shall we do now, Mr Fraye?"

Sam says this without moving her lips, and he nods, clearly impressed. "We shall get out and explore." He puts on his RSPCA hat and locks the car. They climb over a stile and walk along a bridle path beside the corn. There's a solitary bird piping its heart out hundreds of feet above them.

"Is that you singing, Mr Fraye?"

"I thought it was you, Miss Tabuh – having a lark."

It's neither of them; this time, it really is a bird singing – just because it's happy to be alive. Sam hopes to heaven that Lola's still alive.

"We must be positive!" insists Mr Fraye. He strides out with great confidence, which is all a big bluff because he hasn't a clue where he's going.

Sam makes a suggestion. "Maybe we could cut *through* the corn?"

It's a daring thing to do. Farmers don't take kindly to people trampling their crops and they often carry guns. But it would save time.

"Good idea," says Mr Fraye, who's afraid of no one. He pauses to re-light his pipe then drops down on all fours. "Easier this way," he says.

They crawl along in silence. If you were the skylark, all you'd see is a parting in the corn headed by a plume of pipe smoke going round and round in ever-decreasing circles. Mr Fraye is about to admit defeat when Sam whispers excitedly, "There's a *man* asleep in the corn!"

There he is, all dressed in yellow. Not a scarecrow, but a tramp. When they rouse him, he says that he knows of the experimental station – it's *thatta* way.

"Not thissa way?"

"No, sir," he points his muddy finger, "behind those trees, sir. Those trees that are playing pass the parcel with the sun, sir."

Mr Fraye gives him a coin for his trouble but the man hurls it into the corn. If you ever cross this field on your hands and knees, you will find the coin and know all this to be true.

"Speech is free, sir," says the tramp. "The Grimm lies over yonder."

With that, he adjusts his bright rags, lies back in the golden corn and becomes invisible.

The Grimm Experimental Centre sits like a ghastly secret encased in concrete at the bottom of the valley. Mr Fraye straightens his hat and looks Sam in the eye.

"It is very important … hmm … that you have faith in my Grand Plan. *I* think it is going to work and if *you* behave as if it's going to work, it will."

He insists they march down the hill with their shoulders back and their heads held high. By the time they reach the laboratory, any thoughts of failure have gone from Sam's mind.

A man in a white, blood-flecked coat opens the door. He is Dr Pringle and he has piggy eyes.

"Ye–s? What do you want?"

"RSPCA. I have reason to believe you are in possession of a Great Ape for which you have no licence."

As Mr Fraye takes Dr Pringle to one side to discuss the matter, Sam nips in unnoticed and tiptoes through a door marked PRIVATE. Beyond it is a peeling corridor which stinks of something nasty; the formaldehyde used to preserve organs in jars. There's a closed door to her left. It has no window, but, wafting from underneath, she can smell the unmistakable odour of caged animals. She enters cautiously, afraid of what she'll find. Rack upon rack of rats, jam-packed together; dogs and cats incarcerated in crates and, right at the back, there's a cage. There sits Lola, cramped in the corner with her face in her hands.

Lola has a metal collar around her neck. She's chained like a slave. No amount of orang-utan sleight of hand could help her escape, no matter how opposable her thumbs. She has given up. She can see no way out; her spirit has broken.

Sam touches her through the bars, but Lola doesn't look up. She has been drugged to keep her quiet, like a mad woman in an institution. Desperate to make contact, Sam finds the toy monkey and pushes it into the cage. It drops in front of the orang-utan with a soft plop.

"Lola ... it's Monkey."

Lola peers through her leathery fingers at her favourite toy. She bends forward, sniffs it, scoops it up and presses it to her chest. She looks puzzled; maybe apes dream and she thinks Sam is an illusion.

"Lola, I'm here."

The sight of Sam blasts the fog from Lola's head and she begins to hoot. The hooting turns into the haunting cry of a mother whose heart is tearing in half because she can't hold her child. The dogs, the cats and the rats join in and the cacophony brings the furious Dr Pringle running into the room with Mr Fraye charging after him.

"What's that girl doing here? Get away from the cage!"

Pringle tries to wrestle Sam away, but she digs her heels in.

"She's *my* orang-utan. Aunt Candy sold her to you without permission!"

Mr Fraye gets out his pencil and begins to fill out a bogus form. "As Chief Inspector of the RSPCA, I insist that you sign this animal back to its rightful owner or face the consequences."

For a few seconds, Pringle looks as though he is going to back down, but he's suspicious. "If you are from the RSPCA, where's your van, *Inspector* Fraye?"

"None of your business, Dr Pringle."

Pringle strides over to the telephone. "I'll ring the RSPCA and check your ID. Can't be too careful, can we, Inspector?"

If it hadn't been for the beagle in the cage opposite, who knows what would have happened.

"Put the phone down," it growls. "There's a good man."

Dr Pringle swallows hard. He stares at the beagle then he stares at Mr Fraye, who pretends to be as shocked as he is.

"My word, Pringle. A talking dog!" What kind of experiments are you conducting here?"

"Terrible things go on," weeps a white rat. "They say it is for the greater good, but it's not for the greater good of us rats."

"We have *feelings*," sings a chorus of cats.

Dr Pringle's eyes are bulging like boiled eggs. Lola clears her throat and with great passion, she pleads with him.

"I know that, deep down, you're not a bad man, Dr Pringle; you're a good man. If someone locked your mother in a cage and experimented on her for the greater good it would kill you, wouldn't it? Sam is my child. You are killing me, Dr Pringle."

Pringle is shaking so hard, his trouser bottoms are flapping. Lola puts her hands through the bars and begs. "Let me go, Dr Pringle. If you have a shred of compassion in you, let me go."

"Let her go, or you spit on your own mother!" squeaks the rat.

Dr Pringle – who is a bit of a mummy's boy – finally crumbles. He scrabbles around for his keys and tries to undo the padlock on Lola's cage.

"Allow me," says Mr Fraye.

Lola and Sam are reunited. There's no point describing the scene, because no matter how I arrange the words, it's impossible to convey the joy they feel, wrapped in each others arms. If you ever lose your orang-utan, you'll understand.

Mr Fraye is releasing the rats. Being a sensible man, as well as a compassionate one, he gives them plenty of time to run away before he releases the cats and the dogs and a pair of capuchin monkeys he found cowering in another room.

By now Dr Pringle has crawled inside a cupboard and closed the door, so, with a broad smile, Mr Fraye locks him in and ushers Sam and Lola back into the fresh air. "Come along, ladies. Mission accomplished."

They walk back to the car. The capuchin monkeys are swinging in the trees. The dogs are barking with joy and cocking their legs against every tree they come across. The cats have curled up in the corn as if nothing has happened, because cats are not of this earth; they're made from shadows and shimmers and some strange slinky liquid unknown to science – not even to Dr Pringle. One little rat remains on the bonnet of the Morris Minor. It washes its whiskers, announces that life is wonderful, then it shoots off into the corn to raise a new generation.

Lola is sitting in the back of the car like an old relative looking forward to a Sunday drive. Sam is so happy, her eyes fill with tears. She isn't one to cry, as you know, but as she pulls out her hanky, something falls onto her lap. It's the cat charm Kitty gave to Ruth Abafey – she must have slipped it in Sam's pocket.

"Very pretty," says Mr Fraye. "It looks like Bastet, the Egyptian cat goddess."

If it belongs to Kitty, and if Mrs Reafy is to be trusted, the charm might have absorbed Kitty's emotions; maybe Sam could find her through psychometry. She will try later.

They arrive back at Mr Fraye's. In case you're in any doubt about his character, let me tell you that as well as being the perfect gentleman, he's the perfect host. He and his wife have no qualms about letting Sam share a bed in their spare room with an orang-utan, never mind that the sheets are from Harrods.

It's now a quarter to midnight. Snuggled up to Lola, Sam is having a quick look at the witch doctor's list. She's pretty sure Mr Fraye's name must be near the top – and of course it is – but she can't find Kitty Bastet anywhere.

She holds the cat charm, closes her eyes tightly and concentrates.

THREE LUCKY CHARMS

THE WISHBONE

This is the bone overlying a bird's breastbone. It's the custom to dry it for three days – three being a magic number. Two people then pull it apart. The one who gets the long half will have their wish come true.

THE HORSE SHOE

These protective amulets are often nailed onto houses, barns and stables. It's said that no witch will pass under one. The crescent shape is linked to the pagan moon goddesses, the Irish Sheela-na-gig and the Blessed Virgin Mary.

THE FOUR-LEAF CLOVER

Clover usually has three leaves, so a four-leaf clover is considered a lucky find. It's a genetic variation, like six-fingered human hands and multi-toed cats, and is believed to bring the finder health, wealth and happiness.

THE ECCENTRICS CLUB

"**I** had the strangest dream," says Sam over breakfast, "about a place called Eel Pie Island. I don't suppose a place with a name as silly as that can really exist though."

Mr Fraye passes the marmalade to Lola, who spreads it on her toast with her thumb.

"Hmm … yes, it does. It's on the River Thames, near Twickenham."

Eel Pie Island used to be a popular resort for boating parties that had come to sample the famous eel pies.

"They don't make pies there any more," says Mr Fraye. "The hotel has gone. The eel population has declined dramatically. Pollution, I'm afraid." He chews his cereal carefully. "There are only about fifty houses on the island, mostly inhabited by boat builders, craft workers and the like."

"Pop musicians," adds Mrs Fraye, who rarely speaks, but serves and smiles.

"Yes, and them. Ah, well, I suppose they have to live somewhere."

He knows a great deal about the place and Sam is curious to know if there's a particular reason for this.

Mr Fraye knocks his pipe out into a large glass ashtray. "There's a bird sanctuary at its southern end. I do a bit of twitching on the quiet."

"I have to go there," says Sam.

"You enjoy bird watching? Let's make a day of it. We might see a great crested grebe."

But Sam isn't interested in going to Eel Pie Island to spot great crested grebes. She's hoping to find Kitty. "She might know where my father is. Mr Fraye, did you ever meet my father?"

No, but he'd heard of him. His sister had mentioned John Tabuh years ago when she thought he was a murderer and again recently, on the phone, when she realized to her shame that he wasn't.

"We can approach Eel Pie Island in the Morris," offers Mr Fraye. "But ... hmm ... it can only be reached by footbridge or boat, I'm afraid."

"I don't mind walking." Sam gets down from the table. She's already dressed, but there's the small – or rather large – matter of Lola. Naturally, Lola must go to Eel Pie Island too, but Sam is concerned that an orangutan may attract the wrong sort of attention.

"She could go in disguise," suggests Mr Fraye. "Mrs Fraye could lend her an outfit. With a little ingenuity and a large hat she could pass for someone's grandmother."

Giggling to herself, Mrs Fraye takes Lola by the hand and, together, they go through her wardrobe. Lola is used to dressing up. She takes great pleasure in trying on the vast selection of hats on offer. With the addition of a pair of glasses, she is transformed into a passable human being; but the illusion isn't quite complete.

"It's the way she walks," says Sam. "Old ladies just don't walk like that."

Mr Fraye insists his Aunt Lillian did, especially after her operation; but Sam isn't convinced. "I don't suppose you've a wheelbarrow? That might solve the problem."

Mr Fraye won't hear of it; it would never do to push your granny in a wheelbarrow. "We have a wheelchair," he says. "A folding one. We bought it for Lillian but she refused to get in it."

Rather than bore you with the way Mr Fraye hit his head on a beam while trying to get the wheelchair down from the loft, and how he pinched his thumb as he forced it into the back of his car, let's move on as swiftly as we can through the traffic and down to the Thames. Sam can see Eel Pie Island from the window. Mr Fraye parks near the footbridge and unfolds the wheelchair for Lola. He puts a rug over her knees to hide the red hair sticking out of her stockings.

Mr Fraye is so kind, but the truth is that Sam wants to find Kitty by herself. It's time for Sam to move on. She's not sure where she's going and it's a scary thought, but she has her protective oil and witch's cord, and she hopes the witch doctor's notebook will guide her. She'll never find her father if she stays put.

"Mr Fraye, please don't be offended, but I think this is something I have to do alone."

"Ah," he replies, "I did wonder."

"Did you?"

He nods sagely. "But will you be all right on your own? I could wait here, if you like." He pauses. "Or … not," he adds.

"I'll be fine, really. Lola will look after me."

Again, he nods. "Of course. But if ever you're in trouble… Well, you only have to call and I'll come and collect you both." He slips a coin into her pocket. "For the telephone."

"Thanks for everything, Mr Fraye. I could never have rescued Lola without you."

"It was a pleasure. An absolute pleasure, and I hope you find who you're looking for. If you believe you will, you will. Shoulders back, head held high, remember."

As Sam pushes Lola's wheelchair across the footbridge, she realizes she's forgotten to ask Mr Fraye the three questions. But sometimes there's no need to ask directly – he's given her the answers through his deeds: talking doves are just an illusion. The reality is, though, there's no scientific explanation as to how he came into her life just when she needed him – was that magic?

She turns to wave goodbye, but he's gone. The coin is burning a hole in her pocket. She takes it out and a quick glance tells her this is no ordinary coin.

* * *

When Sam held the cat charm last night in the hope of finding Kitty via psychometry, nothing happened at first. It was only in her half-asleep, half-awake state that the name Eel Pie Island sprang to mind. It was such a strong feeling, she sat up in bed and, unable to stop herself, shouted, "Eel Pie!"

It woke Lola, who hooted anxiously, but when she realized that the outburst had been caused by her darling girl, she gathered Sam in her arms, and together they fell back to sleep.

There was a dream about a painted barge covered in cats. There were so many cats, it looked as if the deck was lined with fur. It vibrated with the sheer volume of purring. It was dark and the barge was strung with green fairy lights; only they weren't fairy lights; they were cats' eyes.

Sam pushes the wheelchair up a ramp and explains to Lola that they're looking for a barge with cats. The orang-utan has taken Mrs Fraye's hat off and is licking the cherries which decorate the brim. Sam puts it back on her head and ties it firmly under the chin.

"You're supposed to be in disguise, remember?"

Lola hides her face in the rug, but she's smiling. She likes it in the wheelchair. Orang-utans aren't very keen on walking.

There are several houseboats moored at the water's edge. Some have dogs and Sam tries to steer clear of these. While it's easy enough to fool people that she's taking her granny for a stroll, she can't fool the dogs; they have an excellent sense of smell, and grandmothers smell nothing like orang-utans.

Sure enough, as they turn the corner, a burly hound with little red eyes gets a whiff of ape and barks loudly. Sam breaks into a trot. "Next time I take you out, remind me to rub you with Ruth's oil, Lola!"

Once the dog is far behind them, Sam stops to catch her breath and is greeted by gales of laughter coming from a blue barge. Attached to its mast is a huge inflatable bird held together with patches from a puncture kit; it swoops in the breeze, trying to escape from its tether. Sam guesses it's an albatross. She once read a poem – The Rime of the Ancient Mariner – in which a sailor shot an albatross and was cursed forever, because seafarers believe the birds are the spirits of drowned mariners.

She's just wondering how such superstitions come about when several men dressed as pirates rush onto deck armed with bows and arrows which they fire at the inflatable bird. Most of the arrows miss, but suddenly, there's a loud pop followed by a chorus of hurrahs as the air escapes from the albatross, causing it to fold like a pancake.

"That was lucky, my hearties!" cries the captain.

"That was *very* lucky, Captain!" agree the rest. They all perform the Sailor's Hornpipe, kicking each others' buttocks with gusto as if to celebrate a great victory.

Suddenly, they realize they're being watched.

"Ah," says the captain to Sam, "you mustn't worry, you know."

"Mustn't I?" says Sam.

There's a chorus of mumbling from the crew. Oh, no, she shouldn't worry. That was the whole point of shooting the albatross; they did it to prove that no bad luck would befall the sailors, and to make a mockery of the ancient belief.

"How can you be sure?" asks Sam. "You've only just shot it! Isn't it too early to tell?"

Not at all, they reply. We shoot the same albatross every year and nothing's happened so far. True, the captain has corns, but that's not bad luck; it's because he wears pointy boots.

The captain and his crew are all members of the Eccentrics Club of Great Britain, a group that gathers on the blue barge every Friday the thirteenth to deliberately flout superstition.

"Come aboard!" says the bo'sun, "There're only eleven of us, so if you two ladies would join us for lunch, we can smash the theory that thirteen diners is an unlucky number."

"I'd love to," says Sam, "but my granny's rather shy. I think she'd prefer to sit by herself on the deck if you don't mind."

Nobody minds. They carry the wheelchair onto the barge, park Lola in the sunshine and take Sam down below. The entrance to the galley is blocked by a ladder propped up at such a shallow angle, she has to limbo under it. The pirates encourage her with handclapping and chanting: "Under the ladder! Under the ladder!"

"Isn't it unlucky to walk under a ladder?" she asks.

"Nonsense!" cries the captain.

"Rubbish!" roars the bo'sun. "People only assume it's unlucky because a ladder bears a resemblance to the gallows. But it's *not* the gallows, is it? I bear a resemblance to a pirate, but I'm *not* a pirate, am I?"

"No, you work for the Council," snorts the captain. "There are no pirates in the council."

The bo'sun stops clapping and half closes his eyes.

"There are no pirates ... but there are sharks!"

Sam is about to ask the bo'sun to explain himself when she sees a black cat being chased by an old man in baggy shorts. He's leading a conga of ladies who are yelling instructions at him.

"Faster, Albert! Puss is getting away!"

"You catch him, we'll stroke him!"

"Almost got him... Dang! He's gone under the seat."

Sam kneels down and peers at the cat. It peers back and she strokes its head.

"You didn't ought to do that!" wheezes Albert sarcastically. "Stroking a black cat? That's dicing with death, that is!"

Sam scoops the cat up and rocks it like a furry baby. "Superstitious nonsense," she says.

"Of course it is!" agree the ladies. "We stroke that cat on a regular basis and no harm has come to any one of us, has it, girls?"

"No, no harm ... although Gladys did slip over outside the butchers."

"Yes, and Sylvia Pugh was struck by lightning."

"And Mavis Meredith's boarding house slid down the cliff into the sea."

But none of these tragic events were in any way brought about by stroking black cats; and as if to prove it, they line up and take it in turns to caress the captured cat until the bell rings for lunch.

There are thirteen chairs, but as Lola isn't joining them, the cat is placed on the spare seat next to Sam to make up the numbers. By each chair is an umbrella. The captain sits at the head of the table and as soon as Sam is seated, he bellows, "Brollies up!" There's a whooshing sound as eleven umbrellas are opened and the odd scream as someone is poked in the eye.

The bo'sun nudges Sam with his elbow. "Put your umbrella up. And the cat's while you're at it."

"Why? Does the roof leak? There don't appear to be any holes."

"The opening of an umbrella indoors is dreadfully unlucky!" mocks the captain.

"Ludicrous!" shouts the bo'sun.

"Folly!" wheezes Albert. "I always open my umbrella indoors and I've never had an accident because of – arghhhhhh!"

As he speaks, the leg of his chair falls off and he's deposited on the floor, grabbing the tablecloth as he falls, causing the crockery to slide off and smash.

Sam rushes to help him up. "No broken bones, touch wood!" she says, tapping the table, which outrages the seated members of the Eccentrics Club.

"*Don't* touch wood! We don't do anything that's supposed to be lucky."

"We don't believe in it," agrees Albert, who now has nowhere to sit and is trying to share a small-bottomed chair with the large-bottomed lady next to him.

Sam says that surely Albert was lucky not to be hurt, but he insists luck didn't come into it. The fact that he fell has *nothing* to do with the umbrellas; the leg of his chair had woodworm.

It's not easy eating a meal while holding an umbrella, and the pie tastes odd to Sam.

"That's because it's Mag-Pie," says the bo'sun.

"*Magpie* Pie?"

"Yes, that's why it's mostly gravy and not much meat. There isn't much meat on one magpie."

"Why not make it with more magpies?"

The bo'sun rolls his eyes. "Don't you know the rhyme about magpies?" He starts to sing:

One for sorrow, two for joy,
Three for a girl and four for a boy.
Five for silver, six for gold
Seven for a secret never to be told.

There's a round of applause, and the captain leans across the table and explains that to see a single magpie is about the unluckiest thing that can happen, so imagine how unlucky it is to eat one. Sam puts her fork down. "It tastes awful."

"Have some wine," says the bo'sun, slapping her on

the back and pouring the pale green liquid into her glass.

"Is it unlucky wine?" she asks.

"It made from four-leaf clovers," he whispers, "which *would* be lucky, only we pulled a leaf off each one, so then they were *three*-leaf clovers."

"How unlucky can a wine be? Cheers!" hoots Albert, deliberately spilling the salt.

"You have gravy round your face," says Sam.

"Do I? Does anyone have a mirror?"

The big-bottomed lady produces one from her handbag. Albert looks at his reflection and, having taken care to wipe off every trace of magpie gravy with the corner of the tablecloth, he smashes the mirror to pieces with a ladle. "Seven years bad luck, my friends?" He grins.

"Not on your *Nelly*!" holler the guests in unison. "Well done!" "Bravo!"

The black cat climbs onto Sam's lap, lured by a scrap of magpie meat, and sits there purring.

"This is such a sweet cat, Captain. Does it live on this barge?" asks Sam.

The captain shrugs his shoulders.

"I don't know. We only hire the barge. It might do and it might not."

"Not!" shouts Albert, who's had too much clover wine. "That cat doesn't live here, it lives on the Cat Barge."

"The Cat Barge?"

Yes. There's a barge full of cats of all shapes and sizes moored somewhere round about. Albert can't remember where exactly, but he remembers seeing it once.

"When he was drunk!" says the big-bottomed lady, upon whose lap he is now sitting.

"That cat," continues Albert, "lives with the Cat Woman. But I can't tell you what she looks like, because … because…"

The lady snatches his glass away. "Because you're drunk, that's why!"

"No, no, no … because she wears a *mask*."

A mask? A shiver runs down Sam's spine. "Did she tell you her name, Albert? Was it Kitty?"

"I never asked," he replies. "It's very rude to ask a lady her name."

"No, it's rude to ask a lady her *age*!" insists the woman, whereupon Albert promptly tries to guess how old she is, causing great offence. The rest of the ladies leap to her defence, assuring her that she doesn't look a day over ninety, and, while the captain and the bo'sun try to stop them lynching Albert on the ladder with his own tie, Sam slips away from the table with the black cat in her arms.

With any luck, she will be able to follow it back to the barge.

HOW TO READ HIEROGLYPHS

GLYPH	SOUND/LETTER	GLYPH	SOUND/LETTER
	glottal stop, often used as *a*		*ch* (as in lo*ch*)
	e (or *i* or *j*)		*s*
	a		*z*
	w, or *oo*, *u*		*sh*
	b		*k, q*
	p		*k*
	f, ph		*g*
	m		*t*
	n		*tch*
	r		*d*
	h		*dj* or *z*
	h		*l*
	o		

KITTY BASTET

The black cat sits in front of Lola's wheelchair and washes its whiskers. When Sam releases the brake, it trots off down the towpath with its tail held high. Sam hurries after it, but the wheelchair isn't easy to steer. It keeps veering towards the water like a wayward supermarket trolley and she's afraid that she'll tip Lola into the Thames, or lose the cat.

She shouldn't worry; this Friday the thirteenth is a lucky day for her. The black cat doesn't climb up a tree, nor does it disappear under one of the many overturned canoes on the slipway; it heads straight for home.

Following its silent paws, we arrive at a place untroubled by houses and left to grow wild. Apart from the whine of mosquitoes rising in clouds above the river and the monotonous *squeak, squeak* of Lola's wheelchair, all is peaceful. Deserted.

There, to the left, is the Cat Barge. It is moored alone, its hull bumping against the bank behind a lacy screen of cow parsley. If you look closely, you'll see that the barge is decorated with hieroglyphics, and although the paint work has faded, the gilt on the figurehead is too bright to look at when the sun strikes it; shield your eyes – it is Bastet, the Cat Goddess.

Lola has slipped out of the wheelchair and is sitting in the long grass with her arm around Sam. They watch as the black cat leaps effortlessly onto the barge and sinks into a sea of fur. There are so many cats, the outline of the barge is fuzzy with whiskers.

There's no sign of Kitty yet. Sam puts her finger to her lips, beckons to Lola, and they climb on deck. That part is easy; it's knowing where to put your feet once aboard that's the problem. the barge is carpeted with cats and it wouldn't do to tread on that huge tabby one because it is bound to let out an ear-splitting... *MIAOWWWW!* The startled tabby cartwheels through the air, hissing and spitting, causing the other cats to explode simultaneously like a furry firework display. The fallout of fur is building up to unleash a gigantic sneeze – Sam has to pinch her nose... But someone's coming! Sam stands like a statue; Lola ducks and hides among the cats.

A woman rushes up from below deck, the sleeves of her long robe frothing around her fingertips. Her hair is waist length and dark and although her figure is youthful, it's impossible to tell how old she is because of her mask. It's tight-fitting – almost like a second skin – with the features painted on in Egyptian style. Only her eyes are animated;

troubled eyes that flick from cat to cat, wondering what's caused all the excitement.

The masked woman clutches a kitten to her breast. It's so young, its eyes are still blue; but to its mistress's shock, it has already mastered human speech, because suddenly, it gazes up at her and in a snuffly voice says: "Hello, Kitty!"

The woman holds the kitten at arm's length, stares at it quizzically then presses its face close to her ear. Its eyes widen and it speaks again: "Look behind you, Kitty."

The woman turns and is so startled to see a girl in a ringmaster's hat, it throws her off balance. Sam catches her as she falls.

"You *are* Kitty, aren't you?"

The woman doesn't reply.

"You are Kitty Bastet?"

Perhaps it's not Kitty. Or perhaps it *is* Kitty but she can't remember who she is. Perhaps her memory never returned – or is she playing games? Suddenly, the woman speaks.

"Who in Ra's name are *you*?"

"My name is Sam. Sam … Tabuh."

She hesitates with her surname because she has been brought up as Sam Khaan. She'd kept her mother's maiden name. She was known as Sam Khaan at school but now she wants to be Sam Tabuh.

The woman's mask remains expressionless, but behind it, her mouth drops open in disbelief. A shudder escapes through the mouth slit. "You are not Sam. You're an illusion!"

Sam takes a blue pencil out of her pocket and rubs it with her fingers; the pencil turns red. It's basic magic: the red pencil had a thin tube of blue paper over it. Sam slips it off and puts it in her pocket faster than the eye can see.

"*That* is an illusion, Kitty; I'm real."

She takes off her hat and points to her wild, blonde streak "See? Now do you believe I'm John Tabuh's daughter?"

Kitty claps her hands to her mask and shakes her head in denial. "No, you are a … ghogle!"

Kitty struggles to find the right word; although most of her memory has returned, there are peculiar gaps in her vocabulary.

"A ghogle? Don't you mean ghost?"

"You died in a fire when you were a booby. I was up a ladder, I couldn't reach you. The flans were too fierce. I screamed out to Lilo, 'Save the booby!' But the flans blew out the top widow. I remember falling … falling."

She meant flames, not flans. Widow meant window. Saving the booby? Ah, the *baby*. Sam finds it hard to keep a straight face. Kitty squats down, her fingers over the eye-holes in her mask and groans. "Have you come back to haunt me?"

"How can I haunt you? I'm not dead! The reason Lola and I are here is to ask if you know where my father—"

"Lilo? Is Lilo here too?" Kitty thought she'd died in the fire with Sam. She'd grieved for both of them.

"Yes, *Lola*'s over there, trying to hide among the ginger cats. You can't miss her – I had to disguise her as a granny, and the blouse is rather bright."

"But I do miss her," wails Kitty.

Lola swings across the deck and throws her arms around Kitty, who is overcome with emotion. "Oh … *oh*! My darling pet grape! My sweet meringue-utan!"

Sam notices tears spilling down the elegant nose of the mask. She pretends to watch the seagulls and waits for the crying to stop. "Now do you believe I'm who I say I am, Kitty?"

Kitty dabs her mask with her sleeve. "I want to believe it more than anything but I dare not. What if this is just a beautiful drama and I wake up? My hat will break. I'll go mad."

"Let's do a deal," says Sam. "I will trust that you are Kitty if you trust that I am Sam."

"But I'm *not* Kitty; I am Fey Ra! High Prancess to the Giddiness Bistet."

Sam has been wondering for some time why Kitty's name doesn't appear on the witch doctor's list. She has a quick glance in the notebook. There's her real name, smouldering away at the top. Fey Ra, Priestess to the Goddess Bastet.

"But you can call me Kitty if you like," announces Fey Ra.

She holds out her arms to embrace Sam. "I primrosed your father I'd look after you, but I failed – I'm so sorry."

Sam puts her arms stiffly by her sides. As I've explained, she can't recall ever being held by a person, and although Kitty held her when she was a baby, she's forgotten it and the embrace feels awkward. Lola comes to the rescue and puts her arms round both of them.

This is not the first time Lola has come to Sam's rescue, and now it is time for you to learn about her Heroic Deed. Kitty didn't witness it – she'd already jumped out of the window – but I can tell you that it was Lola who lifted Sam out of the burning crib and it was then that Sam dropped her silver rattle.

But how did the flames start? Why was Kitty up a ladder? Who was the blonde woman Ruth Abafey saw running from the scene?

"Ruth who?"

Kitty can't remember her at all. Sam sits her down.

"*Try* Kitty. Concentrate! She's the witch who pulled you out of the wharf. You left this under her pillow." She shows her the cat charm. Kitty touches it with her fingertips.

"So *that's* where it went. I never knew the witch was called Ruth."

"Why did you leave without saying goodbye to her, Kitty? Where did you go?"

"To look for you!"

Kitty tells Sam exactly what the witch had told her; the blow to her head had deprived her of speech. For a time, she couldn't remember who she was or how she came to be in the witch's waiting room. Then one morning, her memory began to return; there had been a fire in the warehouse. She remembered who started it.

"It was Candy Khaan!"

Sam feels as if she's been hit on the head with a frying pan. "*My Aunt* Candy?"

"Yes! Your Aunt Candy has the most violent teapot—"

"I know she's violent," grumbles Sam. "I lived with her for twelve years."

Kitty throws her hands up in disbelief. "You did *what*? But I looked for you there! Hope against hope, I went to St Peter's Square to see if Lola had managed to rescue you and take you to Candy's."

But the windows were boarded up. No one answered the doorbell. Kitty thought Candy had flown, like John Tabuh.

"I was there all the time," says Sam. "I don't know how I came to be there though…"

She breaks off. Something Aunt Candy had said suddenly begins to make sense. *Your only friend, the orange monkey, turned up with you on my doorstep like rubbish blown in from the street…!* Aunt Candy was the woman Ruth saw running away from the burning warehouse. She'd slammed the door behind her so that Kitty, Lola and Sam would be trapped in the flames. Lola had climbed out of the window with Sam in her arms and followed Aunt Candy home. They arrived safe and sound at St Peter's Square, and despite Aunt Candy's fury, she was no match for an orang-utan with a grudge; she had no choice but to let them in.

Sadly, Kitty hadn't known this. Consumed by grief, guilt, and utterly confused – for her memory would never be quite the same – she went to live as a recluse on Eel Pie Island, where no one would ever find her.

Or so she thought.

The mind-reading trick

The masked magician guesses a secret word which someone has written on a piece of paper – how?

THE SECRET

You need: a pencil, paper, a white envelope, lighter fuel, matches, a fireproof bucket full of sand.

NB Ask permission to use matches and lighter fuel if you are a minor or an arsonist.

1. Choose a volunteer. Explain that you can read their mind.
2. Ask them to write a word down on the piece of paper – they mustn't tell you what it is.
3. Ask them to put the paper in the envelope and seal it.
4. Pour lighter fuel over the envelope; it will go transparent so you can see the word written on the paper inside.
5. Memorize the word, put the envelope in the bucket of sand and set fire to it.
6. Reveal the secret word to your amazed audience.

CHRISTA

No matter what opinion you might have formed about John Tabuh, you should know this: it was *Kitty* who persuaded him to leave his baby daughter in her care while he went to Scotland. He would never have gone if he'd thought Sam was at risk. If only he could see her now, eating oranges with Lola below deck on the barge.

"So he thinks I'm dead too, Kitty."

Kitty nods sadly. "As for your poor mother – the grief must be killing her."

Sam juggles a handful of oranges and explains that there's no chance of that; her mother died when she was born. Aunt Candy told her.

"Oh, *did* she?" Kitty starts muttering in Ancient Egyptian: "Oh, mighty Bastet, by your infinite grace protect the sanity of this unhappy child!"

"I'm fine about it, honestly," insists Sam. "I never knew my mother; I've had thirteen years to get used to the fact that she's dead."

"It's *not* a fact!"

Sam continues to juggle oranges as if she hasn't heard correctly. "What's not a fact?"

"Your mother didn't die in childbirth."

"How did she die then?"

"She didn't." To Kitty's knowledge, Christa left the warehouse in a box, but she was alive and well at the time.

The oranges plop to the floor and the colour drains from Sam's face. You'd think she'd be delighted to hear that her mother was alive, but the truth – if it is the truth – takes a while to sink in.

"Say something," Kitty implores.

Sam is speechless. If her mother is alive, why has she never tried to find her? Does her mother think she's dead too?

"There's a very good raisin—" begins Kitty.

"What good reason could there be for my mother to leave the warehouse in a box!"

"Well … ooh… There was a good reason. It'll come to me in a minute…"

Is Kitty struggling with her memory or is she afraid to tell Sam the truth? Sam grits her teeth.

"Try to remember! Did Aunt Candy know my mother was alive?"

No, Aunt Candy was tricked into thinking Christa was dead. For once, she hadn't lied to Sam.

"Who tricked her? Tell me, Kitty!"

"Your father, your mother and, er, me."

Why would they do such a thing? Why would anyone

want to fool Candy into thinking her own sister had died? Kitty holds up her hands:

"Candy brought it on herself. We had to make her believe Christa had been killed."

Killed? What dreadful secrets had gone up in smoke all those years ago? John and Christa aren't here to explain; it's down to Kitty to reveal everything.

She admits to Sam that the witch doctor really had sent his son on a global quest. That much is now indisputable. Unfortunately, things didn't go quite as John had expected. Hardly surprising. The chances of crossing the Pacific in a mwa sawah and surviving are very slim. The witch doctor must have known the canoe would capsize, so, given that he was desperate for his only son to step into his shoes, why would he send him to his inevitable death?

I suspect Yafer Tabuh *knew* a ship would be passing the right place at the right time to save his son from the shark-infested water. He could read the patterns of the waves. Even if the ship was far out to sea, its ripples could be read at the upper end of the Sepik, and he could judge its position with amazing accuracy.

In fact, John had told Kitty that his mwa sawah capsized on the third day of his journey and that he and Lola had been rescued by an ocean liner called *The Trinity*. John had worked aboard the ship until a dreadful incident occurred, forcing him to flee to London. There he'd met Bart Hayfue who'd given him Kitty's address.

"What dreadful incident?" asks Sam. "Did he tell you?"

"He refused, so I asked the ancient spirits."

So Bart had been right. Kitty *did* believe she could communicate with the spirits. Trying to sound as sincere as possible, Sam asks her what they'd said. Kitty lowers her voice.

"Murder by magic!"

When Kitty told John what the spirits had written, he couldn't look her in the eye. He claimed that automatic writing was a load of nonsense and insisted on showing her a mind-reading trick to prove that although it made him *appear* psychic, it was just an illusion.

"Was it the trick where you have to write something on a piece of paper and the magician sets fire to it and guesses what you've written? asks Sam.

"Yes – argh! You read my mind!"

"No, I didn't. He wrote it down in a notebook I found in the attic."

She still doesn't know how the notebook came to be in the trunk or how John Tabuh came to be a magician. I do, but now isn't the time to share it with you. I'm happy to share the secret of the mind-reading trick though – no doubt you found it at the front of this chapter. I thought twice about telling you. Once you know how the trick works it's so obvious, it's disappointing. But I need you to understand why John Tabuh became so sceptical. The more he learnt how illusions were done, the more he felt there was no such thing as real magic; all was trickery, manipulation and deception.

His English mother was partly to blame. She was determined to bring John up the western way. She didn't have long to live; she knew the world was changing and wanted her son to be prepared. That's why she taught him to ask questions, why she told him that science and psychology were behind most of the phenomena his father called magic – most, but not *all*. Sam opens the shell locket and shows Kitty the photo inside. "Is this his mother?" she asks.

"Yes, that's Freya. When she died, John lost faith in his father because he failed to bring her back from the dread."

"Do you think it's possible to bring someone back from the dead, Kitty?"

Kitty isn't sure, but John told her that when he was thirteen, Lola was hit by a poisoned dart and died in his arms. Sam interrupts the story.

"And didn't he beg his father to bring her back to life?"

That's what she'd dreamt and Kitty says yes. Seeing his son's sorrow, the witch doctor took Lola into his hut and chanted for two days. When he called John inside, Lola was alive.

"See what power I have, my son!" he'd boasted. "I can raise the dead."

But when John's mother died, the same magic didn't work and John was left with nothing but her photo and three questions:

1. Did Lola really die or had she just swooned?
2. Did the witch doctor simply give her an antidote for poison?
3. Had the witch doctor swapped the dead orang-utan for a live one?

151

"I wonder if John's found the answers yet?" sighs Kitty. "He was supposed to be asking three questions his father gave him: What is magic? What is real? What is—"

"Illusion," says Sam. "I know."

But there's one illusion she knows nothing about; her mother's death. How was it faked? She won't find out this afternoon. Kitty is dozing off; she tires easily. She says she has a weak heart, something to do with smoke inhalation. She must lie down in her cabin.

"Do you sleep with your mask on?" asks Sam.

"What mask?"

It could be a weary attempt at a joke. But trust no one.

THE MAGIC CHAMBER TRICK

The masked magician's assistant climbs into a box. The lid is closed, and with a wave of a wand the magician says, "Be gone!" The box is tilted towards the audience with both hands and the lid is opened. Hey presto! – the box is empty. How?

THE SECRET

You need: a large cardboard box, extra cardboard, strong tape, black paint, a little friend.

1. Cut out the bottom of the box leaving a lip on three sides.
2. Cut a false bottom from another piece of cardboard. Fit it in the box and attach with a hinge of tape. Tape on a handle.
3. Cut or tape together a one-piece cardboard top.
4. Paint the whole thing black.

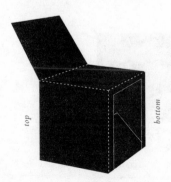

continued over ☞

HOW TO DO THE TRICK

Your magic chamber has a false bottom. When you tip the box forward, the box slides over your assistant, who pulls the hinged bottom shut by holding the handle. Your assistant is now crouched down, hidden behind the box, but to your audience, she's vanished!

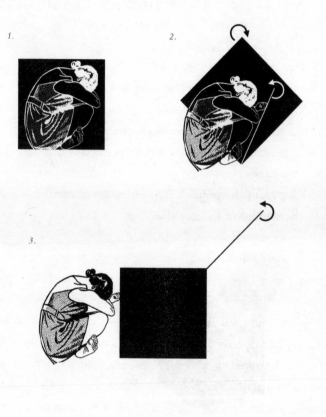

1.

2.

3.

THE MAGICIAN'S ASSISTANT

It is dawn. The Cat Barge has grown a platform of foliage near the top of the mast. It's Lola's nest; she is asleep inside, cuddling her monkey. In the rainforest, she'd have slept in the trees, building a new nest every day. She's used to sleeping in Sam's bed now, but, last night, she wanted to sleep under the stars.

Kitty is up before Sam. Maybe she's an early riser or maybe she didn't want to be caught without her mask on. I know the feeling.

Sam is still asleep. In the night, she dreamt that her mother was lying in a box painted in the Egyptian style. She was wearing pink gloves and her hands were crossed over her heart. She was alive and beautiful – not a bit how Aunt Candy had described her. Sam had cried out, "Mother!"

She'd woken in a sweat then struggled to go back to sleep, desperate to return to her dream. Instead, she slipped into a nightmare: she thought she saw her mother in the same box, but this time her gloves were purple with blood

155

and, when Sam cried out, the woman snapped open her green eyes and snickered, "Surprise... I'm *Candy*!"

Sam sits upright and screams. Lola is below deck and by her side before you can say *Pongo pygmaeus*.

Kitty appears with a cup of coffee. "What's wrong? Have you had a night horse?"

Sam grabs her by the shoulders. "Did my mother bleed to death? Was she stabbed through the heart?"

"No, there was no blood – it was red oink."

"*Red ink?*" It makes no sense. How did Kitty even know her mother?

Kitty perches on the end of the cabin bed and adjusts her mask. "Drink this and I'll tell you."

"I hate coffee."

Sam drinks it anyway. She takes a great gulp every time Kitty comes up with a new revelation; it helps to wash down things that would otherwise stick in her throat. I will now tell you exactly what Kitty told Sam as the sun rose like a fried egg over Eel Pie Island.

When John and Lola first arrived at the warehouse, Kitty kept her distance. Like many artists, she needed solitude to create and what she created was mostly cat-sized sarcophagi – highly decorated coffins similar to the ones found inside pyramids. The warehouse was home to lots of cats. If one died, Kitty mummified it and placed it into a sarcophagus, along with a carved mouse and a tin of tuna to be enjoyed in the afterlife. It bothers me that she forgot to include a tin-opener, but perhaps, if there *is* an afterlife for cats, there's someone there who opens tins for them.

While Kitty practised her art at one end of the warehouse, John practised magic at the other. But as the Dark Prince's doves escaped yet again, splattering droppings all over her sarcophagi, she decided enough was enough; she wasn't prepared to put up with random acquaintances of Bart Hayfue's cluttering up her warehouse with magician's paraphernalia. It just wasn't on.

Kitty didn't say any of this though; John was so handsome, she would always forget what she'd come to tell him off about. He was so charming, he only had to catch a woman's eye and she wanted to mother him or marry him. Kitty wanted to mother him, and when John told her he had no mother, she felt it was her moral duty to care for him.

Although he was managing to scrape a living by performing illusions on the street, John's lack of income bothered him. Kitty said it didn't matter, she could keep them both by selling her carvings; but he was fiercely proud and insisted on paying his own way. One night, unable to sleep for worrying, he confessed that he needed to think of a way to raise enough money to travel the world. His father had given him some pearls to sell, but these were for emergencies. Kitty didn't want him to leave and asked him why the hurry. He was on a mission, he said. He'd been away for two years already and hardly begun. If his father died before he completed it, the consequences would be too terrible to contemplate.

Kitty put her mind to the problem and had a

brainwave. She'd make him a magic box; a sarcophagus large enough for a woman to fit inside. He could use it along with a sword to create a death-defying illusion. And that would be just the beginning! Together, they would create a fantastic magic show: she would make his props, he would invent new and wonderful illusions. They would invite an agent to see his act, right here in the warehouse.

Forget the streets, the agent would be so impressed, he'd book John into all the best theatres. There would be a real stage. A beautiful assistant. He could join the Magic Circle and become the greatest magician in London. He would be invited to travel far and wide – all expenses paid – and, in between shows, he could visit the people on his father's list. How famous he would become. How proud his father will be.

John, who was unduly modest about his talent, wasn't sure if any of this would happen but Kitty seemed so certain, so excited, he was willing to give it a try. But where to begin?

First, he needed a glamorous assistant. John wondered if Lola could take on the role, but apart from the fact that she didn't look her best in a sequinned gown, it was decided that it would be better to employ her in other ways, for the following reasons:

1. Orang-utans are shorter and more agile than human assistants and can be easily hidden in places an audience would never expect.

2. Orang-utans are excellent climbers and can hide up in the roof, manipulating mirrors, hanging upside down by their feet, if necessary.

3. Orang-utans are intelligent and, having very long arms, can be trained to release trap doors and operate secret compartments that a human assistant could never reach.

Lola could help perform all sorts of tantalizing illusions that could never be accomplished if she weren't an ape – and not realizing an ape was on stage (for John would take care to keep her hidden), no one would ever guess how the tricks had been done.

Lola was invaluable, but he needed to find a beautiful human assistant. Apart from passing props and climbing into boxes, he needed her to act as a distraction and misdirect the audience's eye away from him while he was performing his magic. Kitty knew someone who would be ideal for the job; someone who'd worked in a circus and was particularly flexible. However, she was hesitant to suggest her because the woman was a little unhinged, to say the least.

"Let's risk it," said John. "She can't be that awful."

Famous last words, Dark Prince! John might have been brought up the Western Way but he was far too trusting where women were concerned. He believed they were all essentially good, like his mother; but this woman wasn't. Her name? Candy Khaan.

John hired her on the spot. Candy wafted into the

warehouse with her blonde hair flowing over her slim shoulders and smiled at him with perfect teeth. When he asked her to climb into a magic box, she folded into it as prettily as a petticoat and he was sold.

They should have nailed the lid down there and then and thrown the box into the Thames. It would have saved everyone a lot of heartache, but Kitty didn't know just how twisted Candy had become.

People don't become twisted without good reason though. Candy had been badly treated by a man in her past. She'd fallen in love with the circus ringmaster. He'd asked her to marry him, but on their wedding day he jilted her for Lorna the Lion Tamer; the humiliation was too much.

Devastated, Candy had climbed onto the trapeze, hung by her feet, then deliberately let go; there was no safety net. As she plunged head-first into the sea lion pool, the audience roared with laughter, thinking she was a clown. No bones were broken but her failed suicide left her with a shattered ego and a warped brain, and she became greedier and needier than ever.

Kitty was soon to learn how dangerous she'd become, but, by then, it would be too late. For a while, Candy managed to conceal her psychotic nature and set about wooing the innocent John Tabuh with all the charm she could muster. Before the month was out, she announced their engagement and moved into the warehouse.

Kitty had taken John aside and insisted the engagement was far too soon. The woman John Tabuh had fallen in love with wasn't the real Candy; it was an illusion. But he couldn't see it. Even magicians can't see beyond the mirror when they're in love.

As soon as Candy had John's ring on her finger, she changed; she became rude and demanding. She would turn up late for rehearsals. She'd ruin tricks and blame it on Lola, but if Kitty complained, John defended Candy, insisting that she was passionate, not aggressive; a perfectionist, not a tyrant. He said it even though she was making him miserable, because he thought he loved her.

When Candy threw a tantrum and demanded new stage clothes, John said she could hire a wardrobe mistress. She suggested her own sister, knowing, no doubt, that she could bully her into producing a lifetime's supply of frocks and a free wedding dress.

Christa was every bit as beautiful as Candy. They were identical twins. Physically, it was impossible to tell them apart, but there the similarity ended. Christa was modest, gentle and full of compassion, and as time passed the scales fell from John Tabuh's eyes and he realized that he didn't love Candy at all; he loved Christa.

John and Christa couldn't stop loving each other. They tried to for Candy's sake, even though she was a monster. Christa knew how hurt she'd been and didn't want to be the cause of more suffering. Kitty encouraged their affair. She'd never seen John so happy and would cover for him while he slipped off to meet Christa at her flat in St Peter's Square.

Candy had no idea what was going on, but one day,

when John had been out on "business", Christa came back to the warehouse glowing with kisses. Candy knew the signs of a woman in love and demanded to know who her boyfriend was. Caught on the hop, Christa said that he was an Intrepid Explorer called Bingo Hall.

Nine months later, she gave birth to a girl; something of a miracle as she'd been told she could never have children. The baby was called Sam. She had her mother's fine features and her father's blond streak in her dark hair, which Christa kept covered with a bonnet; if Candy saw it, she'd guess John was the father and who knows what she would do.

"She'd kill herself!" Christa had cried. Although she loved John with a passion, she insisted their affair must stop and begged him to marry Candy as he'd promised. It was the last thing he wanted but, as he couldn't bear to see Christa consumed with guilt, he agreed.

Unfortunately the truth has a habit of getting out. The baby was lying in a cot in the warehouse – Christa had only left her for a few minutes to fetch some sequins – when along came Candy. Gloating with happiness because John had finally set a date for their wedding, she took the baby out of the cot and whirled her around like an aeroplane. As she did so, the bonnet slipped off.

Only Kitty saw it happen and recoiled in horror. Candy had seen the blonde streak in Sam's hair and realized in an instant that she was *not* the Intrepid Explorer's baby.

She was John's.

How to saw a lady in half

The masked magician's assistant lies down in a box with her head and feet sticking out. The magician appears to saw her in half. The halves are separated, yet she steps out all in one piece. How?

THE SECRET

There are several versions of this illusion. Here, the assistant simply curls up to avoid the blade. The feet are false ones activated by a motor.

THE MAGIC BOX

Let's return briefly to the barge to see how Sam is reacting to Kitty's story. She has finished the coffee and Lola is licking the last drops out of the cup. The cats have settled on Sam like a furry duvet, and if it wasn't for the soporific effect of their purring, she wouldn't be nearly as calm.

Besides which, the collective weight of tortoiseshells, tabbies and Burmese is preventing her from doing much.

"It was a crime of passion," continues Kitty. "Candy was jealous. She saw an opportunity and struck. It happened when John asked her to reverse the box truck with him the next moaning."

By which she meant rehearse the box trick, an illusion that is simple but ingenious:

1. Lovely assistant climbs into box. Lid is closed.
2. Magician plunges *real* sword into the box – seemingly straight into assistant's heart.
3. Magician spins box, then opens it.
4. Assistant steps out smiling and unperforated.

This trick has been performed many times but rarely with a real sword. Usually, a magician uses a trick sword; the blade snaps back into the hilt under the slightest pressure so it can't pierce the victim. Or he swaps the sword for a rubber one. If a real sword is used, the box is made big enough for the assistant to roll out of the way of the blade.

John's trick was different. His box was very narrow, even for someone as slim as Candy. The sword was real; there was no room for even the tiniest assistant to escape the deadly blade by shifting sideways.

In fact, the box was deeper than it looked; an optical illusion achieved by painting lines on the lid which tricked the eye into thinking it was flat, rather than bowed.

Kitty had tailor-made the box to fit Candy. It was just deep enough for her to grab hold of two rings screwed into the underside of the lid, hidden in the lining. These rings gave her enough leverage to flip herself over so that her legs were at the *opposite* end of the box. To picture the movement, imagine a snake doing a head-over-heels.

John could then thrust his sword into the box knowing that Candy's heart was up the other end and that the blade would slip safely through the gap between her knees. He'd then spin the box, giving Candy time to flip back again. When he opened the lid, she was in the same position as when the audience last saw her; they'd never work out how she'd cheated death.

Timing is everything; if you practise the manoeuvre twenty times a day for weeks on end, you'll escape without a scratch. But if you're a novice? The trick is lethal.

With that in mind, Candy interrupted her sister from her sewing and told her that she couldn't *possibly* rehearse the box trick today, she had to shop for wedding shoes. Would Christa be an angel and stand in for her? Oh, please, darling, before someone else buys them. If Christa wore her costume – the pink silk with the matching gloves – and just climbed into the magic box and kept her mouth shut, John would never realize they'd swapped places. "It's perfectly safe," she told her. "It's only a pretend sword. Just breathe in and stay still." She never mentioned that the only way to avoid being stabbed was to grab the rings and flip herself over – a move her sister could never have mastered.

Christa didn't have the heart to say no. She let Candy lace her tightly into the costume and hurried to the rehearsal. Little did Candy know that Kitty had overheard her giving Christa the wrong instructions, and as soon as she left to go shopping, Kitty ran to the make-shift stage in the basement to warn John. But to her horror, Christa was already inside the box and there was the Dark Prince, sword raised, ready to plunge it straight through the lid.

"Stop!" Kitty screamed. "It's not Candy in the box! It's *Christa*."

She opened the box and helped the bewildered Christa back onto her feet. She'd been seconds from death, and when she learnt that Candy had plotted for her to die under John's sword, she collapsed. The Dark Prince was aghast. Why would Candy do such an evil thing to her own sister?

"She saw Sam's blonde streak," Kitty told him. "She knows you're the father, John."

Christa, somewhat delirious, began to panic. "We have to convince Candy that he isn't or she'll kill herself!"

It might seem odd that Christa was so concerned about her sister's welfare after what she'd just done. Plotting to kill someone in cold blood is bad enough; tricking your fiancé into doing the dirty deed for you is unspeakable. Even so, Christa felt she was to blame, despite John insisting it was all his fault. Seeing her in such distress and not knowing what to do, he asked Kitty for help.

Kitty's plan was bizarre, but there was a chance it might work. She fetched red ink, black ink and an onion; props they would use to trick Candy into believing John had killed Christa. There was no time to explain the logic behind it; they just had to follow her instructions. Christa was to climb back into the box and play dead. John was to rehearse the lines he would say to Candy. Meanwhile, Kitty busied herself with the details necessary to complete the illusion.

When Candy returned, she found John Tabuh slumped over the box, grieving for his fiancée.

"I have killed Candy, the only girl I have ever loved!"

Red-eyed and weeping (thanks to Kitty's peeled onion), John wondered aloud how the trick had gone so fatally wrong. Then, in a dramatic gesture, he threatened to fall on his sword, insisting that life wasn't worth living now his beloved Candy was dead.

Delighted that she meant so much to him after all, Candy wrestled the sword away, flung her arms around him and confessed to the swap. "Darling, it's *Christa* inside the box, not me!"

John pretended to be greatly surprised, peered inside the box and scratched his head, his eyes darting from the "dead" twin to the live one. Faking confusion, he raised the lid just enough for Candy to see Christa's bleeding "corpse" (clever use of red ink).

Now John ranted about having blood on his hands. What had he done, he asked Candy, that was so unforgivable, she'd tricked him into killing his own wardrobe mistress?

At the mention of the word "mistress" – a word Kitty had told John to stress – Candy bellowed: "*Mistress?* I'll say she was your mistress! You are the father of her brat!" And she yanked off Sam's bonnet to expose the blonde streak – only to find that it had gone! Not for a second did she suspect that the streak had been disguised with black ink.

"The baby has no blonde streak! You're paranoid – mad!" Kitty shouted with such conviction, Candy began to wonder if she *had* imagined the whole affair. Now she must pretend the whole thing was a tragic accident or John would call off the wedding.

"Poor Christa!" she cried, her body wracked with fake sobs. "I never asked her to swap places, she insisted! She wanted me to have those shoes; that's the kind of sweet girl she was. I told her, if you must do it, be sure to lie in the box with your head at the *safe* end."

Kitty wanted to scream "Liar!" but she bit her tongue. If Candy knew she'd overheard, she'd also know that Kitty would have rushed straight to tell John. He'd have stopped the trick and Christa would still be alive. Candy had to believe her sister was dead. To bang the point home and to make herself look unbiased, Kitty accused them *both* of murder and said she was going to the police.

John stood in Kitty's way – and a fine piece of acting it was – saying he'd rather die than go to prison. Again he threatened to fall on his sword. This time he actually nicked his chin on the blade, whereupon Kitty rushed to his aid with a plaster and withdrew her threat. As both women fought to tend the bleeding patient, John announced his master stroke – the twist in the illusion that would allow him to marry Christa and leave the country without Candy ever knowing. All this so that he wouldn't break his fiancée's heart.

There was, he claimed, an ancient chant that his father had used to resurrect Lola. It didn't work on people, but he believed there was another chant that did. He'd been given a list of mystics, one of whom must know this chant. With that in mind, John planned to travel the world with Christa's mummified body in the magic box until he found someone to resurrect her. As soon as she'd come back to life, he'd come home and marry Candy. There was only one condition; she must never tell anyone how Christa died, or there could be no happy outcome.

Although John made it sound as if resurrecting Christa was simply a matter of time, Candy wasn't convinced. But he kept stressing that he was putting himself out to get her off a murder trial and that Christa wouldn't be lying dead if Candy hadn't made her feel obliged to swap places for the sake of a pair of shoes.

Rather than upsetting him by saying, "What if you fail?" she wailed, "Can I come too?"

He wouldn't hear of it. "The world is a dangerous place," he said. "I would never forgive myself if anything happened to you."

John warned that he might be gone for years and that if he didn't return, it wasn't for want of love; he'd simply succumbed to a tropical disease, drowned in a swamp or been eaten by a tiger. Seeing her face fall, he added hastily that, for all he knew, the chap who knew the chant might live nearby – in Watford, perhaps – in which case they'd be married by Christmas. He then asked Kitty to look after Sam until he'd tracked down Bingo Hall, to whom he would return the baby – Bingo was the father after all. Naturally Kitty agreed, as it was her idea to say this in the first place. All that remained was for John to kiss Lola and Candy goodbye.

"But where shall I go?" Candy cried. "I can't stay here with the ghost of my sister!" She was afraid it would haunt her, perhaps.

"Move into Christa's flat at the weekend," said John. "Until then, stay here. Kitty will keep the ghost away while you grieve."

Grieve? Candy Khaan's heart was hardly bleeding for her sister; she stuck her tongue out behind her hand, painted on her most alluring smile and begged John not to go; what would she do for *money*? There was no reply. The Dark Prince had vanished in a puff of smoke.

And so had his magic box.

THE CUP AND BALL TRICK

Using three cups and three coloured balls, the masked magician makes the balls pass through the solid bottoms of cups, jump from cup to cup, disappear from the cup and then reappear. How?

THE SECRET

There are many variations of this illusion. This one uses sleight of hand.

1. A ball is shown to be transferred from the right to the left hand, whilst really, it is retained in the right by finger-palming.

2. A cup is then lifted to show there is nothing underneath it and, when it is put down, the finger-palmed ball is released under the cup.

3. The ball is now shown to have vanished from the left hand and the cup is lifted to show the ball has "travelled" there.

KATY JONES

"**O**h! So my father kissed Candy goodbye but he never kissed me," sulks Sam, ignoring the enormity of what she's just been told and fixating – as people do – on the smallest of details.

"He wanted to kiss you," insists Kitty, "but we'd just managed to convince Candy that you weren't his booby. A display of affection towards you would have ruined our illusion."

"So where did Mum and Dad go?"

Back to Christa's flat in St Peter's Square. Candy had been told that John had gone there to hunt for Bingo Hall's address. In reality, John and Christa had gone to the flat for two reasons:

1. To make travel plans: Christa had hastily copied down the names on the witch doctor's list into a new notebook in case the tropical climate faded the ink and made it illegible. The original

notebook was stored in a trunk in the attic, safely hidden in the goatskin pouch. Kitty had promised to come to the flat with further items necessary for their journey abroad, her excuse to Candy being that she'd gone there to mummify Christa.

2. To get married: the plan was to slip away and get married in secret. They would then sneak back to the warehouse, collect Sam and the trunk from Kitty, and leave the country to complete John's mission. They would then return to his father and settle down as a family until the old man died, whereupon John would take over as witch doctor.

Those were their plans. They left the flat to get married, leaving Candy to move in as John had told her to. But then things went horribly wrong. All John and Christa's intentions were destroyed by the warehouse fire.

To be fair to Aunt Candy, when she'd left the flat in St Peter's Square that morning, she had no intention of starting an inferno. She'd been drinking, and the more she drank, the more it seemed like a good idea to visit Kitty to see if Bingo Hall had taken his brat or if John had been in touch. Picture this scene at the warehouse: Sam is asleep in the crib, tired after her morning bath. Lola is washing nappies. Kitty is standing on the top rung of a ladder with a blowtorch, putting the finishing touches to the Egyptian temple she's constructing.

It's a magnificent work of art – over twenty feet high

and hung with elaborate curtains, only they're drooping because the heavy fabric has split one of the curtain rings. As Kitty doesn't have a spare ring, she'll have to solder the broken one together. It'll take forever to take the curtains down, so she decides to fix the ring with her blowtorch while they're still hanging.

We've all done it, haven't we? Taken the shortcut. Fine if you've just burnt the toast; you can scrape the cinders off and no harm's done. But what if you're up a ladder with a blowtorch and a drunken contortionist arrives unannounced, demanding to know if her dead sister's brat has been claimed?

What if that same contortionist looks in the crib, sees the blonde streak in the baby's hair, now that the ink's washed out, and realizes she's been tricked? What if she demands to know the truth and rocks the ladder so violently, the blowtorch sets the curtains on fire?

The warehouse fills with smoke; the flames spread. Kitty jumps out of the window. Candy escapes through the back door and is followed home by Lola, who climbed out of a window with Sam in her arms. Everything is destroyed except for a silver rattle – leading the newly-wed Mr and Mrs Tabuh to believe that their baby had perished in the fire.

Unable to find Kitty or confront Candy, and prevented from getting into the flat because it's boarded up, they leave the country without their trunk, which remains in the attic. If only we could put them out of their misery and tell them that their daughter is alive and living on a barge, and is desperately trying to find them both. Right now, Sam is doing her best to persuade Kitty to ask the ancient spirits where her parents are.

I wouldn't believe in automatic writing but for the fact that this book is the work of someone else entirely. I'm scribbling away like a slave, but who put the thoughts in my head? My muse? The spirits? Who knows. The real author refuses to take any credit, but, believe me, I don't have time to invent all this stuff. I'm merely a conduit, like Kitty.

For some reason, Kitty is reluctant to contact the spirits on Sam's behalf. She says her pen has run out of oink. When Sam offers her a pencil instead, she says she has a hat ache.

"A headache? Poor you. When the pain goes, will you try for me then, Kitty?"

"The pain never goes."

Kitty's trying to wriggle out of it, so Sam goads her. "You can't do it, can you? You're not the reincarnation of an Egyptian priestess at all."

"Yes, I am." Kitty's insistent in a way that's wholly believable. Reincarnation could be proved, she says, if the dates and facts of her past life could be linked to a genuine historical character – it's just that no one's done it yet.

"But how do you *know* you're the reincarnation of an Egyptian priestess, Kitty?"

"Get dressed and I'll tell you."

Sam's outfit needs a wash. Kitty takes her clothes, which are folded neatly at the end of the bed, and gives her a robe. It's too large, but it will do until the green trousers and sparkly blazer are dry. Having changed, Sam goes up onto the deck to find Kitty doing the washing in a bowl. Lola has her own bowl and is dunking her woolly monkey up and down in the suds. It's an unusual sight – an orang-utan, a masked woman and a girl in a ringmaster's hat washing their smalls – but it's a homely scene; the ideal opportunity for Kitty to tell Sam about her childhood – which I will now relate.

Kitty's real name was Katy. Her mother was a fortune-teller, her father trained horses, and they lived in a caravan. Being poor and having two other babies to feed, they were delighted when a rich, childless couple – Mr and Mrs Jones – asked to adopt their youngest daughter.

Katy Jones had a normal, happy childhood until the age of nine when she had an accident which changed her life. She tripped over a cat on the stairs, landed on her head and, when the doctor arrived, was pronounced dead. It was a terrible shock for the Joneses, but nothing like the one they were about to receive.

When the doctor returned to lay out Katy's body, he found her sitting up in bed, laughing merrily as if she had never died. Thrilled as Mr Jones was to see his adopted daughter alive, he was furious with the doctor for making such a callous mistake and demanded an explanation.

Either the doctor had been mistaken or there was none – he swore on his mother's life that the last time he checked, Katy's breathing had ceased. It was a miracle; he gave up medicine and entered a monastery where he took a vow of silence.

However, the accident on the stairs wasn't without side-effects. Although Katy remained well, a trip to the British Museum revealed that all was not as it seemed. For the moment she entered the Egyptian Gallery, she went wild. Normally a quiet child, she now clung to the mummy cases and screamed that she wanted to be "with her own people" in a voice that her adoptive mother didn't recognize. At first Mrs Jones thought Katy must be referring to her real parents – but no.

In the middle of the gallery there was a model of a temple dedicated to the goddess Bastet. Katy sat down in front of it, declared that *this* was her real home and refused to move. To calm her down, Mrs Jones gave her a pencil and paper and suggested that she made a drawing of the temple. Katy began to sketch with great concentration. Suddenly, as if her hand was being moved by some unseen force, she scribbled down a series of hieroglyphics. She couldn't understand them at first and insisted on showing them to the curator who translated: *Welcome, Fey Ra! Welcome high priestess, handmaiden to Bastet; we are your servants.*

Katy never forgot the experience and, ever after, insisted on being called Fey Ra. The Joneses didn't like it, but as she refused to answer to "Katy", they nicknamed her Kitty Bastet, partly because of the goddess and partly because the episode had been triggered by tripping over the cat.

The automatic writing persisted into Kitty's teens. Mrs Jones took her to a neurologist, a psychologist, and finally, a psychiatrist, who suggested (as Bart Hayfue had) that Kitty had a split personality. He prescribed drugs, but Mrs

Jones wouldn't have it; apart from periods of scribbling in a trance, Kitty was normal. Her antics upset nobody, so they left her to it, hoping she'd grow out of it, like acne.

She didn't though; she made frequent visits to the British Museum where she learnt to read hieroglyphics properly. The curator was amazed at how quickly she picked it up, but, as Kitty tells Sam, "I wasn't learning a new language, I was remembering my old one." Sam can hardly dismiss this. Hadn't she picked up the witch doctor's notebook, chanted in Motu and understood every word?

Let's return to the present. Lola is hanging her monkey out to dry on the rigging. Kitty is emptying the soapy water. Sam is reflecting on Kitty's story and is prompted to ask: "But where does the automatic writing come from?"

According to Kitty, this universe contains psychic ether which stores information from the past, present and the future. Our ancestors could access it using natural energies that we have lost touch with.

"You haven't lost touch with the spirits though have you, Kitty?"

Kitty wipes her hands on her long, dark hair and falls to her knees. "They've *abandoned* me!"

She'd tried to contact them. She tried when she thought Sam had died in the fire; she'd asked the spirits if the baby's soul was at peace. But they hadn't replied.

"That's because I wasn't dead!" says Sam. "Ask them where my parents are … please?"

Kitty shakes her head. "If nothing happens, you'll think I'm a fraud. You'll be disappointed and cry."

"The last time I cried was over a butterfly," says Sam. "And that was a waste of tears because it was the start of something good, so I don't cry any more."

"You shouldn't hold back your tears," says Kitty. "They might set the magic in motion. Tears are strong stuff. They're full of comicals."

"Chemicals? Then I'll save them for a special occasion."

There's a pause and Sam is about to ask "What is magic?" but she surprises herself and asks a far more personal question. "Kitty, may I see your face?"

Kitty doesn't let her mask slip but her ears move up a notch, suggesting that her real eyebrows are raised in horror. She runs below deck and battens down the hatches. Sam feels bad for asking. "Was I rude, Lola? I didn't mean to be. Only I'm sure Kitty's hiding something from me." She calls through the hatch. "Kitty, come back. I'm sorry. You don't have to show me your face."

"I don't have a face. It melted in the fire."

Sam calls to her again. "It can't be worse than Aunt Candy's. She wears a mask made from powder and lipstick, but I can see straight through it. Her real face looks like an unmade bed. Kitty, at least you have lovely hair!"

Flattery gets her nowhere; Kitty stays where she is for the rest of the day. Sam assumes she's gone to sleep, so, to pass the time, she practises making sailor's knots with Lola. By late afternoon the washing has dried. Lola fetches it down and folds it, then forages for foliage to build a new nest at the top of the mast. Sam climbs after her and they curl up together in the bowl of leaves and fall asleep.

Sam dreams again. She sees John Tabuh wheeling his magic box through a vast desert. He's being stalked by a sphinx, which steers him into an oasis. In the middle of the oasis, there's a man sitting cross-legged on a mat under a yellow stripy umbrella between two stone crocodiles. He holds a ball in his palm. In front of him are three cups; one red, one green, one black. He says to John Tabuh, "Oh, young magician (for I *know* you are a magician), watch as I place this ball under one of these cups. Now I will move the cups. If you can guess which one the ball is under, you may keep it; put it in your mouth, it will slake your thirst. If you guess wrong, one of my crocodiles will eat you and the other will eat your wife (for I *know* she's inside the box!)."

John Tabuh knows the cup and ball trick but, for some reason, he chooses the wrong cup and Sam, who also knows the trick shouts, "No, Daddy!" in her sleep.

Down below, someone is calling "Sam! Saaaam!" It's Kitty; she has come out of hiding. She's waving a piece of paper covered in hieroglyphics, which, loosely translated, say that they must visit a cross-legged man who sits in the shadow of the sphinx. It seems that the spirits have broken their silence.

Sam must go to Egypt.

HOW TO HEAL WITH HERBS

ALOE VERA

For healing
wounds and burns

ECHINACEA

Helps to prevent
colds and flu

FENNEL

A tonic for the
digestive system

FEVERFEW

Reduces fevers
and headaches

GARLIC

Anti-viral and
anti-fungal.
Kills intestinal
parasites

OREGANO

Good for chesty
coughs and
asthma

THE PILGRIMS

Egypt is a big place. You could search your entire lifetime for a man sitting under a stripy umbrella and never find him. Ah, but say you're in possession of the witch doctor's notebook; all you have to do is study the list of names and, if you have the gift, your eyes will be drawn to his portrait, complete with stone crocodiles. He's called Yerba Hufat and he lives in the Black Desert.

"If the sand's black, the umbrella should be easy enough to spot," announces Sam confidently, snapping the notebook shut.

Kitty harumphs. "Not if it's a black umbrella."

"It's *yellow*," Sam insists. "It was yellow in my dream."

"What if the sand isn't black?" says Kitty. "Say it's yellow. We'll never find him."

She doesn't seem very keen on going to Egypt. Sam thought she'd jump at the chance; it's where her people came from, isn't it?

"I should have gone years ago," replies Kitty. "But

John Tabuh arrived, so I put it off."

"So why not go now?"

There are problems. Although Kitty's an excellent sailor – a skill she learnt from her adoptive father – the barge would never make it to Egypt. Anyway, what would they do for money?

"We could sail the barge to France and sell it," suggests Sam. "Then we could afford to hire a car, drive it through Italy and pick up a good boat from there."

"All that travelling ... my weak heart," mumbles Kitty.

She's stalling for some reason, but Sam has made up her mind. "If you won't come, I'll go on my own. I'll find a way, I always do." She goes down into the fo'c'sle to pack her belongings:

1. Clothes
2. Witch doctor's pouch
3. Divining rod
4. Witch's cord
5. Protective oil
6. Mr Fraye's coin
7. Various magic tricks
8. Shell locket...

Oh no! Where's the locket? Sam put it under her pillow last night; but it's gone.

"Lola, where's my locket?" she cries. "Look in the other pillowcase."

Unfortunately, Lola's pillowcase has been worn thin

by so many cats' claws it explodes in a puff of feathers, just as Kitty walks in.

"What *are* you doing?" She sneezes so violently, her mask blasts forward and she has to clamp the chin down.

"Looking for my locket, then we're leaving," says Sam.

Kitty nods her head, then, in a voice that even Lola doesn't recognize, she says, "Fey Ra wants to go home."

It could be the voice of the priestess or a ventriloquist, but whoever it is, Kitty has changed her mind. She's coming to Egypt after all. Sam is relieved. She's an independent girl but there are certain things she needs an adult for, such as selling barges and hiring cars. Besides, it will be more fun with all three of them.

"Kitty, that's brilliant! But what about your heart?"

"Still beating… Any sign of your locket?"

It has to be here somewhere. They turn the barge upside down but it's vanished. In a final attempt to find it, Sam tries the divining rod. It points at Lola, but a thorough search through her fur reveals nothing.

The passage to France goes without a hitch. They manage to sail the creaking barge across the Channel, through the French canals and up the river without springing a leak, falling overboard or capsizing. It's a slow haul but, finally, they reach their destination and dock at Biarritz, near the foot of the Pyrenees Mountains.

The plan is to shop for supplies then put the barge up for sale to fund their trip, but Lola has fallen ill. She's been off her food for days. Sam thought it was just seasickness but now she's rolling around on dry land, coughing and clutching her stomach.

"Maybe she has a purr ball," says Kitty.

Sam isn't sure if apes get fur balls, but she knows cats eat grass to cure themselves, so she puts Lola into a wheelchair and strolls along the mountain track to look for suitable herbs. Ruth Abafey had told her about the healing benefits of certain plants and she drew them in the witch doctor's notebook; but none of them looked like any of the flowers growing here. It's no good, she'll have to take Lola to see a vet. She's trying to remember the French for "My orang-utan is sick", when the silence is broken by the arrival of a truck full of invalids, coughing, wheezing and complaining. They are pilgrims on their way to Lourdes.

"Is there a vet in Lourdes?" Sam asks.

"You don't need a vet," booms the driver. "You need a miracle. Hop in!"

"I'm not sick," explains Sam. "It's my orang-utan."

The driver turns to his passengers, who are twitching and groaning. "Anybody know if the Blessed Virgin heals apes? Speak up! I can't hear you."

"Oh," says a woman covered in boils, "the holy water didn't cure your deafness then?"

"It did! It's just that everyone's mumbling."

"That's because we're *ill*!" moan the pilgrims.

They look so sick, Sam's reluctant to go with them. The driver bangs on his steering wheel. "Get a move on, love. Time is money."

She and Lola squeeze in between a man with a twitch and a woman with warts. Afraid that she'll catch something, Sam dabs protective oil on her wrists. The pilgrims seize on it immediately.

"What's that? Holy oil? Is it better than holy water?"

"It's only herbs," says Sam. "But if you think it'll help, maybe it will."

The driver snatches the bottle and rubs some on his eyes. "I was blind – hey! Now I can see!"

"Really?" cry the pilgrims.

"Nah. I'm still blind. Only joking!"

An argument breaks out. Which stupid idiot booked the blind driver? What's the point of going to Lourdes for a cure if they're all going to be killed on the road! Sam tries to calm them down.

"Shhhh! Think of your blood pressure. Tell me about Lourdes."

Apparently, it all began when the Virgin Mary appeared before a peasant girl and told her to dig a well. A blind man bathed his eyes in the holy water that was drawn from it, and miraculously, his sight came back.

"And that," interrupts the driver, "is why the sick, the lame and the hypochondriacs have gone there ever since."

"Do you believe in miracles?" asks Sam.

"Oh, yes," he bellows, then he whispers to Sam. "'Course not, but don't tell anyone. A million punters want me to take 'em to Lourdes at forty euros a trip. It's a right little earner."

"You're not really blind, are you?"

"There are none so blind," he says, "as them who can't see. Know what I mean?"

One of his passengers has overheard. "What *do* you mean? Are you calling us stupid because we believe in miracles?"

"Ignore the driver," yells a man with gout, "he's talking out of the back of his head!"

"At least he's *got* a back to his head!" grumbles a man who hasn't.

They carry on moaning until, finally, they arrive at Lourdes. Sam helps Lola into the wheelchair and takes her to a pool of holy water in a secluded spot. She encourages her to sit in it.

"That's right, Lola. Splash it all over. We'll bring some back for Kitty, shall we? It might heal her burns."

Just then, a vision appears before Sam, but it isn't the Virgin Mary. It's Monsieur Hubert Faya – Inspector of Miracles. He doesn't look very pleased.

"Excusez-moi, mademoiselle! What is that gorilla doing in my well?"

HOW TO WITNESS A VISION

Is seeing believing? Can you trust your own eyes? Let's see.

1. Concentrate on the four dots in the middle of the picture for 30 seconds.

2. Close your eyes and tilt your head back. Keep them closed.

3. You will see a circle of light. Keep looking at the circle and a vision will appear.

THE INSPECTOR OF MIRACLES

Sam gives the Inspector of Miracles a steely stare. "She's not a gorilla, she's an *orang-utan*."

"Oh?" he says. "Pardonnez-moi! I suppose that makes it all right then, does it?"

Shielding her eyes from the sun, Sam looks around for prohibitive notices. "I'm sorry, Monsieur Faya, is there a sign that says No Orang-utans?"

His reply is somewhat sarcastic. "Mais non ... then I haven't got a leg to stand on."

"No leg? Perhaps you should hop into the well," Sam retorts.

Monsieur Faya allows a small smile to perk up his moustache and his manner softens. "Ah, well, I suppose an ape is entitled to a miracle as much as I."

Unfortunately, the holy waters don't seem to be doing the trick for Lola. Her cough seems to be even worse. Sam is concerned. "How long should I leave her in there?"

The inspector puffs out his cheeks. "She is not a piece

of laundry. Divine intervention doesn't have a washing cycle."

He sits down on the bank and adjusts his hat and, at that moment, Sam has the strangest feeling that she knows him from somewhere.

"What?" he says. "Does my hair look silly?"

"No, I'm sure I've seen you somewhere before, that's all."

She sits down next to him, kicks off her shoes and dangles her toes in the water. To her surprise, he looks over his shoulder like a furtive schoolboy, unlaces his own shoes and slips off his socks, as if it's the most daring thing he's ever done. "Forgive me, but I'm sure God never intended for us to wear brogues," he sighs.

If God exists, he's the one Sam would really like to question: *Are you magic? Are you real? Are you an illusion?* Maybe Hubert Faya could enlighten her.

"Do you believe in God, monsieur? Only I'm not sure Lola does, in which case she won't be entitled to a miracle, will she? What time does the vet shut?"

Hubert Faya looks at his watch. "Cinq heures et demi." He refuses to be drawn into whether or not he believes in God but says that miracles have happened to people who have no faith, therefore they might also happen to orang-utans.

Sam watches Lola paddling pathetically in the water and hopes he's right.

"Do you believe in miracles, Monsieur Faya?"

The inspector chooses his words carefully. "It's my job to make sure miracles are genuine. To do that, I must remain completely unbiased as I try to find the answer to three questions: 1. Was there really a disease? 2. Was there a real recovery? 3. Is there a natural explanation for the recovery."

The inspector explains that anyone who claims to be miraculously cured must be tested by many doctors and scientists. Their case then goes before a committee who ask all manner of questions. If there's *still* no scientific explanation for the cure, the church declares it a miracle.

"The church has the final say, not the scientists?" asks Sam. "Is that fair?"

The inspector shrugs. "To be fair to the scientists, it's true that one generation's miracle is another's medical fact: diseases that were once deadly are no longer so. It is also well known that the body can heal itself; there are at least three cases a year where tumours disappear spontaneously. Marvellous, I grant you – but miraculous? At the end of the day, mademoiselle, it is not up to science to say whether God performs miracles any more than it is up to religion to establish that water freezes at zero degrees." He dips a toe in the water, closes his eyes, and folds his hands, as if in prayer. "Perhaps the holy water will get rid of my bunion."

Monsieur Faya sits in silence, but his lips are moving. If he's praying, Sam can't make out the words. Perhaps he's reciting the French national anthem. After a while he stops, stares at his offending bunion and sighs. "Ah, not to worry; I will just have to buy more forgiving shoes."

"Were you praying?" asks Sam. "Do prayers increase your chances of a miracle?"

"Or is it because those who pray are positive thinkers?"

ponders Monsieur Faya. "If your faith is strong, you enjoy positive emotions such as hope and joy. This is good for your health." His smile fades. "On the other side of the coin, a lack of faith can lead to negative emotions – anger and sorrow which shrivel our cells and poison our heart and stomach."

Sam frowns. "Are you saying that if I don't believe in God, I'll get sick?"

The inspector shakes his head so vigorously, his hat falls into the water. "Did I mention God, mademoiselle? I think not, I mentioned *faith*. I did not express a view about whom or what one ought to have faith in. That is for you to decide." He leans forward, fishes his hat out of the holy water and examines the brim. "Would you believe it?" he says. "There was a stain just there and it has gone." With some reluctance, he dries his feet on his handkerchief and puts his socks back on. It's time for Sam and Lola to go.

"There's just one more thing I'd like to ask you before we go to the vet, Monsieur Faya."

"Oui, mademoiselle. Fire away!"

"Have *you* ever witnessed a miracle?"

The inspector pulls his socks back off – it's obvious there's no quick answer to this question.

"No one likes to think he is a foolish man," he says. "But somebody once made a fool of this Inspector of Miracles." He tells her the following tale.

"Some years ago, a gentleman arrived at Lourdes pushing a curious box on wheels. He claimed that it contained the body of his wife who had recently died and

whom he had loved beyond compare. He'd come here –
he said – in the hope that the miraculous waters might
bring her back to life, for his father had told him that
resurrection was not impossible. A crowd began to gather
on the banks. He called them together, commanding his
audience like… like…"

"Like a magician?" suggests Sam.

"Like Jesus."

The man had waded into the holy water with his dead
wife in his arms and bathed her. Nothing happened and, as
the tension increased, the man prayed out loud, inviting the
crowd to join in, which they did to the point of frenzy.

As the praying reached fever pitch, the dead woman
began to move her graceful arm, then, slowly, she rose
like Venus, smiling and waving. Transfixed by what they
had seen, the crowd fell silent for a moment, but then the
whispering began. "She's alive! The waters have brought
her back to life!" Giving the man a round of rippling
applause, the sick claimed they felt better than they had
done for years, the deaf claimed they could hear and the
lame threw their sticks in the air. Even the Inspector of
Miracles admitted he was impressed and, for the first time,
he felt unable to remain unbiased – he had witnessed a
miracle along with the ecstatic masses. And five hundred
people can't be wrong … or can they?

Yes, they can. Five hundred, five thousand, five million
– it doesn't matter. The size of the crowd has no bearing
on the truth. Five billion people can be simultaneously
horribly wrong.

This was all John Tabuh was trying to prove when he stood on a rock and announced they were suffering from mass hysteria. He said that he had deliberately tricked them and that his wife wasn't dead in the first place; it was an illusion. He'd done it to show them how easily people can be fooled into believing what they want to believe.

"You shouldn't have blind faith even in your father!" he insisted.

This was the worst thing John could have said. In all innocence he was talking about his *own* father, but everyone thought he was talking about God.

It affected the crowd in various ways. Those whose faith was unshakeable wanted to lynch John Tabuh for his blasphemous behaviour. Those who were a bit shaky lost all hope in a cure and went home. A few grateful cynics thanked Mr and Mrs Tabuh for exposing Lourdes as a con, but the remaining crowd soon turned into an angry mob. The Inspector of Miracles called the gendarmes before someone was hurt. John and Christa were bundled into a police wagon and carted off. At this point, Sam confesses to the Inspector that the couple who'd been arrested were her parents.

"Mon Dieu!" he says. "I am sorry to hear that. I thought they did a brave thing but at the trial, the judge took a very different view. He felt that John Tabuh had set out to tarnish the reputation of Lourdes, for which he was given four years in prison. Personally, I thought the sentence far too stiff."

"And my mother?"

"Two years in a correction centre after which she was taken in by nuns."

Monsieur Faya wasn't sure what had happened to them after that. Rumour had it that they'd fled the country, but he couldn't say where they'd gone.

By now, it is almost 5.30. Shaken by the news of her parents' misfortune, Sam hadn't noticed the time and now she's worried that the vet will be closed.

"This is my fault," says the inspector. "I have kept you too long. I may be able to help you though. There is a local girl who has a reputation for healing animals. I can't promise anything, but the farmers have every faith in her. They say she works miracles with pigs and sheep. I remain unbiased, but who knows? Perhaps she can cure orang-utans also."

The girl's name is Athea Furby. Sure enough, she's on the witch doctor's list, just above a little doodle of a man wearing a suit.

But no socks.

HOW TO MAKE A DOVE APPEAR

The masked magician produces a shallow pan and removes
the lid to show it's empty. The egg is cracked into the pan,
which is in turn set fire to. To put out the flames the magician slams the lid on the pan. When the lid is removed, a
dove flies out. How?

THE SECRET

A prop called a dove pan is used. This
is a shallow pan with a matching lid
which has a very deep rim that fits
inside the pan when closed. It can be
used to produce birds, roses – anything.

1. The rim of the lid conceals a
   second identical pan or "liner"
   that fits snugly into the
   mainpan.

2. When the lid is slammed onto
   the pan, the liner drops into
   the main pan.

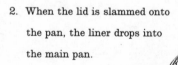

3. The liner is loaded
   beforehand with a dove. When
   the lid is removed it flies away.

ATHEA FURBY

The Inspector of Miracles points Sam in the direction of Athea Furby's humble home. It isn't far, just a short walk round the mountain. You can't miss it; the front garden is decorated with goat bells.

It's hard work pushing an orang-utan uphill. Sam's sweating, unlike Athea Furby, who stands serenely by a picket fence in a crisp, white apron holding a jug of sweetened lemon juice. It's almost as if she's been expecting them.

"Bonjour! Would you like some citron pressé? It is thirsty work pushing an ape up the Pyrenees, non?"

"I'm just grateful she's not an elephant," puffs Sam.

Athea laughs lightly and fills two glasses with juice. Lola doesn't want any.

"She's not well," explains Sam.

Athea nods sympathetically. "That is why you have brought her to me, non? Let me see what I can do." She places her hand on Lola's brow. Athea Furby is only fifteen but her eyes are wiser than her years, illuminated perhaps by something she can see that remains invisible to the rest of us. Sam watches her intently. Does she heal with herbs?

"Non, just hands." For such a slight girl, Athea is surprisingly strong. With little effort, she lifts Lola onto her lap as if she weighs no more than a cat.

"Voilà," she murmurs. "Close your big brown eyes." She rocks Lola in her lap, her bright cotton skirt spread out in the grass and, as she rocks, the brass goat bell around her neck tinkles rhythmically. Sam feels herself getting sleepy, seduced by the *clang, clang, clang* – but she *must* stay awake.

"Lola isn't dying is she, Athea?"

"Not dying; but she has been there once before, I think."

Thoughts of poisoned darts and resurrection chants swirl around Sam's head – but how could Athea know?

"Why do you say that, Athea?"

"I feel it."

Is she feeling the scar on Lola's chest or is she bluffing?

"I feel it now," repeats Athea. "I know what is wrong … it is not so serious." With both hands locked under Lola's rib cage, she suddenly squeezes hard. There's a loud belching noise as something shoots out of Lola's mouth into the undergrowth. The orang-utan inhales deeply, then downs the citron pressé in one gulp – she's cured.

Sam looks among the wild flowers for the object that was stuck in Lola's throat. It's lying among a clump of poppies.

"My locket!"

She wipes it clean. The photo inside is damp around the edges, but it will dry in the sun. She shows it to Athea.

"My grandmother. This little boy ... that's my father."

It's impossible to keep the air of wistfulness from her voice. Athea detects it immediately but doesn't pry, she just sits there and threads daisies.

"He's a magician," adds Sam. "He calls himself the Dark Prince of Tabuh."

Athea smiles knowingly. "Ah, oui. My mother spoke of this extraordinary man. They met long ago but she never forgot him. In fact, her dying words were these: 'Now I know the answers! If only I could have told John...'"

Sam stays silent, deep in thought. Something is bothering her. Athea is too young to have met her father, yet her name is on the witch doctor's list. Suddenly it clicks – there can only be one explanation.

"Was your mother called Athea too?"

Yes, she was also Athea the healer. It seems she passed her gift on to her daughter. "Like your father did to you," says Athea. "You are a magician too, I think. Can you turn this daisy chain into a dove?"

"If I had a dove," says Sam, "I could fool you into thinking I could; but it would be just an illusion. I can't make doves out of thin air."

"*That* would be magic," says Athea. "Real magic."

Lola is stealing peapods from Athea's garden. She pops each one carefully, slides the peas into her fist then eats them one by one, like sweets. Sam can't understand how Athea knew exactly how to make her well again.

"Is what you do real magic, Athea?"

"Me? No, anyone can do it if they have the right touch.

I have been healing animals since I was little. I am not sure how – it is instinctive."

"Or paranormal?"

Athea dismisses the notion airily. "Non, non. What I do is primitive. All ailments give the patient certain characteristics, a combination of clues which point to where the problem lies. Maybe I assess these things faster than most, that is all. I could teach you what to look for if you like."

"I'll pay you for it," says Sam.

"Non!"

But Sam insists. "I can never repay you for saving Lola…" She unclips the witch doctor's pouch and takes out the oyster shell. It contains three pearls, remember. It is rare for an oyster to contain *one* pearl – but three? That's unheard of.

The oyster is long gone, of course. The pearls are packed between the shell halves in fur. Sam removes one and hides it behind her back with the daisy chain.

"I can't give you doves, but I can give you … this."

She fixes the chain around Athea's neck. She has woven the pearl into the middle between two daisy stalks; it glows like a tiny moon.

"It is too much!" gasps Athea.

"I'll swap it for your pearls of wisdom. Teach me how to heal animals. If Lola gets sick again, I need to know how to help her. There may not be a vet where I'm going."

Athea promises to teach her what she can and they spend the afternoon together, discussing among other things:

1. How the paleness of the tongue suggests a sluggish liver in cats.

2. How to take a shrew's pulse.

3. How to burp an owl that has a pellet stuck in its throat.

4. How to turn an unborn squirrel round the right way by massage.

5. Where to press to relieve an egg-bound duck.

6. How to drain a rabbit's abscess using vibration.

Sam is particularly fascinated by the laying on of hands. According to Athea, you can channel positive energy into the patient through your palms. This, she says, has a physical effect on the diseased organ, encouraging it to heal itself.

"This positive energy, is it a kind of electricity?" asks Sam, remembering the highly static Mrs Reafy and wondering if she's still arguing with her spoon.

Athea can't be certain, but whatever it is, it's powerful; you must adjust the dosage according to the creature in your care. An elephant needs a lot more positive energy than a butterfly, but an elephant beetle needs more than a shrew – even though the beetle is smaller, its wing-case is as tough as armour.

By now, Lola is full of peas. There are no pods left on the bush and she lies, stretched out in the sun, with her hands folded peacefully over her belly.

"Do orang-utans need more positive energy than people?" asks Sam. "I'm just asking because, although Lola's shorter than me, she's much stronger."

"I've never healed a person," says Athea. "I have Lourdes on my doorstep, the competition is too stiff! But I think orang-utans can be healed with *less* power because they are not sceptical. People expect me to fail, but Lola, she trusted me. That is half the battle."

Even as they speak, a shepherd is driving down the mountain with a sick ewe in his truck, in the hope that Athea can heal it. If you listen hard, you will hear the crunch of wheels against the chalky road and the plaintive bleating of the suffering sheep. Athea squeezes Sam's arm. "Let us tell the shepherd that *you* are Athea, the healer."

"Me? But what if I fail?"

Athea laughs as if this is an impossible notion. "Sam, you can do it. Believe it and so will the sheep."

The shepherd stops his truck and carries the ewe over his shoulder into Athea's front garden. He tries to balance it on the grass, but it collapses onto its left side, panting heavily. The shepherd tugs at his beard.

"She has been like this for days. She gave birth to twins but they were stillborn."

Athea is willing Sam to do something, to take charge. She gives her a nudge.

Sam kneels next to the ewe, places her right hand on the gritty wool of its belly and closes her eyes. She can feel something that shouldn't be there, despite having no knowledge of sheep anatomy. Now she hears two drum beats – big drum, little drum – the rhythm of the oars pushing against the muscles of the river – big drum, little drum. She pulls steadily, slowly – big drum, little drum – she hears the cry of a crow and, as she opens her eyes, the ewe expels a scrawny, wet lamb into the grass.

There hadn't been twins, but triplets. The lamb is alive,

but it's so small and feeble the shepherd wonders if it's worth keeping. It will be too much trouble to rear. The lamb can't speak up for itself, so Sam gives it a voice.

"You are my shepherd; I put my faith in you."

The shepherd cleans out his ears with a stick, but he's sure he hasn't misheard; his ewe has given birth to a talking lamb! He throws his hat high in the air. "It is a miracle!"

The ewe, who is feeling much better, licks the lamb clean.

"This lamb is a sign," insists the shepherd. "I will never take it to market. Merci, Mademoiselle Athea ... bless you!"

He kisses Sam on both cheeks. She feels guilty about the ventriloquism, but the real Athea smiles behind her hand as if to imply that she's done nothing to reproach herself for; the ewe and the lamb have been saved and so has the shepherd. He's poor, but now that he thinks he has a sacred lamb, people will flock in droves to buy his ewe's milk.

It's time for Sam and Lola to leave. Kitty will be wondering where they are. Hopefully, she will have got a good price for the barge and they'll soon be heading for Egypt.

The shepherd offers Sam a lift. She sits in the back of the truck with the sheep. Lola insists on holding the lamb in her lap – it's doing well.

"Don't forget your wheelchair," laughs Athea. "Lourdes has more abandoned wheelchairs than it knows what to do with!"

It could be because miracles happen every day – but you'd have to ask the inspector that.

HOW TO WALK THROUGH A SOLID WALL

The stage floor is covered with a carpet. A solid brick wall is wheeled on, cased in a steel frame. The masked magician stands on one side of the wall. Screens are placed at either end so there can be no escape. The magician waves over the screen on one side of the wall and shouts, "Here I am!" The

next minute, the magician's hands are waving at the other side; "Here I am now!"

The screens are drawn away and there is the magician on the other side of the wall. How?

THE SECRET

The wall is built over a trap door in the stage. Although the carpet under it is seamless, it has enough "give" for the magician to crawl through. The trapdoor is then shut and all is as before!

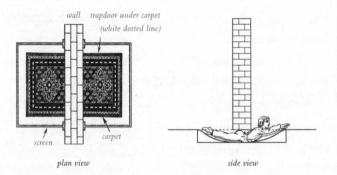

wall   trapdoor under carpet
(white dotted line)

screen   carpet

plan view   *side view*

THE TRINITY

"Do you think it was a coincidence that the lamb arrived when it did, Kitty?"

Sam doubts that she really healed the ewe; she suspects the lamb would have been born anyway. Maybe Athea knew that.

Kitty shrugs. "What does it matter? Just be pleased it happened."

"Fancy there being triplets."

"Triplets? Yes … fancy."

An old lady has expressed an interest in buying the barge, complete with feline passengers. Her name is Madame Fifi-Elisa Ary and she's gone to the bank to withdraw the money in cash. She's taking her time though. Kitty glances at her watch again.

"I hope she shows. I hope she isn't a time-waster."

Just as they're about to give up on her, Madame Ary comes bumbling back, apologizing for her lateness loudly in French; there had been a long queue at the cash desk.

Suddenly, she sees Lola; but her eyesight is not what it used to be: "Is that the captain?" she exclaims, polishing her glasses. "Such fine red hair. Is he a Scotsman?"

"She's an orang-utan," Sam explains. "The barge has no captain, madame."

Now that she's taken her glasses off, Madame Ary looks a bit like Effie Ray, the woman Sam met on the tube. Bart Hayfue would say that the similarity is unsurprising: old ladies look much the same, only the headscarves change – but what does he know?

The barge is sold and Kitty and Sam have enough money to go to Egypt. They hire a camper van and drive across Italy and down through Calabria. Kitty has brought her favourite cat, Khensu, along. She couldn't bear to part with him, even though he sprays everywhere. When we love someone, it's amazing what disgusting habits we're willing to tolerate.

The journey takes several days and it's all very jolly, if a little cramped; the camper has a chemical toilet and tiny beds. They sing, sleep, stretch their legs now and again, and everyone eats lots of pasta, but nothing happens that concerns us, so let's leap forward to the exciting bit.

Kitty and Sam have left the van behind, hired a yacht and set sail from the coast of Capo Spartivento. Everything goes swimmingly until the third day when they hit a storm – and a very large rock – in the middle of the Ionian Sea.

The storm and the rock appeared from nowhere. There was no mention of the freak weather on the shipping forecast, no blip on the radar to alert them to the mountainous obstacle they have just smashed into; it's as if both phenomena have been deliberately put in place to test them.

The yacht has snapped in half like a biscuit and is about to sink. Sam, Kitty and Lola are up to their waists in the water, clinging to a rock; it's too slippery to climb. Khensu is perched on Lola's head like a Russian hat. Luckily, the witch doctor's notebook is safe in a plastic bag inside Sam's rucksack. Kitty feels her fingers slipping and starts to panic.

"Aghhhh! We're all going to drone!"

Sam puts her hand over Kitty's to stop her sliding off the rock. "Don't give up! Mr Fraye says if we believe in the Grand Plan, it'll work."

"What's the Grand Plan?"

"I'm … working on it."

Kitty starts praying in Ancient Egyptian. Sam struggles to think of an ingenious way to save them all, but hope is fading. An hour passes. Lola's teeth are chattering and Sam's lips are blue. Just as they are all about to lose their grip, an enormous ship appears through the mist.

"We're halluminating," groans Kitty.

But this is no hallucination; this is *The Trinity*, cutting through the waves towards them.

"You see, Kitty," says Sam, "it's part of the Grand Plan!"

Or was it all part of the *Grandpa* plan? A lifeboat has been launched. The shipwrecked four are pulled out of the sea and wrapped in fleecy blankets. Once aboard the ocean liner, the ship's doctor wants to examine them, but they protest so loudly it's clear that none of them is at death's door. After a reviving cup of tea, Sam asks to speak to the captain, hoping that he'll be kind enough to give them a lift. In no time at all, she's hustled through to his cabin.

"We need to get to Egypt," she explains.

The captain looks them up and down suspiciously.

"What are you – a circus troop?"

"Y–es, Captain."

It's not true, but it's the easiest thing to say.

"The monkey … does it bite?"

"The orang-utan? No, Captain, she's friendly. Could you give us a lift to Egypt, please? We could pay our way by entertaining your passengers, with magic tricks, if you like."

Upon hearing the word "magic" the livid scars on the captain's chin begin to throb. He thrusts his hands in his pockets, but they're shaking so hard, his loose change rattles. He paces up and down, staring at the ceiling. Then, in a voice that rises to a squeak, he says, "Magic is banned on this ship."

"But wh—"

He waves his hands frantically. "No, don't ask. Don't look at me! I will take you to Egypt on sufferance as long as you perform no … magic … of any kind. You will stay in your cabin at all times except for those times when you will be employed under the ship's cook, and you will not mix with the passengers nor talk to the passengers nor produce animals from under your hat. Is that understood?"

"Aye, aye, Captain."

"Or I'll throw you overboard."

He doesn't really mean it, Sam can tell.

"Oh, we shouldn't like that, Captain. We'll be ever so good, won't we, Lola?"

The captain summons a spotty cabin boy who scuttles in at a ridiculous speed.

"Take them to cabin number 333."

The cabin boy blanches visibly and his shoes squeak as he screeches to a halt.

"C-c-cabin 333?? Are you s-s-sure, Captain? Do I have to, C-c-captain?"

The captain stares at the boy through the wrong end of his telescope and growls like a dog.

"I take it that's a y-y-yes, Captain?" stammers the boy. "Oh, well, You know b-b-best."

He backs off towards the door and makes one last attempt to change the Captain's mind. "I b-b-believe room 332 is vacant and the v-v-view is so pleas—"

For his pains, he's attacked by the captain's paperweight which is hurled with such force it embeds itself in the door, narrowly missing his head.

"Agh! S-sorry, Captain! 333 it is."

Off he goes down the corridor and we must follow this feeble, agitated boy to that cabin.

330 ... 331 ... 332 ... 333.

Here we are. The cabin boy drops the keys on purpose and stands on them. Sam pulls them out from under his shoe and opens the lock. The boy's eyes widen in terror.

"I really w-wouldn't go in, if I were you."

Sam takes no notice. "Why not? Are the mattresses hard or something?"

"M-m-mattresses? It's not *that*, miss. The mattress was replaced after the m-m-murder." He claps his hands over his mouth. "Did I say murder? I meant *Monday*. The mattress was replaced after the Monday."

He is lying.

HOW TO MAKE A GHOST APPEAR

You need: an actor, a bright spotlight, a dim light, a sheet of glass larger than the actor.

1. Position the actor below stage or in the orchestra pit.
2. By adjusting the lights and/or angle of the glass, the actor's "ghostly" reflection appears on stage.
3. The "ghost" is produced due to light bouncing off the actor and hitting the glass at 45 degrees. At this angle the light doesn't pass through the glass but bounces off into the eyes of the audience. The image appears to be on the other side of the glass at the same distance away as the actor – just like a mirror.

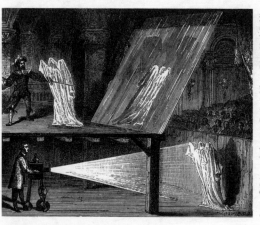

4. The dim light coming through the glass helps the illusion that the ghost is on the stage.

ABU YARFHET

The mattresses in cabin 333 are perfectly clean and bouncy. So why was the cabin boy so jittery? What happened that made the captain quail?

The answer lies with the pastry chef. Kitty is in the cabin drying Lola's fur, but Sam is in the ship's galley helping to prepare apple pies. The chef stands beside her, laying pastry over the chopped apples, tucking them in as gently as if he were putting his children to bed.

"I never had any children," he says, unprompted "Not that I know of, anyway."

"My father doesn't know I exist either," adds Sam.

The pastry chef blows his nose loudly on the tea towel. "Was he a sailor, by any chance?"

"A magician."

What it is about the word "magician"? As soon as Sam says it, the pastry chef drops the fork he's using to perforate the pastry lids and whispers behind his hand, "The captain has banned the M word on this ship." He looks over his shoulder to make sure the vegetable chef isn't listening, but he's busy chopping carrots.

"I hear you've got a big monkey," he mouths. "I've worked here as man and boy and when the gravy chef told me the sailors had rescued a monkey along with yourself, I thought, *Aye, aye, that's history repeating itself.*"

Sam is tempted to say, "She's an *orang-utan!*" But now is not the time to be pedantic. Now is the time to listen to the pastry chef's tale. It could just be a sailor's yarn, but stranger things have happened at sea.

"We were in the Pacific Ocean," begins the chef, "coming back from Australia. It was a Tuesday, because that's the day the captain likes a hearty pudding and I was stirring sultanas into the spotted dick when I heard that the lifeboat had gone out—"

Sam begins to feel a little light-headed. She can smell the familiar green smell that she smelt when she first opened the witch doctor's pouch and she can hear the *plop, plop, plop* of the mwa sawah paddles plunging into the Sepik. Perhaps it's just the scent of the steam rising from the huge vat of peas and the sound of potatoes being dropped into a pan. The call of the Torresian crow? The whistle on the kettle, surely?

The pastry chef is telling Sam that he can still remember the day *The Trinity* came to the rescue of a youth and his monkey who'd capsized in a dugout canoe. As the youth was penniless, the captain said he could work his passage by assisting the ship's magician – the original assistant having been left at the last port suffering from scurvy.

The magician's name was Abu Yarfhet. He was a good illusionist but a bad person. He was seedy, greedy, vile and vicious. It's never easy working for a boss like that, but John Tabuh did his best – in fact, he did better than that. He learnt the tricks with ease; within months, he was his master's equal. Abu Yarfhet wasn't bothered about that – nobody wants a butterfingers assisting them – but what he couldn't tolerate was John's popularity with the ladies.

John didn't deliberately encourage the adoration of his fans, but he only had to push his elegant fingers through his glossy hair and they would swoon. Women would shamelessly move their chairs to get a closer look at him. They'd crane their necks and wave the old magician out of the way in order to get a better view of this ravishing boy.

Abu Yarfhet grew to hate John to the point of psychosis. He made him feel ugly. After the show, Yarfhet would stare in the mirror and blame his lack of popularity on his nose, which was bulbous and pitted like a strawberry. He told himself that if he'd been born with a handsome nose, like John Tabuh, women would love him too.

He was deluding himself; women would still have recoiled. Woman are blind to ugly noses but they can always spot an ugly heart. Abu Yarfhet's heart was as ugly as they come.

"He was a cruel man. Nobody mourned his passing," whispered the pastry chef.

Abu Yarfhet is dead? Yes, indeed! Did John Tabuh have anything to do with it? The pastry chef shakes sugar over the pies and sucks his teeth noisily.

"An illusion went horribly wrong."

Yarfhet and young Tabuh had been performing a trick involving matches and a banana at the captain's table when, suddenly, Yarfhet lurched and knocked John's hand, causing the match to set fire to the captain's beard. Happily, John Tabuh had the good sense to dowse the flames by dunking the captain chin-first into his trifle – much to the amusement of the audience.

The captain's beard never grew back and his chin was charred, but that wasn't the full extent of the damage. Yarfhet was banished to his cabin, but the ladies begged the captain to let John stay, insisting he was blameless and that they wanted to have him for pudding.

Having spent a delightful evening being petted by the richest women in the world, John returned to cabin 333, which he shared with his master. By now Yarfhet was extremely drunk and when he was drunk, he got punchy. He hid behind the door and as John Tabuh entered, he cracked him on the back of the head with a whisky bottle.

The blow wasn't enough to knock the lad out, so as he fell, he pulled the witch doctor's pouch off the table and it spilled its contents, including the shard of human thigh bone. As Yarfhet blundered towards him, John grabbed the bone automatically and cursed him in Motu.

The effect was immediate; Abu Yarfhet was dead before he hit the floor, his face fixed in a pop-eyed grimace. Did the curse kill him? John thought so, but a heart attack can be caused by many other things; bad luck and bad living to name but two.

John tried the resurrection chant, terrified that he'd be under suspicion of murder if he failed to revive Yarfhet. Unfortunately, it didn't work. Perhaps he'd chanted it too quickly. Or too slowly. Or maybe the chant was useless – he couldn't know. All he knew was that he had to get off the ship before the body was found.

The following morning, the ship docked and by the time the corpse was discovered, John Tabuh was miles away. Disguised in Yarfhet's ill-fitting stage outfit, he fled to London using the dead magician's passport and money. Lola went with him, hidden in a magic box.

Some of this Sam learns from the pastry chef; some of it she discovers later in life. "But *why*," she asks, "is the captain afraid of magic after all this time?"

The vegetable chef has finished chopping carrots and is earwigging into their conversation, so the pastry chef builds a tower of pies to hide behind and mutters, "There are *hauntings*. They say that the ghost of Abu Yarfhet resides in cabin 333; at night he haunts the ship, performing the most mischievous tricks."

"Such as turning the Duchess's wine into vinegar," interjects the vegetable chef.

"This is a *private* conversation!" scowls the pastry chef.

But the vegetable chef won't go away.

"Such as putting a live eel in the stew. Putting the ship's wheel in reverse. Creating illusions of icebergs. Scaring the ladies with a foghorn. Tugging the captain's chin."

"Ah, the poor captain; he's afraid the ghost of Abu Yarfhet haunts him because he sided against him when the trick went wrong and favoured the handsome assistant. He fears he's going mad."

"Do *you* believe in ghosts?" Sam asks the pastry chef.

"Yes, he does," interrupts the vegetable chef. "Sailors believe in all sorts. We sees things at sea that landlubbers never sees."

"I can see that your carrots are chopped too thickly!" snaps the pastry chef, hustling Sam towards the door so that they can finish their conversation in peace.

"Personally, I have never seen a ghost," he says. "They are the invention of sailors who wish to keep smugglers at bay."

Whereupon he is spirited away by the wine waiter.

HOW TO NAVIGATE BY THE STARS

1. The positions of the stars change throughout the night and throughout the year moving from east to west, like the sun.

2. By learning to recognize patterns of stars at different times, you can use them to guide you.

3. A particular star – such as Polaris, the North Star – should be followed to make sure you're travelling in the right direction.

4. To find Polaris, first find the Big Dipper. Polaris is an extension of the line formed by the vertical side of the Big Dipper opposite the handle.

5. In the desert, the best time to navigate by stars is during the dry season when there are no clouds.

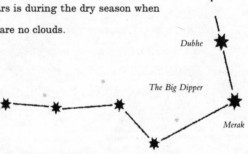

Polaris
(the North Star)

Dubhe

The Big Dipper

Merak

YERBA HUFAT

Put your sunhat on. Apply Factor 50 sun cream and do not paddle in the Nile – there are crocodiles. We have arrived in Egypt. Kitty wants to head straight to Bubastis to visit the ruined temple of Tel Basta, home of her spirit guides, but first they need to find Yerba Hufat, the man who sits cross-legged under the yellow stripy umbrella in an oasis.

But which oasis? A camel seller shows them a map and stabs at an isolated patch of green with his finger.

"You are wanting to go to Bahariya."

Sam assumes he must know his oasis from his elbow, so, having loaded their provisions onto the camels, Sam, Lola and Kitty set off in the direction of the Black Desert with Khensu riding in the saddlebag.

One small problem. When the camel seller said, "You are wanting to go to Bahariya," he wasn't making a suggestion; he was asking a question, only he forget to add a question mark. He'd never heard of Yerba Hufat (not many people have) and he just thought Sam wanted to do the touristy thing and visit the most popular, easy to get to oasis on the map.

Easy to get to? It would have been if Kitty's camel knew its left from its right. It would have been if Sam's camel hadn't just eaten the map. But what's really going to put the kibosh on this expedition is the approaching sandstorm.

This isn't your average sandstorm; this is a wall of sand travelling at fifty miles an hour, sweeping up half-baked lizards and dumping them on top of cacti taller than trees. Sam, Kitty and Lola are sitting under the camels with their eyes closed and their fingers in their ears to keep the sand out. Khensu curls up, ignores the whole episode and goes to sleep.

They sit huddled like this for hours. When the storm finally passes, the shifting sand has altered the landscape beyond recognition. Nobody wants to admit it, but they are completely disorientated. Darkness falls within seconds, as if a mother somewhere has announced that it's time for lights out.

"Can you navigate by the stars, Kitty?" asks Sam.

Of course she can. Mr Jones taught her about the constellations and how to use them as a heavenly map. Kitty climbs back onto her camel.

"Follow that stare!"

"Which star?"

There are no stars. A few grains of white sand have blasted through the holes in Kitty's mask and settled behind her eyelids, making her see stars that don't exist. Sam, being none the wiser, follows behind, with Lola sharing her camel. There's not much room, the camel is badly upholstered, and by morning, tempers are frayed.

"We've been past this same cactus three times, Kitty."

"Nonsense, I know my stares. Keep following, Sam."

"But it's daylight. How can you see the stars in the morning?"

Kitty instructs her camel to stop. Turning her back on Sam, she inserts two fingers under her mask and rubs her eyes. As soon as the sand grains have gone, so have the constellations. "Oh," she says, dully.

"What do you mean, 'oh'?"

They're completely lost. A vulture wheels above them, wondering how long it will have to wait for breakfast. He knows that people – especially young girls – can only live for so long without water. He's never seen an orang-utan before, but it looks juicy. And cats make a good snack.

They're out of water too. The vulture's friends and relatives arrive. This could be the end – but luckily, Sam has her wits about her. While Kitty and Khensu crawl along in the dust and Lola drags her knuckles, Sam holds the divining rod out in front of her and marches forward purposefully.

She marches, head held high, in the name of Mr Fraye. She marches, believing she can do this, in the name of Athea Furby. She marches, hoping for a miracle, in the name of Hubert Faya, and as she marches, the end of the rod starts to twitch. She breaks into a run; she can't stop running – the rod is pulling her along. Now Lola has her arms around Sam's waist, Kitty has her arms around Lola and Khensu and the four of them sweep over the dunes in a desert conga, feet flying across the sand – only now it isn't sand. It's grass!

There is lush green grass and a pool, bright as a giant mirror. It's not Bahariya; this oasis is not on the map. I've looked it up and there is no reference to this particular paradise, no bigger than the gardens in St Peter's Square.

Kitty is afraid it's a mirage and they'll die of thirst, but the water is real. They get down on their knees with the camels and drink. They have just refilled their water bottles when they hear a voice.

"I wouldn't go so close to the edge if I were you. There are crocodilians."

Observing them from behind a palm tree is a man flanked by two stone crocodiles. He's sitting cross-legged under a red stripy umbrella.

"Mr Hufat?" enquires Sam. "But in my dream, your umbrella was yellow."

"It *is* yellow!" he insists, shutting himself inside it. When he opens it again, sure enough, the umbrella is yellow.

"Magic!" he says.

Sam smiles. "Not magic – an illusion."

She reaches behind his ear, retrieves the pencil she placed there a second ago and makes it change colour.

"Look, Mr Hufat. Now it's red … now it's yellow."

Offended that no one is impressed with his umbrella trick, Yerba Hufat takes a ball from his mouth and places it under one of three cups lined up in front of him. He switches the cups round and asks Sam to guess where the ball is.

"Under the green one."

She's right. Declaring that it's beginner's luck, Hufat switches the cups round angrily and asks her to guess again.

"Where is the ball?"

"Under the black cup."

Right again. Exasperated, Mr Hufat tries to outwit Sam six more times but fails miserably.

"I am a fellow magician," she admits. "I know how it's done." Cups and balls is the oldest trick in the book; it's inscribed on papyrus along with tales of wizards turning wax crocodiles into live ones and bringing beheaded geese back to life.

"There's no need to rub it in," snaps Hufat, picking the fluff from his navel.

Sam stacks the cups neatly and, sucking on a blade of grass, considers the geese.

"Mr Hufat, do you think it's possible for a goose to be brought back to life after its head has been chopped off?"

Flattered that his opinion is finally being sought, he cheers up a little.

"That would be a good trick. But that is all it would be – a trick. If a goose lost its head, it would be dead in *this* world but it would have an afterlife in the next."

"Which next world?" asks Sam. "Is there a poultry heaven where beheaded geese and Christmas turkeys go?"

"The Ancient Egyptians call it the Field of Reeds," explains Kitty. "It's like heaven…"

"Only damper," adds Hufat, determined to have the last say. "The geese prefer it damp. Everybody does around these parts. This hot weather gets on one's wick after a while. I'm sick of getting my fingers pinched trying to erect this sun umbrella. I shall be eternally grateful to spend my afterlife in the shade ... assuming they let me in, of course."

In a voice that sounds like Fey Ra's, Kitty adds (and I translate) that first, Ma'at, the Goddess of truth will have to weigh Hufat's heart against an ostrich feather. The god Anubis will check the scales and the ibis-headed Thoth will write down the results in front of twelve great gods who sit in judgment.

"If my heart is light, I will be reborn. Then I will be a spirit member of the starry sky," says Hufat. "Won't that be fun."

"But if your hat is heavy with sin, you'll be gobbled up by Ammit, who is part panther, part hippoo, part crocodoll," Kitty retorts.

Hufat folds his arms defiantly. "That's not going to happen. I'm a good person. I wouldn't hurt a fly."

Not true. Sam has witnessed him swatting six daddy-long-legs which he smooshed into a paste with the red ball, and she's beginning to wonder if Mr Hufat is as harmless as he makes out. There's something about him she doesn't trust. Even so, she'd like to hear his views on what is real, what is illusion and what is magic.

"Mr Hufat, do you think it's possible to bring a dead person back to life with magic?"

He picks the sand from between his toes and sniffs

his fingers. "Most ignorant of little girls, a dead person is as dead as a dead goose! Egyptian magic has a practical purpose – the thousands of healing prayers and chants are used to extend and ease life, not bring it back – that would be sinful!"

Sam hasn't finished with him yet. "But Mr Hufat, is there such a thing as real magic or is it all just a neat trick?"

He slaps his forehead – she is trying his patience. "Thank Ra I was never blessed with a daughter. You are doing my head in. But in answer to your impertinent question, I will say this: magic is the creative force which binds spirit and matter together. Everything has a thread of spirit that connects it to the rest of the world."

He stuffs the red ball into his mouth and says, "Ebil igagibut ogjegs agsorg ebotioms."

Even inanimate objects absorb emotions; something Mrs Reafy also believes. And Ruth Abafey. It strikes Sam that human minds – ancient and modern – all draw similar conclusions about things they can't explain. They all hope for an afterlife; they all want to feel the invisible strings that connect them to their world.

"Indeed," nods Hufat. "Only the symbols change, and the rituals and names of the gods. This limited thinking is hardly surprising given that we are all made of the same ingredients." He draws a circle in the sand. "Each of us is a miniature universe. All that is within us is also without; we are electric and magnetic, just like pebbles and planets. We contain a zoo of bacteria and parasites – even more so in the case of your orang-utan. I *do* wish it would stop scratching."

Sam leaps to Lola's defence. "She has sand in her fur."

"I don't care! She is making me itchy. Any more silly questions? Only it's my bath time. It's hot and I'm starting to stick to my mat."

"Just one more," says Sam. "Has a man called John Tabuh ever been to visit you?"

At the mention of the Dark Prince, Yerba Hufat screws up his face and snarls. "Who is he to you?"

"My father."

"Gah!" Hufat spits into the air, lowers his umbrella and makes a great play of buttoning up the little strap that keeps it closed. He lays it next to him and hunches like a crow. "Yes, I met John Tabuh. He pooh-poohed my umbrella trick. He said it was just an illusion. *That* I could live with, but then he did something far worse."

Sam can't imagine what that could be.

"Don't say he pooh-poohed your ball and cups? If he did, I'm sure he didn't mean to. It's just that he's a magician, and the ball and cups are ... well, they are rather basic. Lola taught me how to find the ball when I was three."

By now, Mr Hufat's face has twisted into a very peculiar shape, as if he's chewing a hedgehog.

"It's nothing to do with cups and balls!" he shrieks. "John Tabuh had the *audacity*, the *gall*, the *temerity*, to doubt the word of Yerba Hufat, despite the reassurance of my very good friend, his father!"

Choking on his own spit, he explains that John Tabuh had asked him if it was possible to bring someone back to life and Yerba Hufat had replied that he could do even better than that; he could bring something to life that had never lived.

"Impossible!" laughs Sam.

This makes Hufat even angrier. He turns and he shouts, "You are just like your father! Are you calling me a liar?"

"No, I'd never say such a thing. It's just that it goes against all the laws of nature."

"Oh!" says Yerba. "You know all the laws of nature, do you? You know them better than Yerba Hufat, who is your elder?"

"But you can't even master the cup and ball," says Sam, under her breath.

"I," says Yerba, thumping his chest so hard that he coughs, "*I* am the greatest magician on Earth! If you refuse to believe I can bring something to life that has never lived, I'll just have to prove it to you, won't I? Just as I proved it to that incorrigible sceptic, your father."

"How exactly did you do that?" asks Sam.

"How exactly did you do that?" mimics Yerba with revolting sarcasm. "I'll tell you how I did that! You see these two stone crocodiles? I snapped my fingers and worked Big Magic. At my command, they sprang into life and grabbed hold of your father's leg with their very sharp teeth. They gave him the most appalling injuries from which he no doubt died. He limped off into the desert with his magic box, and somewhere out there his handsome (*pff!*) but sceptical bones lie, picked clean by the vultures – ha! Good riddance to him!"

231

Halfway through this vicious rant, Khensu begins to growl at one of his crocodiles – it is not as it first appeared. Now that the umbrella had been removed, it's no longer in the shade, and the heat of the midday sun is having the strangest effect on it. It's starting to drip. As the sun continues to beat down, Sam notices a strong smell – like burning candles.

This is no stone statue; it's a real crocodile. It's been coated in a thick layer of wax to immobilize it. As the wax melts from its scaly eyelids, the creature blinks. Khensu leaps in the air; Kitty runs off screaming; Lola swings into the palm tree, and as Sam leaps to her feet, the sinful Mr Hufat commands the crocodile to attack.

"Fetch, Ammit! Eat the sceptical child!"

HOW TO LEVITATE

The masked magician stands at an angle facing away from the audience. Suddenly the magician levitates a few inches above the ground. How?

THE SECRET

audience view

reverse view

1. Stand on the tips of the toes of your foot farthest from the spectator. The angle at which you stand, acting and misdirection all contribute to the illusion.

2. Inform your audience ahead of time that you intend to levitate.

3. Pretend to put lots of care into where you're going to perform.

4. Stress that there are no wires or gimmicks and allow yourself to be examined.

5. Act as if the levitation is physically straining.

6. The audience is misdirected from your actual method because they're busy concentrating on the movement of your feet and the space between the feet and the ground.

7. When "landing" make a point of hitting the ground hard and bend your knees to fool them into thinking you've "levitated" higher than you have. Practise in front of a mirror.

THE CAT CEMETERY

When you're being chased by a carnivore, the natural instinct is to run. But that's the *last* thing you must do: the beast is programmed to chase you and kill you. Crocodiles look sluggish, but don't be fooled; they can reach surprising speeds in short bursts.

Aware of this, Sam faces Ammit and assumes a statue pose worthy of Bart Hayfue. It takes a great deal of courage to do this when confronted by a croc with a head the size of a cello, but her bravery pays off.

Confused that its prey is no longer moving, the crocodile slams on its brakes and peers at her like an old man trying to read a menu without his glasses. Unfortunately, crocodiles are good at pretending to be statues too – it's much easier to balance on four legs.

Knowing she'll be the first to wobble, Sam saves herself using that old standby, ventriloquism. She throws her voice behind her, making it sound as if Yerba Hufat is bleating like a goat. Hearing his favourite dish in full voice, Ammit whips round, runs on his scaly toes towards his master and chases him into the water.

To this day I don't know if Mr Hufat was eaten alive or whether the crocodile took one bite and spat him out; he was rather oily. Whatever happened, his curdling screams could still be heard ten minutes after Sam and friends had escaped on their camels across the Black Desert.

The camels have slowed down to a sullen plod. The plan is to head for Lower Egypt, to Tel Basta, but as I said earlier, Sam's camel has eaten the map. There are no signposts, so it's more than fortunate that they stumble across a tribe of nomads without whom I doubt they would have survived.

Sam's spirits are low. She's afraid her father died in the desert from his crocodile bite and that her mother has died with him, from grief, lack of water and heat exhaustion.

Thankfully that is not the case according to the wife of the chief tribesman, who welcomes the weary travellers to her tent and offers them camel's cheese and figs.

After their meal, Kitty, Lola and Khensu fall asleep against a pile of tasselled cushions. While they sleep, the tribeswoman tells Sam about the time she found a man bleeding to death in the Black Desert. He was in the arms of his wife who was trying to staunch the flow of blood from his leg with her blonde hair.

A nomadic elder had strapped John Tabuh to the magic box and towed him behind his camel. His younger brother carried Christa, and the couple were taken to a tent where they were attended to by the nomadic women.

It was six months before John Tabuh regained full use of his leg, by which time he and Christa had become part of the tribal elder's family. The nomads persuaded them to stay for a further six months and, to repay them for their kindness, the Dark Prince entertained them with magic while Christa made clothes for the children.

"Thank you," says Sam. "Thank you so much for saving them."

The woman hands her a cup of mint tea. "My pleasure. Such charming people. My sisters were in tears when your father left. Compared to John Tabuh, their husbands suddenly looked like the backs of camels!"

Sam leans back against her cushion. "I don't suppose you know where my parents went by any chance?"

"Mexico." The woman smiles. "I wonder if your mother had a little boy or a girl…"

Her mother had been *pregnant*? The news takes a while to sink in. To discover that your father isn't Bingo Hall and that your mother didn't die in childbirth takes some getting used to. Now Sam must get to grips with the fact that, somewhere, she might have a sister or brother.

At first she's excited, then she's jealous. She wants to be the *only* one, certain that if her parents had another child, they've forgotten her. If only she knew that no matter how many siblings came along, John and Christa could never love their first child any less.

If only we all knew that.

If you follow the east bank of the Nile as Sam, Kitty and

Lola did, eventually you will come to Zagazig. Nearby is the ancient city of Bubastis, and there, hidden behind a grove, you will find the sacred enclosure that surrounds the ruined temple of Tel Basta.

Within it lies the shrine of Bastet, daughter of the sun god, Ra, protector of women, cats, children and all that is life-giving; she carries a rattle but I don't know if it's silver. And she has a sister, Sekhmet. According to Kitty, Sekhmet is the opposite of Bastet in every way. She is the wicked sister, the one who revels in darkness.

"Like Candy and Christa," says Sam. "I'm beginning to think life is one big illusion done with mirrors, Kitty … Kitty?"

Kitty doesn't reply. She's kneeling at the shrine with Khensu at her side, offering up this prayer. It's in Ancient Egyptian, so I'll translate it for you.

"Beloved Bast, mistress of happiness and bounty, twin of the sun god, Horus, with your graceful stealth, anticipate the moves of all who perpetrate cruelties and stay their hands against the child of light. Watch over us in the lonely place where we must walk…"

This is as much as Sam hears. In the middle of the prayer, Khensu slips away. It's as if he's evaporated from his own shadow. Sam and Lola go after him in case he gets lost. This is nonsense, of course – cats always know exactly where they are.

They find Khensu in the Cat Cemetery, chattering to himself … or is he communicating with the spirits of hundreds of cats mummified and buried here? His ears swivel, he thumps his tail and he yowls. Perhaps the spirits are reminding him that he isn't just a barge cat, he's a demi-god. Deep down, he's known it all along and he draws himself up proudly like the sacred beast that he is. When Sam calls him, he sticks his nose in the air and ignores her.

"Come on, Khensu."

The feline demi-god won't let Sam near him. Whenever she approaches him, he slides inside a tombstone, soaks into the soil or melts against the moon. Who knows where he's gone, but wherever it is, it's where he belongs. Sam knows he will never come back.

"Goodbye, Khensu... Let's go, Lola. He doesn't want to be found."

Lola will miss him. She's not had a baby to care for since she nursed Sam. Khensu filled a gap that her toy monkey could never fill.

Sam puts an arm around her. "When I find mum and dad, I'll buy you a kitten, Lola. Or a rabbit, if you like. Or maybe you'll fall in love with another orang-utan and have your own baby."

As they walk back to Bastet's shrine, Sam chatters to Lola about the baby orang-utan fantasy. "I could babysit for you, if you wanted to go out. I wonder if you'd have a girl or a boy, Lola... Oh! That's odd. Where's Kitty? This is the right place, isn't it?"

Kitty is nowhere to be seen. She's probably wandered off to see the rest of the temple, so they sit and wait for her. But the minutes turn into hours and still no sign. They search all through the night but Kitty doesn't reply.

"Here, Kitty! Kitty! Kitty!"

A raven-furred cat sits on a tombstone and watches them. It's wearing the bold eyeliner of an Egyptian priestess. The markings on its face bear an uncanny likeness to Kitty's mask. It stares at Sam.

For a split second, Sam believes it might be possible for people to shape-shift into animals – but does it work the other way round? Can animals shape-shift into humans? Would this cat turn back into Kitty? Was Aunt Candy really a python who had turned into a person and was unable to twist itself back?

The cat averts its gaze, bored with the speculation. It's just a cat, Sam tells herself. She takes out a pencil and paper and asks the spirits where Kitty is hiding. Instinctively, she knows she's hiding. She doesn't know why; perhaps it is some kind of test. Or the desire for privacy. Or maybe, like Khensu, she's come to the end of her journey – she's home at last and Sam must carry on without her.

There's no alternative. The spirits remain silent; Kitty doesn't return. Sam has no reason to stay in Egypt. Somehow, she must travel to Mexico to visit Father Bayu. His name is dominating the witch doctor's list – scorching the page. She slams the book shut to extinguish the sparks.

Sam and Lola must make their way down the Nile to Cairo, but the boatman won't allow them onto his raft until Sam pays the fare. He's been tricked before and he's wary of this wild, lonesome girl. Or maybe he's scared of orang-utans.

"Show me your Egyptian pounds, lady!"

"I only have euros, but they're as good as anything."

"No good! No journey!"

She could offer him the second oyster pearl from the witch doctor's pouch, but it would be a waste. The pearl is worth a great deal and she's sure he'll short-change her, so she searches for Mr Fraye's coin.

It's an unusual coin, about the size of a ten-pence piece but heavier. It's tarnished, but when she rubs it on her sleeve, it gleams brightly. On one side there's an orchid framing the embossed head of a hornbill. On the reverse there's a picture of a man in a headdress with boars' tusks in his nostrils. Sam hands the coin to the boatman.

"Will this do?"

His eyes dart from left to right as if it's the currency of the devil. "Get in, get in!" he insists, pulling her on board. "I will take you there for *nothing*, providing you never tell a living soul that I refused to take you in the first place."

Sam promises and the agitated boatman plunges his pole in the water and punts them down the Nile at phenomenal speed, as if pursued by demons. When they arrive at Cairo, he can't wait to get rid of them.

"The airport is *that* way!" He pushes Sam and Lola off the raft and punts away so fast, his arms blur.

The heat is unbearable, but Lola will have to disguise herself as a person or they won't let her on the plane. Sam has no clothes to lend her, so they head for the bazaar to buy a burka.

The bazaar is hot, spicy and loud. There are richly patterned carpets for sale. Chickens, goats, pots, pans, lamps, jewellery and cloth. There's a barrow loaded with spiky-skinned fruit that look like lizards and a barrow loaded with lizards that look like spiky-skinned fruit.

They find a man selling burkas, but he won't accept euros either, so, in a beggar-free corner, Sam takes off her ringmaster's hat and performs a few tricks with Lola to earn some money. In an Egyptian bazaar, nobody cares if you have a pet orang-utan. There are monkeys everywhere, not to mention rats, cats, snakes, camels and dogs.

There are also donkeys – one of which has just collapsed under the weight of its load. Sam has just bought the burka when a shrill cry rings out from a child waving a stick. "He's dead! Now how will we carry pots to market?"

The half-starved donkey is slumped on the dirt floor, a bag of dust and bones. Sam pushes her way through the crowd and asks them all to stand back. At first they take no notice; who is she to tell them what to do?

She must act quickly; showmanship is needed to control this audience. She must be like the Dark Prince of Tabuh and work the crowd. She stands on an upturned mango crate. "Ladies and gentlemen, I will now levitate!"

Sure enough, she appears to have risen into the air – not very high, but just enough to enthral the spice-seller.

"See the magician!" he cries.

Word gets around. Now Sam has the attention of the crowd and, with excellent sleight of hand, she produces two palm fronds from nowhere which she waves hypnotically.

"Magician, magician, see the magician!"

Maintaining an air of mystery, Sam steps down from the

box and walks towards the donkey. As she walks, she chants – but she's not chanting the resurrection chant. She's trying to discover what is real, what is magic and what is illusion, so she's chanting something quite ridiculous:

You put your right leg in, your right leg out,
In out, in out, you shake it all about.
You do the hokey cokey and you turn around,
That's what it's all about!

She hasn't gone mad; she's trying to understand the power of chanting.

1. Is it the actual words of the chant that make it potent?
2. Can you use any old words because the magic in the rhythm of your speech?
3. Is all in the tone of your voice?

It's not for me to say what makes a chant work. It's up to you to experiment and draw your own conclusions; but not now – the donkey is our priority at the moment. It appears to have stopped breathing. Sam is kneeling at its head, fanning it with the palm leaves. Its eyes remain fixed. Sam closes the lids gently with her thumb, then she constricts the muscles in her throat and throws her voice into a clay pitcher balanced on a woman's head.

"Fill me with water!"

The woman smiles awkwardly, hoping she's misheard. But she can't have; everyone is staring at her. The seemingly ordinary pitcher on her head is speaking.

"Fill me with water!"

The woman gives a short, sharp scream as if she's been nipped on the bottom by a dog, hitches up her skirt and runs down to the river to fill her jug.

"Run! Run! Run!"

She returns breathless and passes the jug to Sam who pulls the donkey's drooping lip outwards to form a pouch. She drips the water in and raises its head. The water trickles down the donkey's parched throat.

"It's dead!" cries the child.

Sam lowers the donkey's head, places her hands over its heart and presses – one, two, three ... and release. One, two, three ... and release.

"It's dead!" cries the child.

One, two, three ... release! Sam does it again and again, eyes closed, picturing the cooled blood of the donkey flowing once more through the arteries, lubricating its exhausted engine ... *there*! She can feel a heartbeat. Stand back!

The donkey rocks on its spine, kicks it legs and clatters onto its hooves. It takes a deep breath and lets out a long, low huff through its flared nostrils. The crowd cheers; the donkey is alive! Sam feeds it with slices of melon.

But who's that shouting from the upturned mango crate? It's the boatman. He's dancing up and down and yelling, "Witch! Witch! Arrest her! She's a witch!"

How swiftly the mood of a crowd can change. Despite Sam's protestation that she hasn't brought the donkey back from the dead – all it needed was water and a rest – no one will listen to her.

"Liar! Liar! Witch! Witch!"

The police arrive. Sam and Lola are handcuffed and thrown into the back of a van.

THE VANISHING ELEPHANT

A large cabinet is pushed onto the stage. An elephant is led into it and the blinds are dropped. The cabinet is turned sideways by stagehands and the masked magician waves a wand. Two circular panels are dropped giving the audience a clear view through the cabinet; the elephant has gone! How?

There are two possibilities:

a) The elephant lies down in the cabinet and the floor of the cabinet is slightly raised...

or:

b) When the curtained opening of the cabinet is raised, the audience can see through the circular opening at the back to the rear of the stage, but can't see the elephant because it is standing in the side of the cabinet (now it has been turned) which is wider than the uncurtained opening.

THE FLIGHT TO MEXICO

I t's impossible to pick the lock on the prison cell. Even Lola can't manage it with her opposable thumbs.

"Now what?" Sam sits down hard on the concrete floor. There's no furniture except for a bucket and a bench. Lola upturns the bucket and sits next to Sam.

"Any bright ideas, Lola?"

"Ooo."

Sam wishes the guard would come. If he did, she could distract him while Lola stole his keys, hardly a difficult move for two accomplished magicians.

"Guard… Guard, I need a drink of water!"

Sam bangs on the bars but the man won't leave his desk.

"Quiet, witch, or I'll throw you to the rabble. They will tear you limb from limb."

Sam, who is very attached to her limbs, keeps quiet. At times like this, she really needs to refer to the witch doctor's notebook, but the guard has confiscated her things.

Having finished looking at his magazine, he becomes

bored and starts rifling through Sam's bag. She can hear him talking to himself; he's just found the divining rod.

"Huh? A back-scratcher! Aww... Worhhhhh... That hit the spot!"

Now he finds the witch's cord.

"Now this'll be handy. It'll stop my gown gaping when I answer the door to the butcher's boy... Or I can use it to strangle someone."

He's found the witch doctor's notebook. Sam's heart skips a beat. She squeezes her eyes shut and prays to Bastet, Ra, Jesus, Mary and Allah – *please don't let him destroy it!* Surely there must be one god who will answer her prayer? There seem to be so many gods. Or maybe there *is* just the one and the world is a giant mirrored ball which refracts his image a thousand different ways – who knows.

The guard sniffs the book with his bristly nostrils, "Pooh ... smells funny! Ooh, wonder if it's got any rude pictures..."

He must have opened the book at this point because he screams as if he's been bitten by a cobra and leaps out of his chair. He *may* have been bitten by a cobra – they're ten a penny in Egypt – but I didn't see one, and if it was a snake, why did he curse the book, grab his gun and poke it through the bars at Sam?

When confronted by a man with a bristly nose and a gun, most people faint or scream. But not Sam. She's so angry that he dared to touch her book that she wags her finger at him and, in a voice that isn't entirely her own, she says in Motu: *"Shoot me, shoot me. You can't kill me. I am*

Sam Khaan. If you shoot, your toes will drop off, your liver will shrivel and your children will grow tails!"

I'm not sure if this put him off or not because … look who's here! It's Kitty! She's brought a nice policeman with her who orders the guard to unlock the cell door immediately and release the inmates. Sam could throw her arms around her, but for reasons we've discussed, she doesn't.

"Where *were* you, Kitty? We looked everywhere!"

Kitty shrugs as if she has no idea what she's talking about. "You can't have looked very hard. Maybe you need your eyes testing."

"I do not! My eyesight's fine – and so is Lola's sense of smell."

"Oh … am I smelly?"

To be fair they could all do with a bath, but they'll have to wait until they get to Mexico. They must hurry – their flight from Egypt is in less than an hour.

Boarding the plane to Mexico isn't easy. Paying for the tickets with euros is no problem, but trying to get an orang-utan through customs is never simple. Kitty insists on going through passport control first, because she doesn't want Sam to see her without her mask. She has to lift it up to prove she's the person on her passport photo and, as she does so, Sam watches the customs officer's expression to see if he recoils at her melted features.

I have to tell you he does not. He raises his eyebrows slightly then waves her on. Maybe he's being polite. Maybe he's seen worse. But Sam thinks it's odd that he doesn't react more strongly.

Something else also crosses her mind. She'd given Kitty a bottle of holy water, hadn't she? She wonders if Kitty has dabbed some on her skin and there has been a miracle; but she dismisses the idea. If Kitty's burns were healed, why would she keep the mask on?

Sam has no problem getting through the barrier. She's stolen a passport from a dark-haired girl in the waiting lounge who looks a little like her, and just as the control officer is about to check it, Lola causes a distraction.

Lola is sitting in an airport wheelchair dressed in her burka. All you can see are her soft brown eyes through the slit in the veil – at least, that *was* all you could see; now she's decided to scratch her ear with her foot, revealing a pair of bloomers and extremely hairy legs.

My dear old grandma on my mother's side is fairly flexible but even *she* can't do that – she hasn't got the hips for it. She also has hairy legs and after too many sherries, she'll show her bloomers, and good luck to her. The point I'm trying to make is this: what is considered ladylike in ape society – scratching your bottom, waving your legs in the air and blowing raspberries – is sadly not acceptable in ours. Through no fault of her own, Lola is about to blow her disguise.

If Sam hadn't grabbed hold of her ankles and hastily covered them with the burka, they would have been in big trouble. If she hadn't snapped, "Grandma, put your legs down! Just because you used to be a contortionist, there's no need to show off!" they would not have been allowed to board flight 333 to Mexico.

But they have boarded; they are already up in the air. It's the first time Sam has been on a plane, but the sensation is familiar. She has flown in her dreams – at least, she dreamt that she was passing through clouds, but it was so fast, she hardly seemed to be moving at all. It felt as if she was hovering, yet she couldn't have been because the scenery below kept changing.

Kitty hasn't been on a plane for years and she's extremely nervous. Every time they hit turbulence, she screams, "I'm falling! Help, I'm on fire! There are flans everywhere!"

This has a bad effect on the other passengers. Those who hear Kitty mention the word "flan" start hassling the steward, demanding to know why nobody had served *them* a meal yet. Those with nervous dispositions have fixated on the dreaded words "falling" and "fire" and are peering anxiously out of the windows to see if the engines are alight. Sam tries to draw Kitty into conversation to take her mind off things.

"Kitty, how did you manage to persuade the policeman to release me from the prison cell?"

"Falling! I'm on fire! Extinguish the flans!"

"You're *not* on fire. It's a flashback. Here – blow into this paper bag."

It's not a magic trick, but it prevents panic attacks a lot better than pulling rabbits out of hats. Kitty soon recovers enough to answer Sam's question.

"I told them the dinkey wasn't dud in the first place."

Between you and me, the donkey had been dead; the poor beast had no pulse. Sam knew it, but didn't mention it to Kitty in case it sounded like showing off. I'm not sure it was a miracle though. People are brought back to life every day if a first-aider can remember how to kick-start their heart. What works for us might also work for donkeys.

Back to Kitty. She'd managed to persuade the chief of police that Sam wasn't a witch but the daughter of a magician called John Tabuh. Luck would have it that the chief knew the Dark Prince personally. He'd shaken Kitty warmly by the hand and said, "Ah, I remember John!" He'd been most impressed with him and so had his wife (she had a soft spot for men with thick, glossy hair – a pity, considering her husband was as bald as a baby).

At the time, John had needed money to fly to Mexico. In order to raise sufficient funds, he'd performed the most incredible illusions at the Policeman's Ball. On the chief's recommendation, he received several other major bookings including the palace, where he performed the vanishing elephant trick for the king of Egypt and rapidly became the talk of Cairo.

For once, he hadn't managed to upset anybody, because he avoided asking awkward questions and simply sought to dazzle, which might be a lesson to us all. It seems he was reluctant to leave. But Christa was expecting their baby and his father was expecting some answers, so he had to move on.

Kitty's disappearance at the shrine of Bastet remains a mystery however; she claims she was there all along. This is possible, I suppose. How many times have we hunted for a missing sock in a certain drawer and *known* it wasn't there, only to find it the next day in the same drawer we'd looked in fifty times? Missing Sock Syndrome is a more logical answer than Kitty shape-shifting into a cat, but logic is a strange animal; I wouldn't trust it altogether.

The captain has just announced that the plane is due to land. If you look out of the window, you will see Mexico down below. Fasten your seatbelts, ladies and gentleman.

Arriba!

HOW TO STEP THROUGH PAPER

The masked magician tells the audience it is possible to step right through a sheet of paper. How?

THE SECRET

Copy this template onto a piece of A3 paper and snip through the lines. Stretch it out and you will have a huge hole to step through.

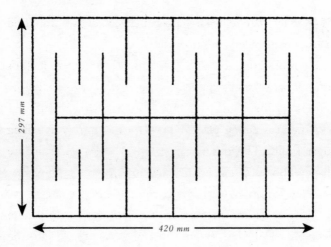

297 mm

420 mm

THE DAY OF THE DEAD

Mexico. We're heading for Janitzio where we must find
a man called Father Bayu.

He is blistering the page at the top of the witch doctor's
list, but Sam doesn't know what skills he has or whether he
is friend or foe.

A fiesta is taking place. The plaza in Quiroga is selling
sugar skulls. The bakers are baking *pan de muerto* in the
shape of bones. There are toy skeletons for sale everywhere.

"Hey, señoritas! You wanna buy *calaveras*?"

The floor is strewn with millions of marigolds. Where
people have walked, the petals have been pressed into the
ground like marmalade shreds; their bittersweet tang is
impossible to escape. The stalls are hung with *papel picado*
– intricately cut tissue-paper banners depicting skeletons
dancing and celebrating. A woman shakes a bag at Sam and
offers her a piece of dough in the shape of a dog.

"*El día de los muertos!*" beams the woman. "We are
remembering the *angelitos* – the children who have died.

Once a year they come back to visit us, so we throw them a party. Won't it be lovely to have them home? I have been baking dough dogs all night."

"Why dogs?"

"I tell you. The dog, he ferries the souls of the departed across the river to heaven."

It seems that in Mexico, death is nothing to cry about. Nor is it ugly or grim. Look at the children's faces as they stuff candy skulls into their mouths and play with their bony puppets – they're as happy and excited as we are when it snows at Christmas.

"Why be sad?" laughs the woman. "Birth leads to life, life leads to death. Death is not the end of the story. It is a fresh start – my father, the tailor, is making suits in heaven and the quality and cut are much better than anything he made in this life."

Sam is tempted to ask, "How do you know your father's heavenly suits are superior?" but it would be disrespectful of her faith. It would be like asking the Pope, "Yes, but how do you know that Jesus is the son of God?"

Whether the dough lady's beliefs are right or not, the idea that we carry on merrily after death and are welcome to come back and visit our relatives is a happy thought – at least it is if you like your relatives. Sam doesn't relish the idea of visiting Aunt Candy ever again. As we speak, she's having a fist fight with a tattooed barmaid in the roughest pub in Kilburn. If there's a heaven, I wonder if there's someone there to serve gin – and if so, is it free?

Sam, Kitty and Lola are in a party mood now; who'd

have thought death could be so exhilarating? Let them celebrate with the Mexicans – let them eat, drink and dance until the moon comes up, and then we will join them in the launch boat and speed across Lake Patzcuaro to the beautiful island of Janitzio.

The sky is frosted with stars. You can see little white houses with bright red roofs. People are carrying candles and copal incense. A path of luminous, curling petals winds its way to the cemetery. Out on the lake, fishermen perform an ancient ritual with their butterfly nets in the mist.

Just as the ceremony is about to end, there's a fierce downpour; the Mexicans call it *aguacero*. Esperanza – the woman who baked the dough dogs – holds her umbrella over Sam and Kitty, but it offers little protection from the driving rain; they're soaked.

Lola doesn't mind, her fur is waterproof. But the water is pouring off the brim of Sam's hat like a fountain. Marigold petals cling to the hem of Kitty's robe and form an orange tide line. Esperanza takes Sam's arm. "Come. Come to my home and we dry off."

She breaks into a feminine trot in her red dancing shoes. They follow her past the cemetery and down the hill to a house that gleams wetly like a freshly iced wedding cake. Esperanza shakes the umbrella, pushes the door open with her wide hips and ushers them inside. "Please, dry by the fire. Go and sit with my family."

But she has no family; at least, none that is alive. Just a homemade altar – an *ofrenda* – decked with candles, garlands and photographs. At the centre is a picture of Esperanza's elderly mother and her father, the tailor. He has his arm around his wife.

"Ah, that is Maricella and Enzo," smiles Esperanza. "Eighty years old and still madly in love. Even more so now they're dead."

She speaks to their photo. "Mama … Papa? This is my friends, Sam, Kitty and Lola from England."

She adds in a stage whisper: "My mother, she love to meet new people. It make her feel young, you know? My father, he not so fussed. He a very quiet man. He only have eyes for Maricella."

She clip-clops into the kitchen and returns with hot soup and red rice on a brightly-painted, papier-mache tray. There is dark café de olla to drink. Lola dries Sam's hair with a towel then helps herself to a bowl of mixed nuts.

"Who is in the other photograph?" muses Sam.

There's another frame on the table with spaces for three portraits, half hidden behind an overblown rose. Esperanza picks it up. "This is the magician's eldest daughter and her two sisters. The twins, they are so cheeky! They die before they is born, so I guess they never have time to learn no manners…"

Sam's blood runs cold. "*The magician's eldest daughter? May I see?*"

Esperanza sits next to Sam and shows her the photo. "There she is, darling, in the middle. Her parents wanted her to be with her sisters."

Sure enough, there's a photo of Sam as a baby, waving her silver rattle. Her mouth goes dry.

"But that's *me*!"

Esperanza polishes the frames with a lace handkerchief and peers at it closely. "No! Is really you? I not recognize you all grown up, but, darling, I very confuse – your father tell me you die in a fire but you not look dead to me."

"I'm not ... it's a long story," mumbles Sam. "What was my father doing here?"

"Oh, he stay here with your mother for a short time after they visit a man call Father Bayu. I do cleaning for Father Bayu and he send them to my home to rest a little while. They give me your photo when they leave."

"They visited Father Bayu?" Sam stares at the photo in confusion. "Esperanza, you said my twin sisters were in the photo with me."

"Sí!" She points with a manicured finger. "You see this little *angelito* on the right? She is your sister Conchita. The one on the left? She is your other sister; the naughty one. She is Consuella."

Sam shivers, but it's not because her hair is damp; it's because the photos of the twins do not exist. There are no pictures of her baby sisters in the frame at all; just two pressed daisies, their pollen trapped like gold dust behind the glass.

"I can't see them."

Esperanza seems mildly surprised. "No? Not even in your mind? Ah, well. They can see you. That is all that matters." She hands the photo to Kitty. "You can see them,

I bet. Don't you think the twins look a bit like Sam?"

Kitty looks, then looks away. She doesn't say a word but she has seen something. Although it's impossible to see her expression behind the mask, her shoulders are heaving. Sam notices immediately.

"What is it, Kitty? Can you see Consuella and Conchita?"

Kitty ignores her and addresses Esperanza. "Why do you welcome Sam's sisters into your home as if they are family?"

Esperanza puts her finger to her lips thoughtfully.

"They *are* family. Conchita and Consuella were a gift to my dead parents; they were born on the day of their own funerals and of my father's funeral."

"I don't understand!" protests Sam. "Why were my sisters born dead? Why would my parents give them to your parents? It all so sad."

Esperanza laughs prettily. "Not sad, darling, magical! My parents couldn't have no more babies after they have me. It make them very, very unhappy. But in the end, their wish come true…"

Esperanza's mother, Maricella, had died a few years back. Her father, Enzo, died shortly after, and it was on the day that he was to be buried next to his wife that the twins turned up.

When Esperanza arrived at the cemetery with the rest of the mourners, she was enchanted to see two home-made caskets – no bigger than shoe boxes – placed in the open grave, one on top of her mother's coffin and one on top of her father's.

In Mexico, if a mother loses her baby and can't afford to

give it a funeral, she will offer the grave digger a few pesos to bury it in someone else's plot; it's considered a great joy for the dead to be honoured with an *angelito*.

"To know that my parents had finally been blessed with twins and were holding them in their arms as the dog ferried them down the river to heaven was a magical moment – the happiest of new beginnings," sighs Esperanza.

"For your parents, maybe," says Sam, "but surely my parents were broken-hearted?"

Esperanza nods. "They were. My brother – he is the gravedigger – he tell me he have never seen such sorrow and I think this is because your parents are not Mexican; they do not realize that their babies are in a happy place. Your father, he was so confused about death – he ask questions, questions, questions. Your mother, she cry tears of milk."

Little wonder. Christa had already lost her first child – or so she thought – and although twins, triplets or even quads could never replace Sam, she wanted more children. Sadly, the twins died before they were born. I don't know why – sometimes there isn't a why – but there was nothing John could do to comfort Christa and nothing she could do to comfort him.

The unhappy couple were so consumed with grief, they became ill at the graveside. Christa fainted and John's leg went into a spasm near his old crocodile bite, leaving him paralysed. The gravedigger, who knew more about death than anybody, was mystified by their morbid behaviour;

how footling were their concerns compared to his? There would always be work for magicians in the afterlife but for a *gravedigger*? Immortal souls needed no burials. He'd be unemployed for eternity.

The Dark Prince and his wife were cluttering up his cemetery. The mourners would be arriving soon for Enzo's funeral, so he threw his spade in the back of the cart, whistled for his donkey and drove them to see Father Bayu.

How to Mend Broken String

The masked magician cuts a piece of string in half, then, with the wave of a wand, it's a whole piece again. How?

THE SECRET

1. Take a piece of thick string, 1 metre long, and cut a 10 cm piece from one end.

2. Loop the small piece of string and nestle it in your left palm with the loop towards your fingers.

3. Show your audience the large piece of string, holding one end in each hand.

4. Using your right hand, take the centre of the string and place it in your left hand, so that the ends hang down.

5. Pretend to pull the centre of the string through your left fist, so it sticks out in a loop, but really, pull the cut piece out. This is what your audience sees. Keep the real centre hidden in your fist.

6. With your right hand, give a pair of scissors to someone in the audience and ask them to cut the string.

7. Take the scissors and cut away all remaining pieces of the shorter string.

8. Hold the string by the ends, letting the centre drop away. The string is restored.

FATHER BAYU

The next morning, Esperanza takes them all to the cemetery. I'm not sure if "happy" is the word to describe Sam as she stands at the graves of Maricella, Enzo and her twin sisters. I'm not sure words exist that can accurately describe her emotions. They have been subtly altered by the essence of marigolds, the taste of dough dogs and the click of Esperanza's red shoes. Death has lost its darkness.

She's uplifted by the thought that although she can't play with her sisters now, it might only be a matter of time. She can hardly wait; she has so much to tell them. She'll plait their hair and read them stories and ... now she's conscious that Kitty thinks she's getting carried away.

"It's not that I'm in any hurry to die, Kitty. I know the afterlife might just be an illusion. If death is final, if there *is* no encore, I shan't be too disappointed. Not knowing just makes me more determined to make my life the greatest show on Earth."

On that triumphant note, she blows a kiss to each baby sister and turns on her heel. "Goodbye for now, *angelitos*! Come on, Lola, let's see what Father Bayu has to say."

Sam has never looked more radiant. You would hardly recognize her as the half-starved, serious little girl you saw through the window in St Peter's Square. Her eyes are bright, her limbs are strong and her hair is long and glossy.

Talking of hair, Sam has been wondering for some time now why Kitty's dead straight Egyptian hairstyle never seems to grow. Maybe she trims it in secret.

Father Bayu lives within walking distance of Esperanza's house. It is a hilly walk – not to be attempted in high heels – so Sam, Kitty and Lola go there alone. They find him tending to his orchid collection in a glass lean-to attached to a stone church. He is dressed in a brown, sleeveless gown tied around his ample waist with string. The gown is so long it covers his feet, so when he walks, he appears to be gliding. For a man who must weigh twenty stone, he's surprisingly graceful; his hands are as elegant as a dancer's.

He acknowledges his guests with a gentle smile and seems both exhausted yet serene. He beckons them over to admire one of his rarer blooms, cupping the bud between his palms.

"Look at that. It has the face of a child, don't you think? Whereas this one…" He moves to the next plant. "This one looks like six baby monkeys clinging to a stick."

Lola, keen to see six baby monkeys, peers at the elaborate folds of the petals and sniffs.

"Good orang-utan," says Father Bayu warmly.

Sam likes him immediately. "Are you fond of orang-utans, Father Bayu?"

"I'm fond of everybody."

He's clearly never met Aunt Candy.

"Everybody? How can you be fond of wicked people?"

He cogitates on the matter then replies, "If people are wicked, it's because they feel unloved. If I add to their sorrow by despising them, they will feel even less loved and become more wicked. I shouldn't want that."

Father Bayu is a psychic healer. Legend has it that he can perform surgery without anaesthetic, pain or blood. He is well known throughout Janitzio, and because he has so many patients, he is in a constant state of exhaustion; but he never turns anyone away.

"I worry we will wear him out," Esperanza had said. "Nobody will go hospital no more. Why would we risk pain and suffering when we have Father Bayu on our door-step?"

He had successfully removed a tumour the size of a grapefruit from Maricella's stomach and, yes, Maricella had been to hospital first, but the surgeon had said it was inoperable.

"Not every psychic healer is to be trusted though," Esperanza warned. "Plenty say they have the gift, but some are frauds. I tell you, I know a guy who plunged his fist into the stomach of a sick boy and said he had removed a tumour. Sure enough, there was something in his hand but it was no tumour – it was goat's intestines! He had hidden them in his hand earlier. I know because my uncle, the butcher, told me so."

Sam thought it was a cruel trick, but Esperanza had laughed her pretty laugh. "You know what is funny, darling? Even though this man was a fraud, the child did not know it and his tumour disappeared! People who do not see through these tricks believe themselves to be healed and, you know what, sometimes they are."

I don't know if Father Bayu is the genuine article or a gifted fraud. Does it matter? A result is a result, no matter how it's achieved. He isn't lying when he tells Sam that he'd cured the paralysis in John Tabuh's leg and brought Christa round and helped her in her grieving.

"Your mother was well on the way to recovery when she left here. Your father will always have a limp, but not enough to bother him. I sent them to stay with Esperanza for a while – to be mothered. Even mothers need mothering sometimes."

Sam and Father Bayu talk at great length, sitting under an orange tree in the grounds of the church. Lola is asleep in the branches. Kitty is picking fruit.

"I was extraordinarily fond of Mr and Mrs Tabuh," Father Bayu continues. "They were good souls, if a little lost. They talked about you constantly, Sam."

"They did?"

"In the most loving way. Know that and you'll never stoop to wickedness."

Kitty throws Sam an orange. She peels it slowly, thinking about what the healer has just said. "Father Bayu, if I hadn't had Lola to love me, do you think I'd have become wicked?"

"It's possible. A child starved of affection may see wickedness as its only playmate; but because Lola loved you, she stopped your heart from hardening. You are not so deeply scarred, all you have sustained is a little scratch."

It doesn't feel like a little scratch. It hurts when Sam remembers her dreadful childhood. It hurts when she thinks of all the years she has missed with her parents. It really hurts when she thinks she might never see them again.

"My scratch feels quite sore sometimes, Father Bayu."

He nods sagely. "Stop picking the scab. Concentrate on doing what you have to do; that is the cure."

"Father Bayu?"

"Yes, my child?"

"I need to know what is real, what is illusion and what is magic. I might get closer to learning the truth if you would try something for me – if you're not too tired, of course."

Father Bayu smiles on the inside. "And what would that be, Sam?"

"I wondered if you could heal Kitty's face? Kitty, show Father Bayu your burns."

Kitty drops her basket of oranges. "Oh, I don't think so."

Father Bayu takes Kitty's arm. "Come, my friend. Let me see what I can do. What have you got to lose?"

Sam urges her to go with him. "Go on! I promise not to look at you."

To her surprise, Kitty allows Father Bayu to lead her away to the inner sanctuary of the church. He closes the door behind him. Lola comes down from the tree and sits next to Sam.

"He seems like a nice man, doesn't he, Lola?"

"Ooo." Lola nods vigorously and spits out a hail of orange pips.

"That's not very ladylike, is it, Lola?"

No, but it's fun, so the two of them suck oranges and shoot pips until the portly psychic healer returns with his patient. To Sam's disappointment, Kitty is still wearing her mask.

"Didn't it work, Father Bayu? Not even a slight improvement? Can I see, Kitty?"

Father Bayu smiles on the outside. "Patience, Sam Tabuh. In time, Kitty will show you her face and you will know the truth about me … about many things."

With that, he genuflects and drifts off to deadhead his orchids.

HOW TO TURN WATER INTO ICE - INSTANTLY

The masked magician pours water into a cup and declares it will turn into ice before your eyes. With a wave of a wand, the cup is turned upside down and an ice cube falls out. How?

THE SECRET

You need: an ice cube, a jug of water, a small dry sponge, a large white plastic cup.

1. Wedge the sponge in the bottom of the cup so it won't fall out when you turn it over.
2. Put an ice cube in the cup on top of the sponge.
3. Pour a small amount of water into the cup.
4. Say the magic word and turn the cup upside down. The ice cube will fall out but the sponge will have soaked up all the water.

BEAU FARTHY

Leaping forward as we must – for life is short – we are
now flying to America. Sam has sold the second pearl
to pay for the flight. There's enough money left to afford a
good hotel and buy new shoes. It's tempting, but as there's
only one pearl left and several countries to visit, they'll
have to check into a cheap hotel and stick with their old
shoes. Lola's happy; she's fond of Mrs Fraye's slippers –
they have fur around the ankles which she likes to pet.

The person who bought the second pearl was a Mexican
jeweller who looked rather like the sort of old lady who
might buy a barge full of cats, except that *this* old lady had a
black twirly moustache (but then so did my grandmother).

Another thing. Although Esperanza had confirmed that
Mr and Mrs Tabuh were heading for America, what she
didn't know was that, on the way, they were kidnapped
by bandits who kept them hostage for months. If the Dark
Prince hadn't spooked them with his famous mind-reading
trick – the one with the envelope and lighter fuel – they

might never have been released. He'd have performed it much earlier of course, but have you ever tried to get hold of white envelopes in bandit country?

We are about to land in Arizona. According to the witch doctor's list that's where Beau Farthy lives, and it's crucial that Sam visits him. There's a portrait next to Mr Farthy's name in which he appears to be holding a cigar or a carrot. Or is it a blowpipe?

Actually, it's a test tube. Yafer Tabuh might be an excellent witch doctor, but he isn't the best of artists. If he drew you a cat, you might easily mistake it for a guinea pig or a moose, or even a hairdryer.

"Maybe Beau Farthy's a plastic surgeon," suggests Sam. "That'd be good, because if Father Bayu was a fraud and your face doesn't heal, he could give you a new nose, Kitty."

"Yes, and maybe he could snip a bit off yours to stop you poking it in my business." Kitty adjusts her mask automatically; it's become a nervous tic. She's ultra sensitive about her appearance. I almost wish Beau Farthy were a plastic surgeon. Plastic surgeons create illusions. They go against the laws of nature and magically reverse time. Sam would have learnt a great deal about what is real from someone who specializes in altering appearances.

In fact, Beau Farthy is an expert in doing the opposite; he keeps people looking exactly as they are for as long as possible – for centuries if necessary. He's a pioneer in cryonics: the art of preserving bodies until science finds a cure for their disease – at which point, they could be defrosted and brought back to life.

"That's the theory, folks!" says Professor Farthy, pushing his fingers through his blond quiff and wiping the excess hair oil down his laboratory coat.

Sam is intrigued. "When – if – you're able to bring the dead back to life because of medical advances, would you call that resurrection, professor?"

He shakes his head irritably. "No, no, I'm not bringing back the dead. I'm preserving the life of the *living*."

"You freeze people while they're still alive?"

Professor Farthy rolls his eyes and rearranges his biros in order of thickness, unable to relax for a second. "What is being alive!" he exclaims. "Not everyone has the same definition of Mr Death."

He sharpens his pencil down to a stub and glares at Lola, who is merrily jumbling up his pens. He bats her away and rearranges them again, then with a sigh of relief, continues, "Death is just medicine's way of excusing itself from problems it cannot fix today. In the West, doctors believe the brain dies five minutes after the heart stops. But that's poppycock."

"Really? Where's your pouffe?" enquires Kitty.

"My pouffe?"

"Your proof," explains Sam. "My friend was hit on the head; she forgets certain words."

Beau Farthy thrusts a brochure into Kitty's hand.

"If that memory of yours doesn't improve none, why not consider cryonics, Mam? In the future, poor memory will be a thing of the past... Dang! Now you've made me forget what I was saying!"

"That our brains stay alive after our hearts stop."

"Indeedy!" beams Professor Farthy. "Many folk have been pronounced drop-down dead only to be revived a whole hour later."

Kitty tells him that a similar thing happened to her after she'd tripped over a cat and fell down the stairs but Beau Farthy isn't interested in anything anyone else has to say.

"The Catholic Church has yet another definition of death," he continues, snatching a red biro from Lola and slamming it back in its rightful place. "It insists that death is the final separation of your soul from your body. But to believe that, you must believe in the existence of a soul. *Pah!*"

"Don't you believe we have souls?" asks Sam.

The professor rearranges a pile of papers on his desk and groans. "I am a *scientist*. I've studied every cell in the human body but I have yet to see the slightest sliver of soul under my microscope."

There's a slight pause, then, as politely as she can, Sam interjects. "But just because we can't see something doesn't mean it doesn't exist, does it? Perhaps it was a really cheap microscope."

He reels back as if she's slapped him in the face. "Not so! My mommy bought that microscope. She always bought me the best!"

He explains mournfully that his mother's generosity was to compensate for the fact that she never visited him at boarding school or sent him cherry pie like the other boys' mothers and that she'd even missed his graduation day.

Sam can only sympathize with him. "I'm sure it was a great microscope. Maybe it's just that no one has made a lens powerful enough to see the human soul yet."

"Until they do, I remain sceptical," insists Professor Farthy. "I'm a scientist, I need scientific proof that the soul exists, which I truly doubt."

He grabs a rack of test tubes from Lola, who is playing a tune on them, then flings himself back in his chair, eyes glazed, mouth gaping.

"I might have proof when I'm dead," he drawls. "But as I intend to have myself cryonically preserved and cured of whatever vile disease carries me off, the truth will be a long time a-coming."

The prospect of immortality cheers him up no end. He vaults out of his chair and asks if they'd like to visit his clients. They are preserved like human ice lollies out the back.

I hope you're wearing a vest. It's bitterly cold here in the Room of Temporary Rest. Although Lola removed her costume after she left the airport, she still has her slippers on, which provide much needed warmth. Sam and Kitty are shivering.

Beau Farthy draws their attention to a row of human-sized churns, dabbing the end of his nose before the drip hanging off it turns into an icicle.

"Each dewar contains one of my clients," he exclaims, slapping the side of the nearest churn and chatting to the contents. "Howdy, Mr Dwight. Brought some visitors to see you."

He undoes the lid. As a cloud of liquid nitrogen escapes, he encourages Sam to look inside. She isn't squeamish, but she hesitates; she's never seen a corpse before. Could it be a more scary sight than Aunt Candy first thing in the morning? She swallows hard then peeks at Mr Dwight.

"He looks very dead to me, Professor."

Beau Farthy waves his arms wildly, shushing her and putting his finger to his lips. "I reject that observation; my patients aren't dead, their lives are on hold. Their brains were still functioning when they arrived, which is more than can be said for some folks."

He smiles sarcastically at Sam. She's tempted to throw her voice and make Mr Dwight say something rude, but she desists; she doesn't want him to lose his dignity any more than he already has, crammed into an ice box like a piece of pork past its sell-by date.

"Mr Dwight is not *dead*!" repeats the Professor, "He's in a state of suspension, like a hibernating turtle. Before his brain stopped, I cooled him down to a temperature at which he no longer requires oxygen; breathing is not an issue for him. His organs remain as fresh as a daisy – have a sniff!"

Nobody wants to, so he closes the dewar lid with a bang and, rubbing his hands together, asks if they'd like to see his horses.

"Do you have stables, Professor Farthy?"

"No, but I sure do have a big refrigerator."

Sam and Kitty are led to another room. Sporting a pair of mittens, Beau Farthy removes what looks like an ice-cube tray from a chiller cabinet. In each section there's a translucent embryo no bigger than the snotty chick in an under-boiled egg.

"Race horses! Future champions. Say, would you ladies like to see my bulls?"

There's no polite answer to that. Sam, Kitty and Lola are treated to the entire contents of the fridge, which contains not only bull embryos but endangered species from around the globe, including the Sumatran tiger and the giant panda.

"Only last year a wild cat was born after its frozen embryo was implanted into a domestic cat − a total success!" whoops the professor. "Which sure does give me hope for Mr Dwight. I see no reason why I can't restore him to the peak of health some sunny day."

Except that Mr Dwight wasn't a wild cat; he was an insurance salesman − and he was a whole lot bigger than a kitten embryo. Sam finds it hard to share Professor Farthy's optimism.

"Have you thawed out any patients yet?"

He avoids the issue by showing them what else he's got in his freezer: three pots of yogurt, half a pizza and rack upon rack of individual human cells stored in frozen vials.

"Looky here now, skin cells! They were grown in my laboratory. Entire organs can be grown − here's a kidney that I made earlier; so sleek, so shiny…" He rubs the kidney lovingly across his cheek then produces a liver. "I could transplant one organ after another, endlessly," he enthuses. "Completely negating the ageing process."

"Have you got any brain cells?" asks Sam.

He looks in the salad box as if they might be in there somewhere, but it's empty.

"I'll grow brain cells in jars and use them to replace the ones that die in my head. I'll build nano-robots smaller than bacteria. They will float around my arteries repairing my body. Hot diggerty, I will be the *immortal* Professor Farthy!"

It's a remarkable vision of the future, but it doesn't appeal to Sam. She worries about Mr Dwight. If he were revived in a hundred years' time, the world he knew would have changed beyond recognition. His friends and family would all be dead. Wouldn't he be lonely? Beau Farthy leans against the chiller cabinet and refuses to catch her eye.

"Friends and family? Never had much to do with them. Too busy putting lives on hold."

"Family is very important to me," Sam tells him. "Did my father ever have an appointment with you? His name is John Tabuh."

Beau Farthy keeps his records immaculately. He whips out his address book and dons a pair of white cotton gloves so that he doesn't soil the pages.

"Tabuh?"

He drags his finger down a list of names, each of which has a list of appointment times against it. "Let me see now. Tabard ... Tabbidge ... ah, here we are!"

There it is, in black and white. John Tabuh had kept an appointment with Beau Farthy two years ago at three minutes past three, third of March. The professor closes his address book.

"Your daddy had an enquiring mind, but he couldn't grasp the notion of cryonics."

"He's a magician," explains Sam.

"That figures – he would keep producing frozen organs from behind my ear. He implied that I could never bring Mr Dwight back to life and I had to remind him that, as a scientist, I knew a whole lot more about life and death than *he* did – that's when he said a strange thing."

"What was it?" asks Sam. "Can you remember? It might be really important."

Beau Farthy remembers only too well. "He said, and I quote, 'Professor, in your opinion, would it be scientifically possible to bring a person back to life by using the power of the *mind*?'"

"Well, do you?" asks Kitty.

The professor thinks for a while then announces that, as the power of the mind has been scientifically proven to heal the body on *occasions*, he couldn't rule it out entirely.

"But I sure hope it doesn't happen too often, or I'll be outta business."

By now, Lola is bored. The conversation is of no interest to an orang-utan, so she slopes off unnoticed, back to the room full of dewars. Meanwhile, Professor Farthy has just mentioned that John Tabuh had been very keen to reserve a dewar for his father.

"He seemed mighty anxious that his daddy might die before he'd fulfilled some mission or other. If that situation occurred, he asked if I could freeze the old man until such time as he'd completed it and then defrost him. I turned him down, of course."

"Why?" asks Sam.

"Your grandaddy would have to get here within an hour of his heart stopping. There's no way he could travel all the way from New Guinea to Arizona in time."

"Grandpa lives in *New Guinea*?" It's the first she's heard of it.

"Sure thing. John said the old man had lived there all his days and would never leave, not *physically* anyhow. He said his father could leave his body at will and travel anywhere he pleased. I call that poppycock but—"

"I call it teleporting," says Kitty, who for once has remembered the correct word.

"Call it what you will," replies Farthy. "Teleportation has no scientific basis whatsoever. Anyone who tells you otherwise is a crank."

Sam doesn't like to hear her father and Kitty dismissed as cranks.

"Aren't scientists meant to keep open minds, Professor?"

He shakes his head in mild despair. "If you keep your mind open, why, it'll let the flies in. Teleportation is a pretty thought and I concede that certain chanting and drumming has been scientifically proven to affect the temporal lobes, inducing feelings of floating outside of the body…" He pulls out a pen and draws a brain on the wall, marking the temporal lobe with a big arrow, then continues. "I'm telling you that teleportation goes against the laws of science. It's just a *hay-lucy-nation*. A strong magnetic field can have the same effect, as can drugs. Under the influence, even sane folk claim to leave their bodies, visit unearthly places and converse with the spirits."

"I converse with the spirits and I'm not insane," Kitty pipes up.

Beau Farthy snorts loudly. "That is debatable, Mam. This is not: teleportation is an *eye-lusion*. Given that Grandaddy Tabuh is a doctor, I'm surprised he has any truck with such nonsense!"

"He's a witch doctor," protests Sam. "Don't you dismiss my grandpa! You might be a scientist but you know nothing about magic."

"Magic?" he scoffs. "Here's five dollars. Go see a magic show. You believe in magic, you'll believe in just about anything. Lookee, little lady, there's a fairy!"

Professor Farthy might be a brilliant scientist but there's no need for him to be so patronizing. He is much easier to bamboozle than he likes to think. Just before Sam, Kitty and Lola leave, he goes to the Room of Temporary Rest to inspect his clients. All is as it should be until he opens Mr Dwight's dewar and finds him sporting a pair of ladies, fur-trimmed slippers on his frozen feet.

They weren't there before; try as he might, Mr Farthy can think of no scientific explanation for them whatsoever and, for the first time, he begins to doubt his own mind.

AN EXCERCISE IN TELEPORTATION

Teleportation is the ability to move matter instantaneously from one point in time and space to another. Some psychics claim to be able to time travel by leaving their bodies. This is known as astral body teleportation. Objects can be teleported visually by doing the following:

1. Charge your physical body with energy and place an object in front of you.
2. Close your eyes and picture the object in front of you in your mind's eye.
3. Visualize the energy around the object blending with your own energy.
4. Visualize the object disappearing.
5. Focus your mind on a new destination six feet in front of you.
6. Feel the object reappearing in that new position. Open your eyes.

Do not be disappointed if you can't teleport straight away – it takes years of practice and it helps enormously if you're a witch doctor, a midiwiwin or a child with paranormal abilities.

RUBY FEATHA

Sam wants to head straight to New Guinea. Maybe her
father has completed his mission and gone home to
live with her grandpa. Maybe they're fishing together in
the Sepik River while her mother sits in the shade in a
pretty hat.

It's a lovely thought, but that's all it is. Kitty advises her
not to be so hasty. "Imagine if you went all that the way
and they hadn't returned? What if your grimfather is no
longer alive? You have to consider that."

"He's alive, Kitty. Whenever I hold his book, I hear his
drum. If the drumming stops, I'll know he's gone – but
when I read the list of names this morning, the beat was
stronger than ever."

Kitty adjusts her mask. "Where next then? Who does he
want us to visit now?"

They must fly to Canada to visit Ruby Featha. I'd like
to tell you that Professor Farthy offered to fly them in his
private jet, but he refused. Although he had no scientific

proof, he suspected they had something to do with Mr Dwight's furry slippers and it had upset him no end.

The last pearl has to be sold. This time, the buyer is an old man, a resident in their hotel. At least, I think he's a man. Old men often look like old women, and he is wearing a skirt. Maybe he has a skin condition and trousers irritate his thighs. But no amount of eczema can explain his enormous hat trimmed with blue-black feathers plucked from the rear end of a crow. The hat is attached to his head by a long pin which has lost its bauble; he wants to replace it with the pearl, or so he says. Who cares if he's lying? They now have the money to catch a plane to Canada.

Rather than bore you with how dull the in-flight salad was and how Lola collected everyone's lettuce leaves and used them to built a nest in the lavatory bowl, causing a desperate queue, let's leap forward once more and join them all in the wilds of Canada, among the deer and the mighty redwood trees.

They ride to Moose Mount on skewbald ponies, and find Ruby Featha sitting in front of a totem pole with a horsehair drum on her knees. She's wearing a modest head-dress but an air of great importance. She is a midiwiwin – a medicine woman, a healer, a spiritual consultant.

It's hard to tell how old she is; her skin is weathered but her posture is youthful. As the most powerful person in her tribe, nobody dares to ask her age. She might be nineteen – she might be ninety.

Sam dismounts and shakes her by the hand. "I knew I'd find you here, Ruby. Grandpa drew you in his book, only in his picture the carving on the totem pole looks like a guinea pig."

"Dear Yafer," laughs the medicine woman. "Art was never his strong point. He meant to draw a horse. The horse is my totem animal. She carries me to other worlds."

Sam's mare snorts softly. Everyone has a totem animal and a power animal, Ruby says. The totem animal links you to your tribe. The power animal represents a special strength or purpose. She moves her arm like a serpent. "My power animal is the snake, all wise, all healing."

"Do you think Lola might be my totem animal?" asks Sam. "She's the one who links me to my family and she's my oldest friend."

Lola removes the woman's headdress and places it on her own head with great seriousness. It's far too small.

Ruby laughs. "Yes, you're right, she is. How lucky you are to have a totem animal with a sense of humour!"

How can Sam discover which is her power animal? Ruby says there's only one way. "I would have to send you on a journey — are you willing to go?"

Sam sighs inwardly. They've only just arrived. "I'm not sure … is it far?"

"Only we've just got off the plane," adds Kitty.

"Ah, but this is a very different kind of plane." Ruby taps her handsome nose. "No tickets required, but before you travel, you will have to be smudged."

It sounds like something that might be done to you by the school bully, but it's nothing like that. Smudging is a ritual designed to purify and protect.

Ruby undoes her power bundle. It clips together with a clasp that looks like a crocodile's claw but could be an eagle's talon – it is hard to tell, they're shrivelled. She removes a feather, a rattle and a seashell stuffed with incense, sage to protect, cedar to cleanse and sweet grass to summon the spirits. I shudder to think what else is in that power bundle, but it isn't a packet of mints and a hanky.

Ruby lights the incense and asks Sam to strip. She isn't shy, but it does feel odd, standing in the prairie in her vest and pants. Take it as a warning: if you ever wish to be smudged, be sure to wear decent underwear.

How to be smudged:
1. Strip to your undies and stand with your arms horizontal and feet apart to form a star.
2. The midiwiwin smudges your right hand with soot and says, "Grandfather".
3. She smudges your left hand with soot and says, "Grandmother".
4. She passes her hand across your hips, down your right leg and says, "Creation".
5. She passes her hand back over your hips and down your left leg.
6. She will say, "Great Mystery!" and wave incense smoke around your head. Try not to cough.
7. Finally, she will say, "Mitakuye Oyasin", which means "All my relations, including stones and animals", in the belief that everything in nature is alive and connected to the same cosmic web – in

other words, that our relatives aren't just people, they're pebbles and bison and maple leaves.

8. You are now ready to go on your journey. I'd take a cardigan if I were you.

Sam is raring to go. "Will I see anyone apart from my power animal, Ruby? Only I'm searching for my mother and father."

Ruby knows this already; she's all-seeing, all-knowing. She takes Sam over to a red cedar tree and they sit beneath it. "You might see your parents. Or other relatives or ancient ancestors. People journey for many reasons: to retrieve a lost soul, to add to their knowledge or to divine answers from the spirits regarding future events."

"How do I get to where I have to go?" Sam's wondering if the tree she's parked under is some kind of mystic taxi rank and that someone will eventually come along and offer her a lift.

"I will guide you. We will pass through the Tree of Life. There are three levels. In the branches is the Astral Temple where the gods and spirits reside. Here you will learn about the future and meet your guide. The Middle World – the trunk – is the Here and Now, where you learn answers to everyday questions such as 'Will it rain?'"

Ruby begins to drum. As she drums, Sam remembers Professor Farthy's temporal lobe and how it has been scientifically proven to be affected by drumming, causing a floating sensation, and as she finds herself drifting away, she hears a tiny voice – her own – calling out, "I want to know what is real, what is magic and what is illusion."

"The answers lie in the Lower World," whispers the drum, "where the dead reside, where lost information is retrieved. Where we learn what ails ussssssssss…"

Was it the hiss of the drum or the rush of the human soul as Sam slips out of her head like a dragonfly shedding its skin. She can see her body still sitting beneath the tree, but it's getting smaller and smaller – neither dead or alive – an empty vessel; all that is vital has been sucked up into the branches. Ruby Featha's chant whirls around her ears:

"The souls of the children perch in the trees,
Like birds, like birds.
The souls of the children perch in the trees,
Waiting to be born."

Something calls Sam's name. It's not Ruby Featha; it's a deep brown voice, old as the earth. It's coming from the uppermost branch and it speaks in Motu. It's a crow, but it isn't any old crow.

It's a Torresian crow.

NUMBER MAGIC

The masked magician asks you to think of a number between 1 and 10 and write it down so it can't be seen. Say your number is 6. First of all you will be asked to double it (12), then add ten to the answer (22), and divide by two (11). Now yell out your final number (11). The magician will then reveal that your secret number is indeed 6! But how?

THE SECRET

It's not magic, just a little-known mathematical law. No matter which number you choose, all the masked magician has to do is subtract five from the last number you shout out: 11 - 5 = 6

The trick works every time.

$$n \ (x2) \ (+10) \ (\div 2) - 5 = n$$

THE SIGN OF THE TRIANGLE

Someone is holding Sam's hand. Strange, because surely to have her hand held, she must have a body – yet her body is still sitting under the tree next to Ruby Featha. If Professor Farthy's mother had given him a better microscope, maybe he would have cried out, "Yes, it *is* scientifically possible to see the soul!"

If he had a decent set of binoculars, perhaps he could see Sam's soul sitting on the bough of the Tree of Life. Maybe the invisible hand she is holding is just a *hey-lucy-nation*, but it feels warm and alive; Sam calls out, "Is that you, Lola. Are you my totem animal?"

It might be a dream orang-utan. Or it might be Freya, the spirit guide; Freya the grandmother. Whatever it is, it's a comforting presence.

Sam feels the draught of wings and the weight of the Torresian crow on her shoulders. As it lifts her off the bough, she feels no pain. She soars through the blinding brightness of the sun – not flying, but being carried and still holding someone's hand. The crow is carrying two souls; to do that, he must be powerful. He must be her power animal, this crow.

Above the tree, on the edge of space, lies the Astral Temple. It's made from clouds unknown to meteorologists – but you have seen them. You've been here before you were born, but you've forgotten. There's a reason for that. If you could remember how beautiful it was, you'd be in too much of a hurry to come back, like Conchita and Consuella.

The crow releases his passengers. Sam falls back onto a soft, furry cushion – it's Lola. She gets to her feet. She turns to face the Torresian crow, but all that's left of it is a bracelet of blue-black feathers around the wrist of an old man with tusks through his nostrils who stands with his arms outstretched.

"Come, little daughter of Tabuh."

In the Astral Temple, it doesn't feel awkward to be held. For the first time, Sam feels it might be possible to bear the embrace of another person. She runs forward. She allows herself to be folded into her grandfather's arms and there she stays until the icy lump in the pit of her stomach melts. The relief is phenomenal.

"Grandpa, is Grandma Freya here too?"

He nods and his hornbill necklace rattles like machine-gun fire as he points to the orang-utan. "Grandma is Lola. Lola is Grandma."

Make what you will of that remark. Is he saying that the spirit of his wife has possessed an ape so that she can protect her granddaughter? My instinct says no, but we're dealing with a witch doctor whose reputation is second to none, so I'm going to ignore my instinct.

"What now, Grandpa?" asks Sam.

The witch doctor removes his headdress – the one with bird of paradise feathers two metres high. "We swap hats!"

It's a fun thing to do and harmless enough. Yafer looks ludicrous in the ringmaster's hat – it's far too small for his hairdo, which looks like a flaming ginger bush. Sam doesn't look much better; Yafer's headdress is so large it slips over her head and lands on her shoulders.

"You'll grow!" he laughs. "But you still have much to put into that little head of yours. You must go to China, to India, to the Antipodes, then you must say goodbye to your old self."

"Can't I stay here with you?"

He shakes his head. "Now where have I heard *that* phrase before? Ah, yes, from my son, the wanderer." He looks at his wrist as if he wore a watch. "I thought he would be back by now."

At the mention of her father, Sam begs the witch doctor to tell her where he is – she's sure he knows.

"*Please* tell me. I've looked so hard, but he always seems to be just over the horizon."

It's no good pleading with Yafer Tabuh. No matter how much he loves his granddaughter, he will not give in to wheedling; he has his plans and he will not deviate from them. He puts a kindly arm around her and they walk up and down.

"Number One Daughter, the more you look for your

father, the more you will find yourself. When you know who you are, he will come to you. He will find himself and *his* father. Then we can all go home!"

He stops walking. Using his forefingers and thumbs, he makes the sign of a triangle.

"There is magic in numbers, child. Your magic number is three: father, mother, daughter. Heart, body, soul. The power of three will show itself to you again, again, again."

"I'm one of three sisters," says Sam.

The witch doctor counts on his long fingers.

"Three is *Big* Magic. One guides you. Two harms you. Three loves you beyond the grave. You must experience all three in equal measure."

"Must I? But what does—?"

The witch doctor presses a finger to Sam's lips. "No buts! It's up to you work it out. Grandpa knows you can do it." He presses his thumb against her forehead, between her eyebrows. "Here is your third eye. The insects have it. All mankind has it. Mostly they are blind, but you possess great vision. By the power of three, you will see what is illusion, what is real and what is magic!"

As he says it, he chants and waves his arms and the faster he waves them, the more they blur into wings and the more he turns back into a crow. Sam is lifted back into the air. She doesn't feel ready to leave, but Yafer has decided it's time...

Down.

Down.

Down.

The Torresian crow drops Sam on the top of a hill. It's so steep, she can't stop running – it's the kind of running that's almost flying and if Kitty hadn't rushed forward and caught her, I think she would have launched herself into the air and flown back to the crow for ever.

How to Walk on Hot Coals

A bed of volcanic rock is alight on the ground. The masked magician summons the gods and walks across it barefoot – yet the feet are not burnt. How?

THE SECRET

Firewalking has nothing to do with faith, willpower or the paranormal.

1. Air has a low heat capacity and our bodies have a high heat capacity, so even if the coals reach 1,000 degrees, a person with normal soles won't get burned if they walk quickly.
2. It's safer to use fuel that has a low heat capacity such as volcanic rock and wood embers.
3. It helps if your feet are insulated with sweat or water.

WARNING: DON'T TRY THIS AT HOME. AT THE VERY LEAST, YOU'LL BURN THE CARPET.

UP TO YOUR NECK IN ANTS

"**A**m I back, Kitty?"

Kitty holds Sam by the shoulders and waits for her to catch her breath. "You never left."

"I *did*. Lola came too. I saw my grandfather. He was as real as you are!"

Ruby Featha stops drumming. "Real? Not an illusion then? Not magic? Are you sure, Sam Khaan?"

Did she have the answer to the three questions? Had she visited the Lower World to retrieve the long forgotten truths? No, she hadn't. Sam's elation turns to melancholy. She's confused.

"It is normal to feel that way," says Ruby. "Sometimes it takes a lifetime to understand the questions, let alone find the answers."

"What if I die never knowing?"

"Nobody dies never knowing," says Ruby. "The dead have all the answers."

Right now that's no comfort to Sam. She'd felt so far

from death, so energetic, so happy, after talking to her grandpa. Now all she wants to do is sleep.

Ruby takes her hand. "Your mind is full, your stomach is empty. Let's eat."

It's impossible to feel miserable for long sitting around a campfire with a blanket around you to keep off the night chill. Especially when you're sharing the experience with your totem animal and a woman who can catch fish with her bare hands.

Lola isn't keen on salmon, but she's happy to stuff her cheeks with berries and nuts. Sam leans back and uses her soft belly as a pillow. "Ruby, how did you get to be a midiwiwin?"

"Some inherit the title – but to inherit is not enough; you must prove your skills." She pauses to poke the fire. "You have to suffer a trauma or an affliction. Suffering provokes your psychic abilities."

Kitty taps her mask to draw attention to herself. "*I've* suffered! I tripped over a cot on the stars and binged my hat when I was a little grill. Then the whorehouse caught fire and my farce was destroyed by the flans. Then I fell into a wharf and almost drained to death. Then I lost my mammary, didn't I, Sam?"

"Yes, and you muddle up your words, especially when you're tired."

"No, I don't."

"You do. You just said mammary instead of memory."

"I did *not*. There must be something wrong with your earring, Sam."

300

Ruby interrupts; it would be a shame for an argument to break out and spoil the evening.

"Kitty, the fact that you have suffered greatly explains your ability to communicate with the spirits. I believe they contact you through automatic writing?"

How Ruby knows this, I don't know. Maybe the spirits wrote and told her. It doesn't matter; at least Kitty feels better for having her skill and her suffering publicly acknowledged.

"I'm glad *someone* recognizes my pain," she mutters.

Sam feels it's only fair to remind her that she's not the only one who's suffered and reels off a list of dreadful things she's had to endure.

1. Being told that her mother had died in hideous circumstances.
2. Being told that her father was a no-hoper called Bingo Hall.
3. Not being allowed to perform magic.
4. Not being allowed to bring friends home.
5. Having to wear circus clothes to school.
6. Being threatened with a teapot.
7. Being locked in an attic.
8. Being made to eat scraps.
9. Being forced to cut Aunt Candy's toenails.
10. Having to sleep in a knicker drawer.
11. Having her orang-utan sent to a laboratory.
12. Never having any birthday or Christmas presents.
13. Having frying pans thrown at her.

No matter how dreadful your own life is, at least you've never had to cut Aunt Candy's toenails. It is no doubt true that suffering shapes us. It may even trigger seemingly paranormal abilities. But could you or I ever possess the wisdom of the midiwiwin; a wisdom so powerful it masquerades as magic?

"What would I have to do to be like you, Ruby?" asks Sam.

The medicine woman smiles to herself. "Learn to leave your body at will and travel anywhere on, above, or under, the earth. Then there's the initiation ceremony, of course."

What initiation ceremony? It all depends which tribe you belong to, but here's a selection of tasks you might be asked to attempt. Do not try them at home – they are dangerous. By the time the ambulance arrives, it will be too late, which will be an appalling waste: I need you later on.

Initiation ceremonies:
1. Being buried up to your neck in an ant's nest.
2. Walking on hot coals.
3. Diving through a hole in the ice.
4. Spending three days in a smoke-hole.
5. Going out into the snow for a week with a wet sheet around you.
6. Being strung up from hooks threaded through your skin.
7. Climbing a rope and staying at the top for nine days.
8. Sitting in a sweat lodge.

9. Wrestling a tiger.

10. Cutting off your little finger.

Years ago, Ruby had gone for initiation ceremony number ten – she only has three fingers on one hand. Much as Sam wants to be like her, she doesn't like the idea of cutting off her own digits.

"It's not the pain," she explains. "But I'm a magician. I need all my fingers to perform."

"So wrestle a tiger," mutters Kitty.

I'm not sure why she's in such a snappy mood. Perhaps she isn't feeling well. She was complaining of chest pains earlier, but then she's always complaining about something.

"There aren't any tigers in Canada," says Ruby. "Choose again, Sam."

Ant's nest. Hot coals. Smoke-hole … how do you choose between them? Is it worse to be bitten by insects, to have your feet fried or to kipper your lungs? Sam can't make up her mind, so she asks Ruby to decide for her.

Ruby Featha touches her third eye and thinks carefully. "Forget the list. You shall have your own *special* initiation, Sam Tabuh."

THE SIGNS OF THE ZODIAC

Each person is born under one of twelve signs of the zodiac. Each astrological sign is believed to represent a certain colour and stone.

Aries   The Ram
March 21–April 19
Colour: Scarlet
Stone: Bloodstone

Libra   The Scales
Sept 23–Oct 22
Colour: Pastel green
Stone: Diamond

Taurus   The Bull
April 20–May 20
Colour: Madonna blue
Stone: Emerald

Scorpio   The Scorpion
Oct 23–Nov 21
Colour: Dark red
Stone: Jasper

Gemini   The Twins
May 21–June 20
Colour: Saffron yellow
Stone: Crystal

Sagittarius   The Archer
Nov 22–Dec 21
Colour: Brilliant blue
Stone: Carbuncle

Cancer   The Crab
June 21–July 22
Colour: Silver
Stone: Pearl

Capricorn   The Goat
Dec 22–Jan 19
Colour: Brown
Stone: Jet

Leo   The Lion
July-23–Aug 22
Colour: Ruby
Stone: Amber

Aquarius   The Water Bearer
Jan 20–Feb 18
Colour: Electric blue
Stone: Sapphire

Virgo   The Virgin
Aug 23–Sept 22
Colour: White
Stone: Pink jasper

Pisces   The Fish
Feb 19–March 20
Colour: Violet
Stone: Topaz

THE EAGLE'S NEST

Here are the details of Sam's initiation ceremony: she must climb the third tree on the third hill at three minutes past three o'clock. There is a bald eagle's nest at the top. She must spend the night in the nest and bring back a feather from its breast.

Kitty is worried. It's not because the tree is tall; Sam is an excellent climber. It's because bald eagles have an eight-foot wingspan, talons like butcher's hooks and deadly beaks. They're flying weapons. She takes Ruby to one side.

"Can't she walk on hot cakes instead?"

"It was hot coals," says Sam. "Stop fussing. I want to do the task Ruby set me. If the eagle turns nasty, I'll defend myself with the divining rod."

She might as well attack a fighter plane with a lolly stick. But it's almost three o'clock. It's too late to back out of it. She remembers Mr Fraye's philosophy and thinks positive.

Lola wants to go with her, but Sam's not allowed to take a friend during this initiation; there are some things you have to do alone. Lola watches anxiously from underneath Kitty's robe as Sam makes her way to the third hill.

She reaches the third tree; it's a pine. It looks easy enough to climb, but as she pulls herself up on the first branch, she feels a sharp pain in her hand; the cones are covered in cruel spines. Blood oozes from her palms. She has no gloves but she does have her witch's cord. She loops it around the branches and uses it to haul herself up – that way, she avoids lacerating her skin.

The tree is higher than the top flat in St Peter's Square. If you fell out of Aunt Candy's kitchen window (and once Aunt Candy almost managed to push Sam out) you'd probably break your neck. If Sam slips now, if the cord breaks... But think positive!

There's no sign of the eagle yet. It has lost its only chick. The chick leant over the edge of the nest – a dangerous thing to do if you can't fly – and fell while searching for its mother.

Sam climbs higher and higher. She hasn't avoided all the cones. Her hands are scratched and blistered but the pain doesn't register. This isn't unusual. In the heat of battle, soldiers are often unaware that they have been shot; it's only when the fighting stops that the pain starts.

Sam has six branches to go. The wind is getting up; the tree is swaying. Breathing deeply to overcome her nausea, she clings to the trunk, looping and knotting the witch's cord with her teeth. Using the movement of the tree as momentum, she lassoes the uppermost branch and, keeping the cord taut, inches herself up the trunk with her feet.

The eagle's nest is right above her head – an untidy platform of twigs and branches knitted with bleached fish bones, snake spines and the regurgitated skulls of rodents. Sam flops into it, exhausted. She lies on her back and studies her hands. "Ouch." She licks her wounds. Her eyelids are heavy. If she loses consciousness she might fall out of the nest like the chick, so she uses the witch's cord to strap herself in.

The clouds sail by, shape-shifting into stampeding buffalo. She counts them: one buffalo, two buffalo, three … thirty … three hundred … until she falls into a deep sleep. Far away in Covent Garden, she can hear Bart Hayfue singing: "When the wind blows, the cradle will rock, when the bough breaks—"

Sam is woken up by an ear-splitting shriek; the eagle has returned. It glares at her, its beak poised like giant secateurs. She can feel the hot steam escaping through its nostrils. Her immediate thought is that it will rip her nose off and throw her over the side. The mother eagle is shocked to find a strange, featherless creature in her nest and, naturally, her first thought is to get rid of it. Aware that the eagle is still grieving for her baby, Sam protects herself by mimicking the cry of the chick.

How does a child born in London know what bald eagle chicks sound like? Easy. Mr Fraye had taught her at the breakfast table. He went through his whole repertoire of birdcalls from albatross to zebra finch and when Sam knocked the top off her boiled egg, he threw his voice into the shell and gave it the cry of an eagle chick.

Those kinds of breakfast antics are not something you forget easily. Sam closes her throat to create the right pitch and starts squeaking like a fledgling. The eagle cocks her head quizzically and the fury fades from her eyes. The thing in her nest doesn't *look* like a chick, but it sounds like one, so she gives a motherly grumble and flies off to fetch it some food.

Five minutes later, the eagle returns with a fish. Sam has no choice but to open wide and let her stuff the slimy, flapping morsel into her mouth. It's big, so she has to chew. Trying not to retch, she swallows the flesh and guts, sieves the bones through her teeth and spits them out.

Satisfied that her chick is full, the eagle puffs herself out, settles like a duvet on top of Sam and dozes off. It's hard to breathe with a fifteen-pound bird sitting on your chest. Sleep is impossible so Sam amuses herself trying to ease a feather from her breast. It's not difficult if you have magician's fingers; she's so gentle, the eagle barely twitches.

Sam whiles away the rest of the night trying to spot the constellations. Kitty has taught her most of them; she can see Pisces clearly from where she's lying. Unfortunately, it reminds her of the fish she ate earlier, her stomach churns and she averts her gaze. Over there is the Great Bear and there's Gemini, the Twins – or is it? There's an extra star. Has Sam discovered a new constellation? The star winks back; it's telling her the secret of the universe in cosmic semaphore. Babies know the secret. We all know it – it's printed on the inside of our skulls; but by the time we've learnt to talk, we've forgotten our first language, Starspeak.

Occasionally we almost crack the code, but something or somebody always interrupts us.

As dawn breaks and the eagle flies off, Sam is on the brink of understanding. She unties the cord. She stands up triumphantly in the nest, certain that the great universal truth – the Grand Plan – is within her grasp, that it's only a fingertip away. All she needs to do is stretch…

"Sam? Saaaam! You can come down now!"

Kitty's voice shatters the peace. Sam loses concentration and the truth slips away. The moment has passed. How frustrating – but at least she knows the answer is out there. She almost touched it. She will be able to reach it when she's taller.

It's much quicker coming down the tree than going up. Sam arrives at the bottom bloodied and disorientated. She's had no water or sleep. She's shivering but smiling. Ruby is waiting for her.

"Is your initiation complete?"

Sam produces the eagle feather.

"Did you find the answers you were searching for?"

"I only found more questions."

Ruby's face splits into a smile. She is delighted with her student. "Then you came closer to the truth than your father did."

John Tabuh had visited Ruby. He wanted to know if it was possible for a person to leave their body and travel at will – or whether Professor Farthy was right. Was it just a *hey-lucy-nation* caused by the rhythm of the drum playing games with the temporal lobe?

Ruby had sat John down under the red cedar tree and offered to send him to the Astral Temple. Although he was sceptical, Christa persuaded him to try, hoping that he might see his father; he missed him so much.

The drum drummed and John Tabuh was surprised to find himself in a place that wasn't entirely in his head. But his father never showed. He was there, but he wasn't at home, it seemed, to a son who hadn't completed his mission.

The witch doctor regarded John's visit to the temple as cheating. It *would* have been possible for him to discover what was real, what was magic and what was illusion right there if Yafer had allowed it, but he didn't approve of short cuts; they taught nothing but laziness.

John was unable to disguise his frustration, so Ruby had offered to guide him to the Lower World instead. He was grieving and she hoped it might comfort him to see his dearly departed. However when he came back, he was even more upset.

He'd seen an old Mexican couple with his twins in their arms; he'd smelled the herbal soap his mother used to use; but he didn't see the girl he wanted to see more than anyone else in the world. Sam guesses it was her, but as she's still alive there's no way he could have met her down among the roots where the dead reside.

"He dismissed the whole experience as a dream," sighs Ruby. "I suggested he walk across hot coals to see if it would bring him closer to the truth, but he said no, anyone could walk on hot coals. They might look hot, but it was just an illusion. The heat isn't sufficient to burn the soles of your feet – not if you walk fast enough."

"He's a magician," says Sam. "He knows these things."

"He doesn't know everything," says Ruby. "He said he was going to China to see what other illusions he could expose. He was convinced that the unexplainable could always be explained and that there was no such thing as magic."

"I hope he's wrong," frowns Sam. "What do you think, Ruby? What is magic?"

Ruby Featha makes the sign of a triangle with her forefingers and thumbs. "Magic is something even the spirits cannot explain. All I know for sure is what it isn't. Perhaps you too will find your answer in China."

Kitty tuts loudly. "We can't afford to go to China."

They'd sold the last pearl to get to Canada. Sam takes off her ringmaster's hat and produces a racoon. "Perhaps I could earn money performing magic tricks for your tribe, Ruby."

"And I can carve you a new tumtum pole," adds Kitty.

Ruby shakes her head. "We do not use money. We could only pay you in beads, bread and kindness."

Beads, bread and kindness are a whole lot nicer than hard cash, but try explaining that to the ticket man at the airport. It's no good looking at the ponies either; they're swift, but unless they sprout wings, they'll never make it to the border, let alone Beijing.

"You can go anywhere if you set your heart on it," says Ruby. She holds the eagle feather up to the breeze and lets it go. "Follow the feather. Mount your steeds."

The feather flies off. They follow it right to the edge of the plain. The wind drops. The feather falters; it floats down into a stream and falls between some rocks. The rocks are too far from the bank for Sam to leap onto them, so Lola is sent to fetch it.

"Quick, Lola! Grab it before it gets washed away."

Lola leaps, lands with one foot on each rock and feels around for the feather.

"HAVE YOU FOUND IT, LOLA?"

No, but she has found something half-buried in the sediment. It's the size of a crow's egg. She washes it in the clear, running water. As she holds it up to the rising sun, it radiates fire.

It's a ruby.

MAGIC CHINESE LINKING RINGS

The masked magician takes six solid steel rings and juggles with them. Then, in a blink of an eye, they're all joined together. How?

THE SECRET

1. The masked magician has a group of three rings linked together and a group of two rings linked together.

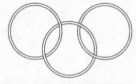 

2. There is also a single ring called a key. This has a split in it, large enough to pass another ring through, allowing him to link up all the rings.

3. The magician hides the split in the key ring using fingers and misdirects the audience with exaggerated hand movements to disguise the trick.

FU BAR YETAH

They sell the ruby to a gold prospector. He wears a ten-gallon hat and a bootlace tie and his boots are high. So is his voice, which makes me wonder if he's really who he says he is.

What does Sam care? She has a rucksack full of dollars, she's off to China.

The marvellous thing about the Chinese is that they happily accept people in disguise. They have a long tradition of theatre in which men play the part of women. Then there are the geisha girls who blank out their real features with ghostly make-up, cherry lips and tiger's eyes. Consequently, when our threesome get off the plane, nobody glances sideways at Kitty's mask or the ginger hair poking out of Lola's dress. Lola carries a fan to hide her face, but really there's no need.

They are met by a small boy dressed in saffron robes. "Greetings, Miss Sam, Miss Kitty, Miss Lola!" He bows and gives them each a paper basket containing a mandarin. He's a shaolin monk and he's come to take them up the mountain to the Hall of the Heavenly Kings.

"Who sent you?" asks Sam. "How do you know who we are?

"My master, Fu Bar Yetah. He tell me to fetch three ladies: lady in magic hat, lady in funny mask and hairy ginger lady."

He explains that his master had been visited by a woman called Ruby Featha during his meditation time and that she had told him of their imminent visit.

"I have come to lead you along the right path," he announces. "My master say there are many paths but not all lead to enlightenment!"

"I've got a weak cart," sulks Kitty, thumping her chest. "Can we hire a rockshaw?"

There are no rickshaws, only bicycles. They hire two with sidecars. Lola drives Kitty but, being a performing orang-utan, she does it standing on the seat with one leg out behind her, then sits back-to-front on the saddle, pedalling with her hands. Finally she drives so close to the edge of the mountain that Kitty screams and jumps out.

"Miss Kitty walks, we all walk!" says the boy. "My master say mountain is too steep for wheel of bike but never too steep for wheel of fate!"

"Is it much further?" grumbles Kitty.

"My master say no destiny is too far if you desire it enough!"

Kitty leans against a tree, puffing heavily. "He says a lot, your mister."

After a gruelling climb, they arrive at a set of golden gates carved with lions' heads. Beyond the gates, in front of a temple, there are rows of monks practising hand-to-hand combat in silence.

The boy folds his arms proudly. "One day, I will be as good as these men. See what I can do already!"

He drops his arms by his sides and breathes in deeply through his nose. His eyes bulge slightly then, without warning, he leaps vertically and lands neatly on his bottom in an overhead branch.

If Sam hadn't seen it with her own eyes, she would have thought it was impossible to reach that branch without a trampoline. Perhaps the boy has springs in his shoes. She examines his feet, which are swinging playfully in the air. He's wearing silk slippers that are far too thin to conceal any trickery. She looks up at him in amazement.

"How did you do that?"

"Ah, many years of practice, Miss Sam!"

He can't be much older than eight – nine at the most.

"You're not old enough to have practised for many years."

The boy jumps down and, landing as lightly as a kitten, explains that his mother left him at the temple when he was a baby. He's been training with the monks ever since.

"I practise morning, noon and night. Master say an iron beam can be worn to a needle if you rub hard. Would you like to see me jump again?"

There's no stopping him. This time, he aims a little too high, misses the branch and falls flat on his backside in the grass. He springs to his feet, his cheeks crimson. "It is all in the breathing," he says, ignoring their giggles.

Sam tries to compose herself. "All in the breathing?"

He nods energetically. "Very special breathing called qi gong. Food and water moisten skin and muscle but only the main breath – qi gong – make the body this strong!" He throws a few kicks at an invisible, midget enemy, then continues. "Before hand or foot strike, first must come breath! It give you courage, strength and energy. My master say if the mind controls the breath, a boy can jump an abyss."

"How useful," mutters Kitty.

She's so short of breath she can hardly stand, let alone jump. The boy is exhausting to watch.

"I can make my breath so fine, I can pierce a wooden board with my finger … have you got a wooden board?"

"Sorry," says Kitty. "It's the one thing I forgot to pack. Have *you* got a wooden board, Sam? No? What a shame. How about you, Lilo?"

No one can oblige, so the boy grabs Sam's divining rod, holds it out in front of him and punches a neat hole through the crotch with his forefinger.

"All in the breathing," he whoops. "That is qi gong!"

Sam takes the divining rod away from him. "*That* is a hole."

It's incredible that his tiny finger managed to penetrate the wood, but how dare he damage her rod! That was a gift from Mrs Reafy! She's really angry with him but the boy is so offended, she apologizes and blames her temper on tiredness. It was a long plane flight and a hard bike ride, and she still hasn't caught up on her sleep after her night in the eagle's nest.

"We're *all* tired," says Kitty.

Realizing he's no longer in the dog house, the boy cheers up immediately. "Ah, you ladies short of energy? I find you some. Come – come!"

Somewhat bemused, they follow him through the golden gates, down a gravel path and across the grass until he stops in front of a large, flowering bush.

"You can absorb energy from all living things," he says. "Sit!"

The three of them sprawl about on the lawn. Lola rolls onto her back and grasps her toes.

"No! No floppy ladies! Sit with legs crossed, back straight and hands like so." He assumes the lotus position and takes a deep breath.

"I can't do that with my legs," moans Kitty. "I should have stayed in Egypt. The worst thing they make you do there is stand with your head sideways."

The little monk ignores her. "Breathe into your belly and absorb the energy from the bush."

Lola stands on her head and looks at him through her legs, Kitty lies down and eats her mandarin but Sam does as she's told. She copies the boy's breathing exactly and, after a while, she can feel the blood cooling her veins and her heartbeat slowing down. Suddenly, she is aware of a couple of bright electric threads, like miniature lights strung on a spider skein. They stretch from the bush to her fingertips.

A flock of finches flies out of the bush and flutters along these two threads of energy. Three of them settle on Sam's shoulder. Another three perch on the boy's head.

"Why?" whispers Sam. "Why are they doing that?"

"They are attracted to the magnetic field. It is same as one they use to migrate."

Kitty sits up. "They're just attracted to the breadcrumps on your soldier."

But there are no breadcrumbs on anyone's shoulder. No one has eaten any bread. After the finches have flown, Sam feels curiously revived. Kitty, fortified by the mandarin and a lie-down, accepts the boy's invitation to see his room, which is to the left of the exercise yard.

It's very basic; the facilities are worse than the ones at their hotel in Arizona. He hasn't even got a bed but he says he likes sleeping on the stone floor; it removes his negative energy.

The only items of furniture are a statue of the Buddha, a candlestick and a jug of water with a lizard swimming in it. The boy does, however, have a fine collection of weapons, all of which could be deadly in the wrong hands. Kitty doesn't approve, and with good reason.

First, he demonstrates how to whirl a wooden staff, knocking Sam's hat off in the process. Having done that, he brandishes his broadsword with such ferocity, he slices the top off the jug, which sends the lizard flying across the room. It lands with a sticky plop against the wall. The boy is incorrigible.

"You want to see me fight with tiger hammer?"

"NO!"

"Ha! I bet you can't do this."

He snatches up his staff and hits himself violently across the chest, splitting the pole in two.

"I wouldn't *want* to do that." Kitty winces.

Sam, who knows a thing or two about trick swords, picks up the staff and examines it. Perhaps it's cardboard painted to look like wood, in which case it would have split with ease. Perhaps it has a false compartment in the middle or a minor explosive device.

She can't find anything dodgy at all. It's a sound piece of wood. The boy had genuinely broken it across his chest.

"Qi gong!" he cries. "What I tell you, Miss Sam? All in the breathing!"

It seems that qi gong is a force to be reckoned with. Sam is keen to master the technique and asks if he wouldn't mind teaching her the basics.

The boy throws back his head and laughs. "How long you plan to stay – your lifetime? Take you many, many years to learn. First you must master Ch'am – this is the calming of body and mind to a single focus. Only then can you endure big elephant pain. Come, the monks will show you!"

Sam, Kitty and Lola follow him into the temple. The boy slips off his shoes and enters, bowing so low his pigtail touches the wooden floor. Sitting on a jade throne is a man with a shaved head and a very round face. In front of him, ten monks are meditating; the boy sticks his tongue out.

"When you meditate," he whispers, "you must put tip of tongue against roof of mouth. You must not let thoughts of dragons playing at your gates distract you. You must be quiet as a junzi strolling in a faraway mountain. You must be as silent as a—"

"Quiet!" bellows Fu Bar Yetah.

One of the monks tuts, his concentration ruined. Seizing the moment, the boy slides on his knees towards his master and, tugging at his voluminous trouser legs, introduces his guests.

"They have come to learn our ways, master."

"Really, Errant Boy?" sighs Fu Bar Yetah, and then, a little more kindly, "To learn about tranquillity, first one must shatter it, I suppose." He beckons to Sam, Kitty and Lola. "Come, friends of Ruby Featha. See what the body can do once it has been mastered!"

He claps his hands. The monks stop adjusting their underwear and picking their noses, jump to their feet and line up in front of a heavily carved trunk. Fu Bar lifts the lid.

Each monk removes a weapon of his choice, including an iron bar, a block of mahogany and a heavy rock. They then assume their positions and wait for the command – all eyes are on their master, who is holding a party popper.

He pulls the string. There's a small bang and the monks fly into action, cartwheeling through the air and flick-flacking across the floor as if they have no bones. After this warm-up, they settle down and focus on their equipment.

Sam watches carefully as the tallest monk grabs an iron bar and, with a blood-curdling roar, smashes it over his partner's skull. It snaps like a candy cane.

Kitty clutches her head. "*Ow!* That must have hurt!"

The monk remains expressionless. Surely a heavy blow like that would cause concussion, unless he's superhuman? Perhaps the bar is made of rubber. But if so, how would it make that metallic clank?

"All in the breathing!" insists Fu Bar Yetah.

The youngest monk is holding a rock. His partner, eyes narrow with concentration, holds out his arm, preparing to chop it in half with his bare hand.

"Heeee-yah!"

He strikes; the rock breaks in two. Sam wonders if it was a fake rock, possibly cut from polystyrene, but it's clear from the sound it makes as it lands that it's not – it's solid. Perhaps it's been tampered with, cracked and lightly glued together so that it falls apart when struck?

"*Bai she xin shou!*" booms the master. "Hand is accurate as spittle of a white snake!"

However, nothing can explain the fattest monk's ability to stand upside down, supported on one finger. Why doesn't it snap under his weight? Sam looks to see if he is wearing some kind of support, a glass thimble perhaps. No, there appears to be no cheating going on.

"Very muscular finger!" beams Fu, "*Cuan xin zhi!* Direct the qi right into finger, finger is as strong as dagger. Finger can pierce heart."

The monks bow to their guests. The show is over. Were they illusions? Were they real feats of strength, or were they Chinese magic?

"Please – examine the weapons," says the master. "They are for real. Shaolin monks do not perform tricks like

323

monkeys, OK? With long training, a man can move mountains."

This is a slight exaggeration, but even so, Sam is in awe of the monks. "Incredible, Mr Fu!"

He raises his neat eyebrow so high, they disappear over the back of his head. "Incredible to you in the West, but in the East? Very old hat!" He leans back in his throne and tells her a story.

"Once, the ancient gods were trying to hide the strongest power in the universe from Man so he could not use it destructively. The first god say to hide it on the mountain top – no good! Man can climb. The second god say to hide it at bottom of the sea – no good! Man can swim. The third god say to hide it in the middle of the Earth – no good either, Man can dig. Finally, the fourth and wisest god of all, he say, 'We must hide the power *within* Man – he'll never think to look for it there!'"

"But you found the power, Mr Fu!" says Sam.

"Ah, not me personally. The power of qi gong is thousands of years old. Master it and it will make you seem superhuman – but only to those with low expectations of themselves. You, Miss Sam, are Sleeping Tiger! Great strength lies within."

"Am I a Sleeping Tiger?" asks Kitty.

"You are Turtle with Head in Shell!" guffaws Fu Bar.

Kitty feels vaguely insulted but Fu assures her that although turtles are helpless on land they are Queens of the Ocean. Given her sailing skills, Kitty likes his metaphor after all.

The monks invite them to the tea house where they all sit on a thick rug around a low table. Lola picks the green tea leaves out of her cup and eats them. Sam asks Mr Fu if he'd be willing to teach her qi gong – just a little bit, because she's in a hurry to find her parents. Has he met her father, John Tabuh, by any chance? Only she's certain he's visited China in the past few years. Fu Bar Yetah presses his fingers together and rests his chin on them.

"Slowly, slowly catchee daddy."

"Sorry, Mr Fu?"

"I met your father last year," admits Fu. "He was most impressed by qi gong and wanted to learn its secrets. He ask if it is possible to breathe qi into a corpse and bring it back to life."

At this point, Errant Boy trips with the teapot and splashes boiling tea over his master's head. Lesser men might have sworn but Fu Bar deals with the pain by taking a deep breath and inflating his stomach like a balloon. His belly is now so full of qi, it shifts the table forward; he's now roughly the same shape as Lola.

"Sorry, master!" fawns the boy. He takes out a white handkerchief and buffs Fu's bald pate until he can see his reflection in it. Sam daren't continue the conversation until he has put his hanky away.

"Do you think it's possible to resurrect a dead person with qi gong, Mr Fu?"

Fu Bar nods his head and the sunlight dances off his glossy pate like a swarm of fireflies. "I do not doubt it – but to learn how takes longer than a dragon's tale. Your father was very keen to learn but he have no time! He and his wife were in a hurry to go to India."

"Ah, Missy Christa – beautiful lady!" sighs Errant Boy.

Sam's heart leaps. "Do you hear that, Kitty? My mother was here! She was alive and well!"

Fu Bar Yetah pulls at his chin and pauses ominously. "Alive? In a manner of speaking."

Sam's smile falters. "What, was she ill? Was she ... dying?"

The master folds his hands and bows gravely. "A mother who loses her daughter dies every day."

How to Lie on a Bed of Nails

The masked magician produces an oblong piece of wood the size of a bed with hundreds of sharp nails sticking out of it. Naked to the waist, the magician lies down on the bed and goes to sleep. The body should be pierced to death, but on standing up, there's hardly a mark to be seen. How?

THE SECRET

This trick has nothing to do with paranormal strength or supreme faith. If there are enough nails, the weight of the body is distributed evenly between them so that the force exerted on each nail is not enough to break the skin. The dangerous parts are lying down and getting up where the weight may be briefly supported by only a few nails – ouch!

BAHUT

We're flying to India to visit a man called Bahut. His name has been throbbing away at the top of the witch doctor's list and the notebook smells faintly of aloo sag; an Indian dish made from spinach, which tastes much nicer than it sounds. Lola is looking lovely in a sari, Kitty is too hot and Sam is fretting about her mother; had she become seriously ill in China?

"Kitty, can't you ask the spirits if my mother is still alive?"

Kitty refuses and fans herself with an in-flight magazine. "Take no notice of Mr Pu. She can't have been that ill if your father took her to India."

"Maybe she was dead when he took her to India."

"Yes, yes, whatever."

Sam is surprised at her callous tone. "Don't you care?"

Kitty gulps hard and stifles a sob. "Didn't mean it. Hate flying … arghhh the plane's tipping! Can't breathe!"

No wonder she's uncomfortable. It must be hard trying

to suck enough oxygen through the nostril holes in her mask, but she still won't take it off.

"You might be cooler if you cut your hair shorter," suggests Sam.

"I like it long."

"It's funny how the fringe never seems to grow at all," says Sam.

"It gets to a certain length, then it stops," Kitty insists.

They travel in silence. Sam practises qi gong in her plane seat. Mr Fu taught her the basics during their two-week stay at the Hall of the Heavenly Kings. He was an excellent teacher, she was a quick learner and by the time she left, she'd learnt how to direct qi into her knees. Her jumps were nothing like as high as Errant Boy's, but that would come in time, Fu said.

"Practise night and day and you will jump as high as the moon hare!" he'd told her. "You very, very good ... for a girl."

They land in India. Sam practises her vertical jumps while they're waiting for the train to Nepal. Lola joins in and trips over her sari. Kitty is irritated by their boundless energy.

"How can you jump about in this heat?"

"It's all in the breathing."

The train is packed and they're pushed into the carriages with sticks by the Indian porters. There's nowhere left to sit, and halfway to Nepal, Kitty can stand it no longer and announces that if they don't get off *right* now, she will die.

"But the train's still moving, Kitty."

"Don't care. Let me through! Let me out!"

She opens the carriage door. Sam can't stop her.

"Kitty – don't!"

Kitty jumps.

The train is going slowly but the momentum is enough to send her flying across the dirt track. Sam fights her way to the door.

"Quick, Lola. Kitty's hurt."

They hold hands and jump. They tumble and roll. Miraculously, neither is injured. Sam dusts herself down and runs over to Kitty who is lying on her front, clutching her face.

"Are you OK? Have you broken anything, Kitty?"

"Don't roll me over, I'm fine."

She's trying desperately to adjust her mask. It had rolled up over her chin as she skidded along the ground. Sam tries to help her up, but Kitty lashes out. "Get off! Stop *fussing*. Go and hire a trick from over there. Leave me alone."

Sam turns round. By the side of the dirt track, there are trucks for hire called tuk-tuks. The man in charge only has one eye. He mistakes Lola for the girl of his dreams and tries to exchange a tuk-tuk for her hand in marriage. He puts his arm around her waist, which Lola doesn't object to, but when he pinches her bottom, she slaps him round the face so hard he swallows his gold tooth. Luckily, Kitty arrives and has a word with him.

"How dare you? Lola is a respectable married lardy. Now hand me the cheese!"

The man nurses his sore cheek. "I am not selling cheese, I am hiring tuk-tuks."

Sam points to the truck keys hanging from his belt. He dangles them nervously at Lola.

"A thousand apologies for pinching your bottom, lovely lady. In order that you do not tell your husband, I insist that you hire this tuk-tuk for free. Please, take it!"

They climb into the truck and head for Kathmandu. At noon, they stop for lunch in the village and notice that a crowd has gathered between the spice stall and the snake charmer. As Sam works her way to the front, she sees a magician in flowing robes standing next to a rope. It appears to be standing up all by itself in a wicker basket.

A small boy standing next to the magician is commanded to climb the rope. As he climbs, the rope sways a little. He climbs higher and higher, then suddenly, he vanishes. The crowd shield their eyes from the sun, trying to see beyond the rope – but the boy has gone! The magician looks up and shouts.

"Come down, boy. Or *I* will come up!"

There's no reply, so he takes out a sword, flourishes it and invites Sam to examine the blade; it's razor sharp. He grips it between his teeth and, with a scowl, he climbs the rope in hot pursuit. The crowd gasps – now the magician has vanished! High above, beyond the end of the rope, an argument breaks out. There's a boyish scream – severed limbs and bloody rags fall from the sky. The boy has been murdered!

Now here comes the magician, feet first down the rope, shaking his fist at anyone who dares to boo and hiss. He folds his arms and waits for silence. He claps his hands and commands the rope to coil back into its basket, which it does obediently. All eyes are upon it. Does the rope have a mind of its own? Might it spring back out and attack them like a cobra?

The magician slams the lid on the basket to prevent the rope escaping, but he can't – something is pushing against it. The crowd draws back, ready to run to safety … and out bursts the boy!

He is smiling and bowing. There's a collective sigh of relief, applause and whistles. The magician bows, removes his hat and passes it round. Kitty, not willing to part with her money, gets back into the tuk-tuk quickly with Lola.

Sam stays in the crowd; she wants to find out how the illusion was done. As soon as the magician has his back to her, she examines the rope. There's a tiny hook pushed into the end. As she looks up, she can just make out a very fine thread stretched between two trees. The magician must have thrown the rope up in the air so that the hook caught on the—

Just then, the magician turns round and catches her fiddling with the rope. Alarm flickers across his face; how much has she seen? He smiles a false smile and tries to shoo her away.

"Nothing to see, dear. Magic show over."

Sam refuses to move.

"It's a great illusion," she says. "I'm a fellow magician, I know how you make the rope stay upright – you throw it in the air and hook it over that wire. But what I can't work out is how you make the boy disap—"

His expression changes. He hisses at her to shut up, but it's too late; someone in the audience has overheard.

"Wire? What hook?"

The rumour spreads fast. The rope isn't really magic – the audience has been duped and they don't like it.

"We want our money back. Fraud! Fraud!"

Mad with rage at the prospect of losing his livelihood, the magician tries to grab Sam and throw her into his basket. Luckily, she does her best ever vertical jump, lands in the waiting tuk-tuk and Kitty drives her off at top speed.

If it hadn't been for qi gong, I fear she'd have ended up in that basket and met a very sticky end with a sword.

Bahut – the man they're supposed to visit next – lives at the foot of the Himalayas by a banyan tree. They don't have his exact address but it seems that the witch doctor leaves nothing to chance: it may have been his will that the tuk-tuk broke down by a well where an old woman happened to be drawing water. She fills a bottle with a bucket and waves it at Sam.

"Would you kindly take this to Mr Bahut? No water has passed his worshipful lips for a week and I am worried that he will shrivel. I'd take it myself, but I only have one leg."

This is an outrageous lie: the woman has two perfectly good legs, but for some reason she's hooked the right one up behind her back and insists on hopping about as if to make the illusion more convincing.

Sam stifles a laugh. "You're not related to a lady called Effie Ray, by any chance?"

"No, no. I am born and bred in India. It is a far more pressing matter that you take this water to Mr Bahut. He is over that hill in a sandy place, under the sacred banyan."

Sure enough, there he is with his legs in the air and his head in the sand, wearing nothing but a loincloth decorated with tulsi beads.

The man is a sadhu – a living idol who spends his days in devotion, in the hope of reaching a state of enlightenment through suffering and denial.

Sam taps him on the shoulder to get his attention. "How do you do, Mr Bahut?"

There's a muffled shriek. His legs collapse and he pulls his head out of the hole, spitting sand and spluttering. "How do I *do*? What in the name of Shiva are you doing, sneaking up on me like that?"

His hip-length hair is twisted into a knot on top of his head and dressed with paste made from ashes and cow dung. Sam hands him the bottle of water.

"Why do you bury your head in the sand? Are you hiding from someone?"

He blows his nose on his loincloth, which has rucked up around his hips like a nappy. "Not hiding," he protests. "Burying one's head frees the mind for *spiritual* concerns. When my head is down the hole, I can slow my heart rate to two beats per minute, simply by altering my breathing – that's practically dead, isn't it!"

Sam is impressed but not altogether surprised. She's already seen what the shaolin monks can achieve with qi gong. She tells Mr Bahut about it, but he just scoffs.

"Qi gong? Ping-pong! All that leaping about and showing off. My way is pranayama; breathing techniques that allow one to endure the impossible... Watch! This is uddiyana bhanda – observe my tummy."

With a sound like a punctured tyre, Bahut expels all the air from his stomach until his internal organs touch his spine. He then fills himself back up with air and asks for a bucket. Kitty moves to one side.

"Why? Do you want to be sick? I know I do."

"No, no, if I had a bucket of water, I could show you the breathing technique of jalandhara bhanda in which I am able to draw a pint of water up my botty."

"We don't have a bucket," says Kitty hastily.

"Didn't the woman by the well have a buck—?" Sam doesn't get chance to finish.

"No!" Kitty reckons this is a trick too far. "Mr Bahut! Why would you *want* to do a thing like that?"

The answer is surprisingly sensible, although the scenario is unlikely to happen.

"If my lips were sewn together and I could not drink, I could absorb enough water through my nether region to prevent me dying of thirst."

It has its practical uses, then. More than that, Bahut says it's just one of a series of techniques that a sadhu must perfect in order to release his body from the restraints of the human condition. Having mastered it, he would then have godlike control over all his organs.

"Does that mean that you can heal yourself?" asks Sam. "Say you lost a leg, could you grow a new one, like a lizard grows a new tail?"

Bahut doesn't answer. Instead he stands up, tucks his right foot behind his ear and balances on his left foot. "Once, I stood on one leg for two years," he boasts.

Fascinated, Lola copies him.

"Didn't you get bored?" asks Sam.

"Not at all. I visited more places in my head than I ever could on my legs. A man who balances on one leg is never lonely; people visit out of curiosity. I have met all sorts. But none more interesting than a magician who turned up a few months ago."

Sam leaps up. "Was his name John Tabuh? Was he with my mother?"

Bahut nods, causing himself to wobble and tip to the left, so Lola kindly props him up again.

"Mr Tabuh and his lady wife were most agitated," continued the sadhu. "There had been a hoo-ha in the village. He had recklessly challenged the resident magician to perform the Indian Rope Trick at dawn, rather than noon."

John Tabuh had watched the trick and worked out how it was done. I will now pass on his observations to you, in case you ever wish to perform it.

1. The glare of the midday sun created a blind spot at the top of the rope, making the boy invisible.
2. The "bloody limbs" were bits of monkey meat wrapped in cloth, which the magician had secreted in his pocket.
3. As for how the boy reappeared – simple! He was

hidden under his master's robes and carried down the rope. The audience was misdirected to watch the *top* of the rope, whereupon the boy slipped unnoticed into the basket.

4. Yes, the rope was supported by a hook caught on a fine thread between two trees.

The magician insisted that the Dark Prince was wrong: the rope trick was no illusion – it was *magic*. But when John asked him to prove it by performing the same trick when the sun was down, he refused. He said he had to visit his aunt. Noon was the only time of day he was free.

"How about tonight then?" John had asked, at which point the magician punched him on the nose for fear that he'd steal his trick and expose it.

"My father would never expose a trick," Sam protests. "It goes against the magician's oath. He was only trying to find out what's real, what's magic and what's illusion."

"I know that to my cost," harumphs Bahut. "Your mother was exhausted and your father asked if I had a bed she could borrow. But my bed is most uncomfortable – ooh … ow … cramp!"

He unhooks his leg from behind his ear, rubs it, then hops into a cave. He returns with a begging bowl and a bed studded with nails, which he throws down, pointy side up.

"I explained to your mother that she was most welcome to borrow this, but unless she mastered pranayama, she would have a most painful night. Only a sadhu in a state of religious ecstasy can endure such torture."

"Nonsense!" John Tabuh had said. "If you distribute your weight evenly, it doesn't hurt."

Unfortunately, Bahut had found this remark more painful than any amount of nails.

"Is it true though?" asks Sam. "Was my father right?"

Lola is about to test the mattress, but Bahut won't allow it. "Don't! You are not a holy, thus you will become holey and a most excruciating experience that will be!" He lies down on the nails and shuts his eyes. "I am not feeling a thing, but that is because my faith is so very strong."

Sam crouches down to see if the nails are penetrating his flesh; they aren't. "Your faith in what, Mr Bahut?"

"That when I die, I will not be reincarnated as a dung beetle. Thanks to my extreme devotion, I can jump the queue and assume a permanent, godlike status in Nirvana, thus breaking the tedious cycle of life and death. Please leave! You are coming between me and my cosmic consciousness."

"Just one more thing," says Sam. "Do you know where my father went?"

The sadhu opens one eye. "Not telling!"

They're about to walk off when he sits up again. "It is the custom to give the sadhu a donation. When you behold him, you receive a spark of his spiritual energy."

He stares pointedly at Sam's ringmaster's hat and presses his palms together. "I'm *supposed* to renounce worldly goods but I wouldn't mind coming back as a slimy slug if you gave me your hat."

Sam hates to part with it but she needs it for a bribe. "You can have it if you can tell me where my father went."

Bahut doesn't hesitate. "Australia. Katoomba – to meet a medicine man in the shadow of the Three Sisters. He said it was a matter of life or death – hat, please!"

Sam gives him her hat. He puts it on and smiles as if he's reached Nirvana already.

"Does it suit me? This hat is something magical, isn't it!"

Magical? Is he using the word loosely or is he wiser than he seems? Sam isn't sure.

"What *is* magic, Mr Bahut? Is it the hat? Or is it something much larger?"

"If the hat fits, *that* is magic," he replies. It could be a very shallow answer or it could be a very deep one, so Sam asks him another question.

"What is real?"

"Dreams are real. I've always dreamt of a hat like this, and here it is in all reality."

"Then what is illusion?"

"Ah," he says. "It is an illusion to think that I will ever give you back your hat."

"Goodbye, Mr Bahut."

They leave him studying his reflection in his begging bowl, under the shade of the banyan tree. As they head back to the tuk-tuk, Sam notices that Kitty is lagging behind.

"You're very quiet today, Kitty."

She's hardly said a word.

"Jet log."

They've done a lot of flying, but is it really jet lag that's bothering her?

Or does she know something we don't?

HOW TO MAKE A CURSE

Curses have been practised in many cultures for thousands of years, their main use being to protect the home, treasures and gravesites and, of course, for revenge. Different countries have different ways of cursing:

- Point a kangaroo bone and recite the curse (Australia).
- Inscribe the curse on a piece of lead, bury it or throw it down a well (Ancient Rome).
- Make a wax effigy of the monster Apep, write his name on it in green ink, wrap him in papyrus and throw him in the fire (Ancient Egypt).
- Take a cursing stone, stroke it then turn it to the left while reciting the curse (Ireland).
- Write down the curse and bury it with an egg or an animal heart (Europe, Middle Ages).

TUHAB

The flight to Australia is far too long. Kitty keeps sighing and thumping her chest, telling anyone who'll listen, "I've got terrible indignation."

Indigestion is a plausible excuse: the meals on the plane are awful. They're flying economy class and eating economy food, with their knees tucked under their chins in economy seats.

Lola doesn't mind. Knees-under-the-chin is a comfortable position for an ape, and it would have suited Aunt Candy, who as we speak is folded in half in her rum barrel. But Kitty isn't a contortionist and she's struggling to breathe. Let's land before she expires and take the train to Katoomba, the home of Tuhab, the Elder.

It's late afternoon when Sam, Kitty and Lola arrive. Tired as they are, it's impossible not to feel uplifted by the scenery. The Blue Mountains are veiled in a sapphire haze caused by the vapour from the gum trees. Even so, after half an hour, Kitty is starting to get impatient.

"It's all very bleautiful," she grunts, "but I'm bored now. Where's Tuhab?"

The sadhu had said that Tuhab would be waiting for them in the shadow of the Three Sisters, which is the name of the giant rock formation in front of them. Sam studies the map again. "Maybe we're standing in the wrong part of the shadow."

"Well, don't expect me to wander round the bush looking for him."

Kitty's very tetchy today and as much as Sam wants to keep the peace, she's determined to find the mysterious Elder.

"There are too many people about here, Kitty. Maybe he's shy."

"But we don't even know what he looks like."

"Yes, we do. There's a portrait of him in this notebook. He has dark, curly hair…"

But that description hardly distinguishes him from half the population of Australia.

Kitty sits down and refuses to move, so Sam takes Lola by the hand and starts walking away. "And he has a spider tattoo, Kitty."

Sam marches off down the path. Kitty groans and gets to her feet.

"Damn you, Yafer Tabuh. Sam? Lola! Wait for me, you nuisances."

They walk into the evening and see no one. Soon it's hard to see anything, it's got so dark. They have no idea where they are, but that's not quite the same as being lost.

"Yes it is," mutters Kitty.

Sam begs to differ. "No it isn't. If we don't know our true destination, we might be in exactly the right spot."

"If that's the case," says Kitty, "I'm going to stop here and go to sleep behind this rock. If your theory is correct, what's the point in taking another step?"

Sam can't argue with that. She takes off her rucksack, props herself against the rock next to Kitty, and closes her eyes. The rock has absorbed the baking sun all day – its red warmth soothes their aching backs and they drift off to sleep. Nearby, Lola has made a nest in a gum tree, which she is sharing with a bright green gecko. It sits on her chest like a brooch.

Around three in the morning, Sam is woken by flying foxes. There are so many bats, they blot out the moon. A wallaby bounces over Sam's feet, kicking up a spray of dead leaves. She needs to stretch her legs. Her right foot has gone dead. She stamps it on the ground. Mid-stamp, she freezes, sensing that something, someone, is watching her.

Tuhab slips out of the shadows, illuminated only by the starlight. He gazes at her, looking deeply concerned.

"You should not be here," he murmurs. "This is a sacred rock. You should not touch it." He refuses to look Sam in the eye, and speaks so softly she can barely hear him. "Everywhere you walk, you leave echoes in the earth. This land, its rocks, its rivers, everything is shaped by the foot-prints of my ancestors."

Sam apologizes profusely. "I'm sorry. I didn't know. I'd never intrude deliberately – do you want us to leave?"

Tuhab nods his head slowly and points to Lola in her gum tree.

"You want us to sit over there?"

Again, he nods, but still he won't look Sam in the eye. Is it shyness? She isn't sure. How can an elder be shy and hold such a position of power? She nudges Kitty, who wakes with a start. She sees Tuhab and gives a muffled squeak.

"Argh … am I dreaming?"

Tuhab scoops up a handful of dust and lets it trickle through his fingers. "The history of this place is called the Dreaming. Dream time is here."

"Oh good. I'll go back to sleep then," mumbles Kitty.

But Sam won't let her. "We're on sacred ground," she explains. "We're trespassing. We have to go and sit over there with Lola."

They follow Tuhab over to the gum tree. Kitty giggles as he tweaks the back of his shorts which have bunched themselves up into an uncomfortable wedge.

"He's not what I expected," she whispers. "He doesn't look very mystical, does he?"

It is true that he doesn't from the back. But maybe it is a double bluff. He gestures to the space under the gum tree and waits for them both to sit down. Kitty pats the earth next to her and, in a somewhat patronizing way, suggests that he sits next to her and makes himself comfortable. Tuhab remains standing and in the manner of an earnest schoolboy performing in assembly for his parents, he points to the triangle of darkly dominant boulders in the distance and began to relate the legend of the Three Sisters.

"They were once three beautiful sisters. A witch doctor turned them into rocks."

"And…?" wonders Kitty.

Tuhab refuses to expand on the story, despite Sam's best efforts to get him to do so.

"A witch doctor? What was his name, Mr Tuhab? He must have been very powerful."

Tuhab, who has been looking sideways at Kitty's mask, quickly averts his gaze. "Not as powerful as me. I could turn three sisters into rocks…"

"Sure you could," laughs Kitty.

The composure of his face changes for a split second, but it's long enough to give Sam a terrifying glimpse into the real nature of this seemingly gentle soul. A shiver runs down her spine. She gives Kitty a warning dig in the ribs, but all subtlety is lost on her.

"Ouch! What did you do that for, Sam?"

He's hiding it well, but Tuhab is painfuly aware that Kitty isn't taking him seriously. Sam suspects this is a grave mistake. Lola, who has woken up and is dangling upside down from a branch can sense the ominous atmosphere and recoils quietly back into the leaves. In an attempt to smooth things over, Sam finds herself apologizing to Tuhab again.

"You mustn't mind Kitty. She's not herself, you know."

Tuhab blinks slowly. "She is not. But who she is, you do not know. That is why she wears a mask."

Now it's Kitty's turn to feel uncomfortable. "What's he on about?" she mutters. "Can we go now, Sam? I'm not sure this is the person we should be speaking to at all."

"Shh – he's on the list," whispers Sam. "He's one of Grandpa's Very Important People."

Tuhab's expression remains fixed, but his ears are twitching and his eyes glitter with emotion. It's hard to read if it is anger or sorrow. Perhaps it's a bit of both.

"People are sceptical," he mouths to no one in particular. "Even my one and only son doesn't believe in my magic."

"You sound just like my grandpa," says Sam in what she hopes is a cheerful way.

He stares solemnly at his feet. "Yafer Tabuh knows how I feel. In dream time he came to me. He also has a son who lost faith in his father. Your grandfather instructed me to work Big Magic on John Tabuh if he came my way…"

"And did he?" asks Sam. "Did you meet my father?"

Tuhab holds up his hand.

"I met him on" – he counts on his fingers, as if to work out the date – "Friday."

Today is Sunday! Sam has almost caught up with her father. She can hardly contain herself. Was he well? Was he happy? How was her mother?

Tuhab ignores all her questions. "No, it was Thursday." He closes his eyes and shakes his head. "I tried to help him, but he was *sceptical*."

"In what way?"

"In every way."

It seemed that John had taken one look at Tuhab and, because he didn't fit his strict template of how a magician should present himself, he made the foolish assumption that he was powerless.

Tuhab produces a long, low growl in the back of his throat that makes the earth vibrate. Is it a growl of contempt? Disappointment? Or is he merely clearing his throat?

"He was polite," admits Tuhab. "But he only feigned respect. When I wouldn't give him the answer to 'What is magic?' he assumed I was a fool and didn't know." He allows himself a brief chuckle. "I could have given him the answer on a plate, but that would have taught him nothing. So I performed my magic on his wife. It will be the making or breaking of him.

Kitty confronts him nervously now. "You haven't hurt Christa, have you?"

Tuhab's eyes grow steely cold, making a mockery of his mellow features. "Why? Who is she to you?"

Kitty stamps her foot. "She is this child's mother!"

Tuhab fixes her with a long stare. There is not a trace of malice in his gaze, which makes it all the more malignant. He is exuding the most calculated kind of calm, the most poisonous peace.

Sam pleads with him. "Where is my mother? Please tell me. I know you know."

Christa is in the big brick hospital – St Vincent's – but only one person can save her. Someone on the witch doctor's list – but which one?

"Which one? The missing one, of course." Tuhab flips back his head and laughs like a kookaburra.

Sam and Kitty back away slowly. Lola fixes Tuhab with a wounded gaze and he speaks to her in a language Sam can't understand; is it orang-utan-ese or is it his native language? She isn't sure, but this is what she *thinks* she heard him say.

"It has to be like this, Freya. We agreed."

There's a mosquito in her ear; she might have misheard.

How to break a curse

You need: a black candle, water, a black bowl.

1. Fix the candle upright in the black bowl using wax drippings.
2. Fill the bowl to the rim with fresh water without wetting the wick.
3. Breathe deeply and meditate until your mind is clear.
4. Light the candle. Visualize the power of the curse cast against you living within the flame.
5. As the candle burns, it will splutter and go out as it touches the water – the curse is broken.
6. Dig a hole in the ground, pour the water in it and bury the candle.

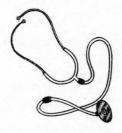

GONE WALKABOUT

Sam, Kitty and Lola catch an early morning train back to Sydney. Nobody sleeps, they're all too worried about Christa.

"Why did Tuhab have to hurt my mother, Kitty?"

"Maybe he didn't."

But if not, why did she have to go to the hospital? When they arrive at St Vincent's, there's some confusion at reception. Kitty asks if they have a patient registered in the name of Christa Khaan, but she's not on their books. Is this the wrong hospital, perhaps? They're about to leave when Sam realizes her mother would have used her married name and marches back up to the desk.

"Do you have a Mrs Tabuh?"

"Ah … yes."

The receptionist puts her head to one side in the manner employed by medical staff who know something dreadful has happened but are not obliged to tell.

"Are you a relative?"

"I'm her daughter and this is Kitty, my friend."

"I'm her gaudy one," adds Kitty.

"My guardian," explains Sam.

The receptionist looks at Lola curiously. "And this lady?"

Lola is sitting in a hospital wheelchair and has pulled the blanket over her head, exposing her hairy knees. Sam pulls the blanket back down.

"This is Grandma Tabuh. She's shy; she hates hospitals."

They're led to the relatives room. The doctor will be with them shortly.

"It's bad news," whispers Sam. "After we've come all this way."

Kitty pats her hand. "Chin up, darling."

She says it with unusual tenderness. There's a tremor in her voice and Sam notices that her hands are shaking. The doctor comes in. He's barely out of medical school and not used to being the bearer of bad tidings. He fixes them with what he thinks is a kind smile, but is more of a grimace – the same face Lola pulls when she's frightened.

"There's been a bit of a blunder," he announces. "Your mum's gone walkabout."

"Gone *walkabout*?"

He waves his hands frantically as if to erase the flippant expression. "Not that she was in any state to walk. She was lying in intensive care. I only nipped out for a quick smoke and when I came back, the bed was empty. Gone off with the fit-looking fella, I reckon. The one with the streaky hair."

"My father!" groans Sam.

"No kidding? The porter saw him charging out of the hospital pushing a box on wheels. Oh no, don't say she was in it! I guess your dad wasn't too happy with my prognosis, but that's no reason to run off with your mother."

"What's wrong with her?" asks Sam.

"Ah, she's pretty crook. She collapsed somewhere in the Blue Mountains. We tried every trick in the book but she slipped into a coma."

"She was cursed!" wails Kitty.

"Ye–s," says the doctor. "That's what your father said. At first I thought he wasn't the full squid. But actually, it's not the first time we've had a curse-case here, only usually the patient is an Aborigine. When someone's been hexed, they collapse, shrieking and writhing, then they stare aghast – like this – pointing at the spirit of the enemy…"

He does the actions, oblivious to the distress he's causing.

"The victim gets sicker and sicker. His pulse becomes imperceptible, and unless he's offered a counter charm, he's not gonna last too long…" he trails off.

"My mum will die?" whispers Sam.

"Yeah. Death is inevitable." The doctor scratches his head. "Funny thing is, there's never any visible sign of disease after they've been cut open – it's like they've died of shock. Or it could be that when the mind has no hope, the body shuts down and commits a form of mental suicide, if you like."

"I don't like!" Sam explodes. "Surely my mother wouldn't be influenced by a curse."

The doctor shrugs. "I can't think of another explanation. I'm kicking myself for not calling security, you know?"

"Perhaps my father took her to another hospital and she's OK."

The doctor shakes his head. "I doubt it. There's no way she'd have survived the trip without intubation. I'm afraid she's a dead woman."

Kitty walks over to the window and lets out a heart-rending sob. "She's *dead*?"

"Yeah. Ah, well, we've all got to go sometime. I'm as cut up about it as you are. Jeez – you shoulda seen me blubber when my pet rat died—"

There's a clatter and a thump behind him. Kitty has crumpled to the floor. The doctor slaps his forehead in despair and panics. "Aw, cripes, not another one! In my lunchbreak too."

He feels for her pulse and bellows for assistance. Two burly nurses charge into the room. Sam rushes to Kitty's side to help her, like she'd helped the ewe and the donkey, but the nurses steer her out of the way. No one will tell her anything.

"What's happening? Has Kitty fainted? Let me through!"

Kitty is rolled onto a stretcher and lifted onto a trolley. The doctor yells instructions. "Let's lose the party mask! Where's the oxygen? Stick this up her nose, somebody."

They're taking her away. Sam hangs onto the trolley.

"Let me go with her… *Please*!"

They won't allow it.

"You stay here with your granny."

Sam sits down, pale-faced and clammy. "This is not good, Lola."

"Ooo, oo."

Lola squeezes Sam's hand. She tries to amuse her by turning a cork from her hat into a cookie but Sam's too upset to appreciate it. An hour passes. A nurse comes back into the room.

"Your friend Kitty's been asking for you. I'm afraid she's had a heart attack."

"Will she be all right?"

The nurse smiles weakly. "I really can't say."

"Can I bring Grandma Tabuh to see her?"

"No," says the nurse. "It's best if you don't because Grandma Tabuh isn't really a person, is she? She's an orang-utan. She shouldn't be here at all. It's against regulations."

Sam pleads. "Where does it say no apes? Kitty has to see her. It'll make her better."

The nurse bites her lip. "All-righty. I'll turn a blind eye. Just this once. Would you like to come this way?"

Sam's stomach lurches as she enters a small side ward. There's a bright floral curtain around the bed; Kitty is behind it. Sam washes her hands with pink disinfectant. Lola washes her feet. The nurse raises an eyebrow but doesn't chastise her. "Shall I leave you guys with Kitty for a bit?"

"Yes, please."

The nurse closes the door behind her. Sam tiptoes over to the curtain, not knowing what to expect. She eases it back on its rail and stares in disbelief.

Kitty's mask is on top of a locker, the mouth-slit twisted into a smile under a long, dark wig. It's as if Kitty has slipped out of her skin and left her old self in a heap. The real Kitty lies facing the wall, her ice blonde hair trailing over her shoulders – why had she chosen to hide it?

"Kitty?"

Slowly, Kitty turns towards her. Sam claps her hands to her mouth in shock – but it isn't revulsion at seeing a face disfigured by fire. Kitty's features are perfect. She looks just like her sister Candy did when she was beautiful. Identical, in fact. But they are not twins.

"Triplets," whispers Kitty, "Me, Candy and Christa. One guides you, two harms you … three loves you beyond the grave…"

Her head falls back on the pillow. Sam sits by her side and holds her hand. Kitty isn't some random Egyptian priestess, she's Sam's flesh and blood – her aunt. Why did it have to be a secret? Kitty shrugs feebly. "You'll see."

Had Kitty worn the mask purely to disguise the fact that she was the eldest triplet, born three hours before Candy, at three minutes past three on the third day of the third month? Or had the mask served a double purpose? Perhaps her face really had been burnt in the fire and the holy water had miraculously healed it. Or was it all down to Father Bayu?

Kitty's too exhausted to explain. She gazes at Sam in wonder, as if she's seeing her for the first time but actually, it's the last. "My beautiful, magical knees…"

"Don't you mean niece, Aunt Kitty?"

Kitty closes her eyes.

"Aunt Kitty? Stay with us – stay with me!"

Sam begins to chant. She chants in Motu. The spell had worked for the butterfly; it wasn't the breeze. Really it wasn't.

Kitty puts her finger on Sam's lips. "Don't you dare bring me back, darling. You have to do the last bit on your own."

How? The doctor says her mother is dead. No one knows where her father is and there's no one left to ask on the witch doctor's list. The last name was torn away.

Kitty smiles briefly. "Follow the leatherback title, Sam."

"What title? What do you mean?"

But Kitty doesn't answer. She has gone. Where to, I cannot say. Heaven? The Astral Temple? Maybe she's in Mexico being ferried across the river. Maybe her soul is being weighed against a feather in Egypt. Maybe she is in Nirvana.

One day, you will know and so will Sam. But right now, she's completely numb. She thought she would cry, but she can't. Kitty's body is still warm, but it's not Kitty any more. It's just a Kitty-shaped illusion, an ashra device. Empty and inanimate.

Death is the perfect disappearing trick, the best sleight of hand, the most subtle piece of misdirection. Sam stands there for a moment, trying to work out where Kitty went. She half-expects her to reappear from behind the curtain, blowing kisses to the audience. She calls out.

"How is death done?"

Indocilis privata loqui. The magician never tells.

HOW TO BREATHE

We breathe in and out over 21,600 times a day, but most of us only use a fraction of our lung capacity. This yoga exercise shows you how to breathe efficiently and slow down your respiratory rate, leaving you calm and relaxed

1. Lie down in complete stillness, close your eyes and become aware of your natural breath.
2. Relax into its smooth ebb and flow.
3. With each breath, say to yourself, "I'm aware that I am breathing in, I'm aware that I am breathing out."
4. Feel the breath flowing in and out of the nose – cool when it enters, warm as it flows out.
5. Feel the breath flowing in and out at the back of the throat and down the throat.
6. Feel the breath flowing down to the chest and into your lungs, expanding and relaxing them.
7. Shift the attention to the rib cage. It expands ... and it relaxes.
8. Feel the breath in your abdomen, moving up as you inhale, down as you exhale. Become aware of the whole breathing process from the nostrils to the abdomen.
9. Bring the awareness back to your whole body and open your eyes.

SANTA YSABEL

A dark-haired figure in a long robe walks beside Sam down to the harbour. It's Lola, wearing Kitty's wig. Sam has no idea where they're going. She has cleared her head of the burden of her own thoughts and is waiting for something else to fill the void.

There's a forklift truck at the water's edge. Two men are loading statues into wooden crates. Once the crates are secured, they are picked up by the truck and loaded onto a ship waiting in the docks. Sam watches until the men disappear for a tea break. The tall, gangly one has left his packing knife behind. She slips it inside her blazer.

Sam climbs into an empty crate with Lola and pulls the lid down. They lie in silence, losing track of time. The men return. She holds her breath. A belt is strapped across the crate to keep it shut, then the truck shoves its metal forks underneath; the vibrations make Lola's teeth judder.

"Shh, Lola. It'll be all right."

There's a sudden lurch as the truck lifts its cargo up into

the air. Sam can see the sky through the slits in the lid. Now the crate is being lowered onto the deck of the ship. She pulls out the packing knife and starts to saw away at the leather strapping. She's struggling for air, so she concentrates on her breathing and slows down her heart rate. Pranayama. Qi gong. Relax.

There's a cry from the docks. "Curly, mate, we're one statue short of a crate. Did someone load an empty?"

Too late; the ship has already set sail across the Coral Sea to the Solomon Islands.

Who knows how long the journey takes. Time has lost all meaning for Sam. She survives by creeping out of the crate at night with Lola and stealing leftover cabbage from the galley. It's the only thing the sailors won't eat.

There's plenty of rum on board too. A tot or two would help to keep out the cold – but what if each barrel has an Aunt Candy folded up inside it, bloated and pickled like one of Professor Farthy's specimens?

Sam is going crazy trying to understand everything that's happened to her. Could the witch doctor really have twisted fate? If so, why would he allow his own grandchild to spend her childhood living with a drunken aunt? Did she have to suffer like that? Maybe she did.

If Aunt Candy had been a kind person, Sam would never have been shut in the attic and would never have discovered who her real father was. And didn't Ruby say that suffering makes you who you are? She leans against a barrel and looks at the photo inside the locket.

"I'm not sure who I am any more, Lola. I've changed, don't you think?"

"Ooo." The orang-utan rakes her fingers through Sam's tangled, waist-length hair.

"Ouch! I know it needs combing, but you're not my mum; she's dead. That's *twice* she's been dead. First it was an illusion, now it's real. Was she as lovely as everyone says?"

"Ooo."

Lola, who has allegedly died only once, isn't giving much away. Sam keeps asking questions.

"Do you think it's a coincidence that my magic number is three and my mother was a triplet born on the third of the third at three minutes past three? I doubt even Bart could explain that away with statistics. I wonder if he's still playing statues in Covent Garden?"

No, he isn't. Nor is Ruth Abafey gathering herbs by moonlight. Mrs Reafy has moved on, and I can tell you with absolute conviction that Mr Fraye has disappeared in a puff of smoke along with the Inspector of Miracles and Athea Furby – the goat bells are still there though.

What has become of the others on the list? Is Father Bayu still tending his orchids? You can search for ever but you'll never find him, or Professor Farthy, or Ruby Featha, or the inscrutable Fu Bar Yetah. Mr Bahut, Tuhab? They have also vanished into thin air.

They haven't died, so where are they? I put it to you that they are all the same person. There is a master of disguise at work. He can appear as any character, wherever and whenever he pleases. He might be sitting next to you right now. I confess I've been on the rum, but I suspect there's an element of truth in my theory. We shall see.

Dawn is breaking. The ship is about to dock in Santa Ysabel. The crates are unloaded, but no matter how long you watch, you won't see Sam and Lola disembark. I misdirected you so they could escape. While you were listening to my theory, Sam lowered a dinghy into the water and the two of them rowed away.

There they are now, bobbing about in the Solomon Sea. It was never Sam's intention to go to Santa Ysabel. She felt strongly that she was meant to go elsewhere – but where? The witch doctor's list isn't giving her any clues. She's relaxed though, like someone who knows fate is out of her hands – unless she is in a trance. The waves drum against the dinghy.

Bom-*bom bomba… **Bom**-bom bomba…*

She closes her eyes. Her hand flops over the side.

Bom-ba, bom-ba, bom-ba … bomba.

She's falling asleep. The witch doctor's notebook slips through her fingers and sinks down to the bottom of the ocean where it's engulfed by a giant clam. If you ever go diving in the Solomon Sea, you must find that clam and persuade him to let you have the book back. Keep it; it has your name on it. But, hark! Is that the cry of the Torresian crow? Sam stirs, sits up in the dinghy and rubs her eyes.

"Where are we, Lola? Which island should we head for? That one, that one … or that one?

Sam hoped the wind or the tide might have chosen her destination, but maybe she can't leave *every* decision

to fate. She stands up and scans the horizon. "Eeeny …
meeny … miny… WOAH!'"

Something strikes the bottom of the dinghy with a
hefty blow and throws her right off her feet. If Lola hadn't
grabbed her ankles, she would have fallen overboard.

"Hold tight, Lola! It might be a shark… Arghhh – here
it comes again!"

Ordinarily, it might well have been a shark – there are
plenty of sharks in the Solomon Sea – but it isn't.

"It's a leatherback turtle!" cries Sam. "It's huge!"

It circles them, then it heads for the third island, its great
flippers sculling through the water. Sam rows after it as fast
as she can, worried that it might get away; but it's in no real
hurry. As the dinghy scrapes against the edge of the reef, the
turtle pokes its head out, blows water from its nostrils, then
submerges. Sam watches it swim back out to sea.

"I'm glad it was a title and not a shark, aren't you, Lola?"
She paddles through the shallows onto the sand, mumbling
to herself. "Did I just say title? No, why would I? I must
have sunstroke. I should never have given my ringmaster's
hat to Bahut."

Shielding her eyes from the sun, Sam surveys the small
island, sheltered by coconut palms and mangrove trees. A
soft wind wafts the scent of sun-warmed wood across the
bay. She's a million miles from St Peter's Square, but she's
never felt closer to home.

"If this is paradise, we must be dead, Lola. Esperanza
was right. Death is a good place; we can make sandpies."

Hand in hand, they skip over the sand into the wilderness.

GHOST WRITING

The masked magician tells the audience there is a ghost in the room and says, "Spirit, I command you to write down the name of the girl with dark hair on this piece of paper." After a short while ... the paper shakes. The magician holds it close to the light bulb – hey presto! – the girl's name has appeared. How?

THE SECRET

The masked magician knew the name of the girl and wrote it on the paper earlier with invisible ink. To make invisible ink, simply use a toothpick dipped in lemon juice.

The magician rattled the paper to create the illusion that a ghost was writing on it and the heat from the lamp made the name appear.

SAN JORGE

Where is John Tabuh? I can tell you only this much: he's on an island, but I never did find out the name of it or how he got there. Maybe he travelled by ship – or did an old lady disguised as a sheep farmer take pity on him and fly him there in her helicopter?

Right now, I'm more interested in his state of mind, which has reached an all-time low. It's no good telling him to cheer up, that it might never happen. As far as he can see, it *has* happened – things can't get any worse.

John had made a valiant effort to heal Christa. He'd put aside his cynicism and drawn on everything he'd learnt on his mission. He'd tried using herbs, but those didn't work. He'd tried the laying on of hands. He'd sprinkled her with holy water – despite the chaos he'd caused at Lourdes, he'd slipped some into his pocket because he liked the shape of the bottle.

He'd tried chanting, but words failed him. He'd sat with a pencil and paper in the hope that the spirits might send him a prescription via automatic writing, but the psychic surgery was shut. He tried qi gong, pranayama – you name it, he tried it. But Christa remained in a coma.

Unable to feel her pulse, John became more and more desperate. He prayed to Jesus, Mary, all the saints. He prayed to Allah, Shiva and Buddha. He prayed to sun gods, sea gods, every god he'd ever heard of, but none of them returned the favour.

He even summoned Lucifer, and when the devil didn't reply, he called upon the spirits of his ancestors. Like my elderly relatives, they were hurt that he hadn't been in touch for so long and didn't see why they should help him out in a crisis.

Christa lay lifeless in his arms. He took out his magic wand, waved it over her body and cried, "Abracadabra! Abracadabra! Abracadabra!"

Nothing happened; he hurled the wand into the sea. There was no such thing as magic. It was all an illusion; that was the reality. He'd lost Sam, his wife, his twins, his father, his orang-utan and his home.

He felt like throwing himself into the sea after his wand. The only thing that stopped him was the thought that he'd have to face his father in the Lower World, and he'd be even more disappointed in his son than he was already. So he picked orchids instead.

John gathered great armfuls and arranged three of the best blooms in Christa's hair. Then he placed her in the magic box and covered her with the rest of the flowers. Satisfied with the arrangement, he felt in his pocket for the list Christa had copied from the witch doctor's notebook, took out his pen and scratched an angry line through each person.

It was only when he came to the last name that John hesitated. This was the name Sam had never seen; it was ripped when she first opened the notebook – the pages had been stuck together if you remember.

It just said Shamanka. There was no portrait, just a rough map of San Jorge. All credit to John Tabuh, he'd managed to find everyone his father had asked him to visit so far – and that was without the benefit of his copied list ever glowing hot like the one in the genuine notebook. He could find this Shamanka if he wanted to.

Did he want to though? Christa was dead. None of the people he'd seen had convinced him that resurrection was possible – quite the opposite in fact. He sucked the end of his pen, cursed his father and scribbled out the last name furiously.

Only it refused to be obliterated. The ink from his pen wouldn't stick to the paper; it formed little blue beads, which popped and vanished. Perhaps there was a drop of grease on the page. He felt with his thumb, but the paper was clean.

He reached for his pencil instead, and pressed so hard he almost made a hole. He blanked out "Shamanka" with dozens of thick black strokes, and when he could no longer see the name, he shouted, "There!" as if to imply that no one could make him do anything he didn't want to any more.

He was about to rip the list out of his notebook and screw it up when he noticed something very odd: his pencil strokes were moving. He blinked, but they were definitely moving. They were forming a fuzzy queue and were sliding off the page. He snapped the book shut to trap them, but they were too quick; they slipped out and escaped across the sand.

John's immediate thought was that he must be seeing things; he hadn't eaten or slept for days. It was a possibility. He took a deep breath and opened the book again.

SHAMANKA!

It was still there, as bold as ever, as if it were screaming at him. The witch doctor *would* be heard – he *would* be obeyed, because he was John's father. But John didn't believe in the old magic. There had to be a logical reason for the ink and pencil marks to disappear, possibly to do with the texture of the paper and the reaction of sunlight on pigment.

The Dark Prince told himself this but something in his subconscious said otherwise. Before he knew it, he was reaching for his knife and looking for a suitable log to turn into a dugout canoe big enough to carry him and his magic box to San Jorge.

The moon is up. A group of Melanesians are waiting for John Tabuh. They don't know who he is, but they've been sitting at the edge of the coral reef for hours, reading the waves. They know the ripples are caused by a small craft with a heavy cargo. By studying the distance between each wave, they've estimated that he'll arrive any minute.

Here he comes now! The Melanesians greet him noisily. They jump into the water and help him drag the mwa
sawah onto the sand, which is littered with pale pink shells.
They're fascinated by the ornate, coffin-shaped box; what's
in it? John Tabuh clutches his heart.

"My wife."

"Ah!"

They can tell by his face that she lies dead inside the box
and are bemused. They don't put their dead in boxes here;
they leave them on the reef for the sharks to take and they
suggest to John that this would be a most charming ending
for his woman.

Or why not leave her body to decompose in the canoe?
That's another tradition of theirs. He could collect her
bones when the birds had picked them clean and make
a nice shrine. There are many such shrines on the island,
some with complete skeletons of their great, great, great
grandfathers; would he like to see them?

John thanks them but says he has other plans. He has
come here to find someone. Is there a Shamanka living on
this island? At the mention of the name, the Melanesians
let out a unanimous shriek, cover their eyes and fall to their
knees. Terrified as they obviously are, John persists.

"Could your Shamanka bring my wife back to life?"

They beat their breasts in anguish. Don't even think
about it! If you ask Shamanka to bring back the dead, you
will incur the wrath of the spirits; they will seek terrible
revenge on you!

John tries to picture what form this revenge might take. He conjures up several images that make his eyes water, but as he doesn't believe in spirits, he says to the Melanesians, "I will sacrifice my soul if Shamanka can resurrect my wife."

He's joking. It isn't a very funny joke, putting himself up for sacrifice, but he's feeling frivolous. It's the kind of euphoria that often creeps up on mourners after a funeral. They catch themselves laughing, yet moments ago they swore they'd never smile again. Grief is so two-faced.

John is certain Christa's resurrection won't happen anyway. She's dead; death is final. But now that he's here, he might as well see Shamanka and get the whole nonsense over with. Afterwards, he will find a beautiful spot and bury his wife the western way. Having done that, he has decided to Live Life Dangerously. He will swim three times a day in shark-infested water. He will eat puffer fish. He will visit the frozen wastes without a coat and while he's there, he will stroke hungry polar bears.

According to Bart Hayfue, if you live this dangerously, statistically you'll soon be killed. It's hard to say how soon though, because luck always comes into the equation. The sharks might be vegans. You might be immune to puffer fish poison. The polar bears might be friendly.

John hopes his luck will run out soon. He can't see the point of living any more, and if he's killed by sharks, poison or polar bears, his father can hardly accuse him of suicide. If he bumps into Yafer in the Lower World, he can tell him with a clear conscience that he suffered a fatal accident whilst engaged in Manly Pursuits. Maybe they'd be able to patch things up in the afterlife and do some bonding.

Please excuse the Dark Prince's mental ramblings; he's grieving, remember. The Melanesians realize this and eventually they dust the sand off their knees and help him carry the magic box out of the canoe.

Women and children arrive with flaming torches. They have heard about the man who has come to sacrifice himself and, as they have no television, this promises to be a most exciting evening. They bring him roasted fish wrapped in leaves. Grubs in honey. A potent drink made from fermented fruit. The elders beat their drums. The magic box is hoisted onto the shoulders of six strapping youths and John Tabuh is swept along by a procession of wailing dancers.

They are taking him to Shamanka's lair.

MAGIC ALPHABETS

Many alphabets said to have magical properties have existed through the ages. They are still used by witches and shamans to write secret notes and to empower their spells.

This Celestial Alphabet contains images believed to have been sent by messenger angels.

Thes	Cheth	Zain	Vau	He
Daleth	Gimel	Beth	Aleph	Zade
Pe	Ain	Sameth	Nun	Mem
Lamed	Caph	Iod	Tau	Schin
Res		Kuff		

SHAMANKA

"**S**hamanka! Shamanka! See the man willing to sacrifice his soul to you. Come out of your cave. Work your big magic. Bring his woman back to life. Come, Shamanka, come!"

The Melanesians are chanting. The elders are drumming. The strapping youths lay the box down by the mouth of the cave and back away. John Tabuh, intoxicated by the rhythm of the drums stands with his hands clasped behind his back to stop them trembling.

Is he afraid? No, but here is a magician who suddenly finds himself not on stage, but in the audience. He's not used to being in this position. What's more, he's the only one who doesn't know what's going to happen next.

You'd think that the Dark Prince – who understands the psychology of an audience better than most – could avoid reacting along with the crowd, but it's proving impossible; the mood is contagious. He waits wide-eyed and breathless for Shamanka to appear.

The moon slips out from behind a cloud and creates a

white spotlight on the sand. On cue, the drumming and the chanting stop. A hush falls over the audience, its many eyes mesmerized by the circle of moonlight. Keep watching … keep watching. The sea holds its breath, listening for the ominous rattle that heralds the arrival of the one who can hold back the tide.

Tsss … tsss … tsss … like the hiss of a serpent slipping out of the theatre wings.

Tsss … tsss … tsss … invisible against the velvet-black backdrop of the night.

Tsss … tsss … tsss … nearer and nearer. Nearer, nearer and nearer…

Aiyeeeeeeee!

Everyone jumps back, afraid to look yet unable to avert their gaze, like rabbits entranced by a stoat. Shamanka is materializing on stage in a whirl of blinding sand. She appears without footsteps or wings, as if she's neither human nor angel: so what is she? She isn't a ghost, yet she wears the luminous mask of a lost soul; are we staring Death in the face?

She's the height of two men. She towers over the crouched figure of John Tabuh. She leaps on impossible springs. Is she subhuman, superhuman? He can't say; he can't speak.

She swoops around the magic box casting a circle, thrusting her fists in the sand. At each point of the compass, flames bloom like cactus flowers. She stamps on the ground. She throws her head back, her spine arches over and her headdress brushes the floor.

She stamps with her hands and her feet, harder and harder. The vibrations shunt the audience backwards. They cling to the sand with their fingers but they can't hold on – they're shifting backwards … backwards … towards the sea – all except for John Tabuh, who wraps his arms around the trunk of a palm and hangs on.

Shamanka stamps and stamps, and as she stamps, the magic box shakes and the lid scrapes and shifts. The islanders grab their children and shoot off into the darkness like rockets, leaving a trail of fading screams in their wake.

Only John remains. The performance is all for him now. As he clings to the tree, watching the box bump up and down all by itself, he tells himself it has to be an illusion. But he can see no strings, no mirrors. Is there a trapdoor hidden in the sand under the box ? Is there a man in the trap, making the box move? Maybe the Melanesians are her stooges. Maybe they told Shamanka he was coming and devised this show together.

This is the most rational answer, but John is wrong. Perhaps Shamanka has misdirected him. She sent the Melanesians screaming and while he was watching them, his eyes were diverted from the box; that's when she put something under it to make it jump.

Wrong again. Shamanka is innocent. She didn't put anything under the box; the turtle did. She crawled out of the sea one night, laid her eggs and buried them on the beach. The box was placed on top of her nest, and now the eggs are hatching. Hundreds of little leathery wings are pushing up through the sand, rocking the box.

Was it a coincidence that the box was laid over the turtle's nest the night the eggs would hatch? It seems unlikely, but maybe there were lots of nests, in which case it wouldn't have mattered where the box was placed. The baby turtles would have shifted it soon enough. Right now, they're flapping across the beach like birds trying to fly through apple crumble. They're racing towards the navy blue blanket of sea, and as the last wave of turtles breaks out from under the box, the lid flies open.

Shamanka stops stamping and stoops so low over the magic box her headdress touches her toes. She stares inside. She stares and stares. The sea spray whispers, "Mother?"

John Tabuh lets go of the tree. He watches as Shamanka kicks off her red fur underskirt and casts it away. It rolls into the shadows. John watches it melt into the darkness... Misdirection! When he looks back, she's half the size, as if she's stepped down from someone's shoulders. Now that she's taken off her headdress, she's no taller than a girl. As she removes her mask of death, a sliver of moonlight reflects in her dark hair – but it's not the moonlight; it's a blonde streak.

John Tabuh breaks out into a cold sweat. It can't be Sam. It can't be ... unless someone has resurrected her? But that's impossible. No one had offered him the slightest hope, least of all without a body. Sam was burnt to ashes in the fire; the witch had said so, hadn't she?

No! Think back, John Tabuh. Ruth Abafey said all that remained was the silver rattle; she never said that the baby had burnt to death – *you* jumped to that conclusion.

A good witch doctor never jumps to conclusions; he reads between the lines.

John Tabuh's daughter is sitting by the magic box staring at her mother's body. He wants to run to her and hold her in his arms. But he doesn't. He stays where he is, clutching his head. The Melanesians have drugged him; he must force himself to think straight. *So help me, Father.*

He writes in the sand with his finger:

S-H-A-M-A-N-K-A

He stares at the girl, stares at the letters. He rubs them out and writes them in a different order.

S-A-M-H-A-N-A-K

A breeze gets up. The letters buzz before his eyes like sandflies. He shields them with his fingers, but they're shifting. He blinks, he blinks again, but there it is, spelled out before him.

S-A-M K-H-A-A-N.

Is there magic in letters? Are these letters magic symbols, magic spells? He takes his father's list out of his pocket. He can barely read it; he's shaking with excitement and this helps to jumble up the letters. He rearranges them in his head.

R-U-T-H A-B-A-F-E-Y … YAFER TABUH!
B-A-R-T H-A-Y-F-U-E … YAFER TABUH!
H-U-B-E-R-T F-A-Y-A … YAFER TABUH!

They don't all fall into the exactly same pattern, but even so…

F-A-T-H-E-R B-A-Y-U … FREYA TABUH!

F-E-Y R-A … FREYA!

Effie Ray? How do you solve that one? Phonetically:

F-E R-A-Y … FREYA!

Out of the corner of his eye, John sees that someone has joined his daughter – someone short and stout and red-haired, like his departed mother.

It's Lola! Shamanka was not as tall as two men. She was as tall as a girl standing on the shoulders of an ape! John has worked that out for himself, but what he can't fathom is how his father has managed to orchestrate fate and time to bring Sam back to him – or why.

Most sons would be impressed at their father's ability to go against the laws of nature and pull off a trick like that. They'd run home and apologize for pooh-poohing the power of his magic, but not John. Right now, he's livid. Why couldn't his father have been a farmer or a tailor or a dentist? Only a witch doctor would send his only son to hell and back in order to learn his trade; only a witch doctor or a psychopath would kill off his son's wife – and to prove what?

Christa lies dead. His daughter is bent over the magic box still. Is she crying? It is hard to tell but Kitty had said never to hold back the tears. John can't bear to watch her grieve alone. He pulls out a silk handkerchief … and another … and another … they're all knotted together in true magician style. He walks over.

"Sam?"

She looks straight through him. "I am Shamanka!"

There's an odd expression on her face, almost as if she's

annoyed at being interrupted. John Tabuh shows her the silver rattle. He knows she knows who he is; he's hoping she'll fling her arms around him and cry, "Daddy!" But that only happens in his dreams. John assumes she's angry with him. He assumes she blames him for not bringing her mother back to life, just as he blamed his father. A good witch doctor should never make assumptions however.

John Tabuh takes a deep breath – it's all in the breathing – and apologizes to Sam from the bottom of his heart. "Sam, I'd sell my soul if it would bring your mother back, but there's no such magic. I've spoken to the wisest people on Earth, but none of them has the power of life over death."

Sam looks at him in despair. How can he have travelled so far and learnt so little? What does she have to do to make him believe in Grandpa? She folds her arms defiantly. "Ah, but you haven't spoken to *me* yet."

She begins to chant an ancient chant. It's in Motu but it means the same the world over. It's the most powerful chant in the universe, because when Sam says it, every woman who has ever loved a child responds as if it were her own little one tugging at her skirts.

"Mother … Mother … Mother?"

The voices of mothers around the globe fill the air. In English, French, Spanish, Swahili…

"I'm here … here … here."

The mother turtle calls, mother seabirds call and not so far away, in Borneo and Sumatra, mother orang-utans croon to their own babies, real or imagined. Newborn or dead. John holds his daughter by the shoulders and turns her towards him. He watches her lips, her throat. They do not move. "I know how you're doing that…"

Now he hears a voice calling from inside the magic box: sweeter than Candy's, softer than Kitty's. John throws his hat on the floor.

"Don't – it's just ventriloquism. I can do it."

He throws his voice to Lola: "Listen to your father!"

But Sam isn't throwing her voice. Behind them, a woman laughs lightly. "I'm here."

Christa is sitting up in the box and smiling. She reaches out and holds Sam so close, she can hear her heart beating.

Bom-ba … bomba! Bom-ba … bomba!

Bom-ba … bomba! Bom-ba … bomba!

Was it a true resurrection? Did the sound of Sam's voice break a curse? Did she heal her mother with psychic surgery? Was a miracle brought about by the sprinkling of holy water?

I doubt it; I'm not convinced that Christa Tabuh was dead in the first place. I happen to know that if you swallow the slime from a certain Australian toad, which has been secretly dunked in your drink, you will fall into a deep coma and appear well and truly dead – especially to a young doctor who's only just passed his medical exams.

There are only two known antidotes to this toad slime; one is stored at the Hospital for Tropical Diseases and the other is known only to me. I'll tell you what it is, in case you ever accept a toad-flavoured drink from a medicine man and find yourself without a pulse.

The antidote is the acid from the bite of a yellow spider

that lives inside a rare species of orchid. These orchids are only found in the Solomon Islands and they just happen to be the ones that John Tabuh wove into Christa's hair.

To this day, I remain sceptical about the resurrection of mortals. But John Tabuh does not; this is the turning point for him. Something far greater than luck or chance has reunited him with the wife, child and father he thought he'd lost for ever.

Was it magic? The Dark Prince thinks he's finally found the answer, but is he right? That is something you must find out for yourself. For now, it's only right that he should go home to New Guinea to show off his beautiful wife and his wisest of daughters to his dear old dad.

In whom he has *every* faith.

HOW TO DISAPPEAR IN A PUFF OF SMOKE

The masked magician takes a bow. There is a thunder crack! Swirling green smoke fills the stage. As it clears, we realize that the magician has vanished. How?

THE SECRET

There are several ways of creating smoke, fog and mist to use as a screen and enhance illusions.

1. Pyro flash cartridges: These produce deeply coloured, dense smoke for 7 to 30 seconds – plenty of time to "dematerialize" right in front of the audience's eyes.

2. Smoke guns: These feed liquid smoke into a heated chamber. It then vaporizes and produces a jet of dense white smoke – a perfect piece of misdirection.

3. Smoke chillers: These use solid CO_2 to produce low-lying smoke ideal for creating the right atmosphere for a ghostly apparition.

4. Dry ice: This produces dense, white, water-vapour smoke, forced out of the front of a kettle – ideal for creating eerie midnight wharf scenes.

5. Liquid nitrogen foggers: These spray a fine mist, which drops the air temperature and causes a low-lying fog, ideal for disguising ... well, all manner of things.

YOUR TURN

What happened next? John Tabuh returned home to his father and was welcomed with open arms. He hadn't failed his mission; he'd swallowed his youthful pride, learnt his lesson and apologized profusely for ever doubting the Old Magic. Even so, John worried that he wasn't fit to walk in Yafer Tabuh's shadow, never mind step into his shoes.

"I'm afraid I'll never make a great witch doctor," he confessed sadly.

To his surprise, his father heartily disagreed. He shook his head so vigorously, he almost had his eye out with his hornbill necklace.

"Number One Son, you have *already* made a great witch doctor!" he guffawed, clapping John so hard on the back, he began to choke on the betel nut he was chewing.

"I'm ... *heuuurch* ... got a nut stuck ... not quite sure what you ... *heuuurch* ... urgle," John choked.

Sam stepped in and gave him the Heimlich manoeuvre. There's nothing magical about this procedure – you don't need to be Athea Furby to perform it. Simply study these instructions:

1. From behind, grasp the sufferer round the upper abdomen.
2. Clasp one hand over the other with the fist in the angle of the rib cage.
3. Pull hard inwards and upwards against the bottom of the breastbone – the sudden increase of pressure in the chest should force the food out.
4. Reassure the patient (unless you're too late, in which case call a witch doctor).

Thanks entirely to Sam's quick thinking, the nut shot out of the Dark Prince's gullet into the Sepik River and he was able to continue his conversation.

"Sorry, Father, what were you saying before I almost choked to death?"

Yafer Tabuh grinned from ear to ear. "I was about to say that you have *already* made the perfect witch doctor!"

"I have?"

"Certainly. With the help of your wife, whom I chose for you most carefully, you have made *Shamanka*!"

He took Sam's hand and held it up in the air. There was a roar of approval from the crowd, who had been gathering on the banks since the early hours of the morning to welcome her. The witch doctor embraced his granddaughter fondly then made the sign of the triangle.

"She who is born to the third triplet on the third day of the third month at three minutes past three will grow to be wiser than her father and her grandfather put together!"

There was another roar of approval and much banging of drums, which sent the Torresian crows shrieking into the sky.

"Shamanka! Shamanka! Shamanka!"

Yafer called for silence. He took off his headdress with the bird of paradise feathers and with great solemnity he placed it on Sam's head, and because she was so much wiser than her years and because her head was so full of magic, it fitted like a dream.

It wasn't a dream though. When Yafer Tabuh finally departed from this world at the age of 105, it was cast in stone that he was not to be resurrected and that his granddaughter, Sam, should inherit his crown. Thus, the little girl from St Peter's Square became the next witch doctor and the Old Magic lived on.

It still lives on. When I count to three, you will be back in your theatre seat. Sit tight, I would hate you to miss the end of the show.

One … two … three…

The curtain falls. The house lights come on. The show is over for the rest of the audience; for you, it's just beginning. They put on their coats and leave, but you stay in your seat until the theatre is empty; there's something you want to know. Soon, the cleaners come to sweep up the popcorn; we don't have long.

I am the Masked Magician and I would like an audience with you alone. Hurry now. Climb onto the stage and slip behind the curtains. I am waiting in the wings. I have something to show you, something you have never seen before, I promise.

Ah, there you are, my courageous companion. Come closer ... excellent, you have a good, firm handshake. This bodes well. You show no sign of nerves, you're not afraid of me – and why should you be? We have travelled the world together, have we not?

You know more about me than I know about you. You gave nothing away throughout our journey. I admire that. It confirms what I've suspected all along; you are perfect for the job.

What job? It heartens me to know that you are full of insatiable curiosity. All will be revealed soon, but I sense there are three other questions you'd like to ask me first.

What is magic? You're wondering if the witch doctor could truly twist fate? I'm glad you asked me that; it means you have a touch of John Tabuh's cynicism, which is good because it makes you ask a question like the next one...

What is illusion? At the back of your mind, you suspect Sam's journey was just a daydream. She is no one special; just a bored, lonely orphan. Influenced by a trip to a magic show with her arthritic old aunt, she invented an exotic pet to keep her company and fabricated a magical family to replace the one she'd lost, casting herself as heroine.

However, you're not entirely happy with this tidy explanation, are you? You've seen how miserable life can be for people with narrow minds so you're keeping yours open. But you're nobody's fool, which is why you'd like to know the following…

What is real? Did Sam really exist? The witch doctor? Did *any* of the characters exist or did I conjure them up one rainy afternoon to entertain you in this old theatre? What's that you say? You want me to show you the thing you've never seen before? My true identity, you mean? I must say, you're very bold. Ah, well. I did promise, I suppose.

Very well, I will take off my mask…

I am Shamanka!

I am Sam Tabuh; see the blonde streak in my hair? Look up into the gods – you will see my assistant. I'm sure you recognize her, even though she is disguised as a small boy.

It is Lola.

We have come from New Guinea to find you. I have no sons or daughters to step into my shoes. Like my dear departed grandfather, I manipulated time and fate and arranged for you to be born. I chose your parents carefully. You arrived on the right day at the right time in the right place, just as I planned. I even chose your name. Shout it out loud! There is magic in it.

Big Magic.

You are destined for great things, my friend. Maybe in this life, maybe in the next. Bad things may happen, but you will overcome them; you will grow wise.

You have hidden powers.

Be on your guard. Some of the characters you will meet will not be who they seem. I have put them there for a reason. You may not understand why now, but you will. Be wary, but do not be afraid. I have provided you with a spirit guide, a totem animal and a power animal. If you don't know who they are, you will find out soon.

You have a unique gift. Never doubt it, even in your darkest moments. I am Shamanka. You are no longer the person you were before our paths crossed.

You are better, brighter, braver.

You are magical.

It is time to start your journey.

WILD BOY

ROB LLOYD JONES

Behold the savage spectacle of the wild boy!

London, 1841. In the seamy, smoggy underworld, a boy covered in hair, raised as a monster, is condemned to life in a travelling freak show. A boy with an extraordinary power of observation and detection. A boy accused of murder, on the run, hungry for the truth. Ladies and Gentlemen, take your seats. The show is about to begin!

"A gripping murder mystery" *Sunday Express*

THE BOY WHO SWAM WITH PIRANHAS

DAVID ALMOND

A life-affirming and fabulously fishy tale about one boy's journey from anguish to joy.

Stanley Potts is just an ordinary boy, but when all the jobs in Fish Quay disappear his Uncle Ernie develops an extraordinary fascination with canning fish. Suddenly their home is filled with the sound of clanging machinery and the stench of mackerel. Stan, however, has his own destiny. As he delves into the waters, he finally discovers who he really can be.

"This book will make hearts sing" *Sunday Times*